Gulf

James McNaught

Contact: bekasume.books@oputsnet.com.au

ISBN: 1-4116-5614-8

Table of Contents

The Mailman

Bluey Walters yawned and stretched. He scratched himself and looked over at the rising sun. It was 6:30 in the morning and already quite hot. He stood on the wide verandah of his Cloncurry boarding home. This was his one stationary investment. It was a large, rambling, weatherboard high set house, stationed on the eastern edge of town to the north of the Townsville road. His block was one acre, with unkempt grass and a gravel drive. The yard had six large shady mango trees and was surrounded by a broken down barbed wire fence. Its paint was chipped and peeling but the high corrugated iron roof still retained its dull galvanized color. The verandah was 10 feet wide and surrounded the house.

Rhonda, Bluey's divorced sister had three rooms for herself and her own bathroom. Nina, the aboriginal cook, lived downstairs next to the laundry. There was a large communal lounge room, a big kitchen and the dining room on the southern side of the house.

Bluey rented rooms to eight tenants, all public servants up in the 'Curry to do their country service; with a view to accelerated promotion. The population changed periodically as the public servants were married or transferred somewhere else.

A good business man didn't ever have idle property. Bluey did not use a room himself. He slept on the verandah in the east, outside Rhonda's rooms. He used her bathroom as well. There was room underneath for the tenants to park and he had a large storeroom down there. His truck was parked and maintained in a large corrugated iron shed, in the yard, shaded by three of the mango trees.

Bluey was 31 years old. His name, in true Australian fashion, came from his bright red hair. He had bright blue eyes and plenty of freckles on his face and body. His face was mostly hidden by a large red beard. At 5 feet 8 inches tall he was a solid man running to fat. His blue Bonds singlet bulged out over the waistband of his bottle green Ruggers[*], the waistband had given up the struggle of holding in his sagging 'slipped chest'. He had worn Stubbies[+] for many years but recently changed to Ruggers. They had a chord around the waist as well as the elastic and didn't reveal too much builder's cleavage at the back when he bent over.

Bluey sighed and enjoyed the balm of the morning. The sky in this part of the country was a rich blue and straggling across it were

---

[*] Ruggers are Australian shorts with an elastic waist a tie cord and side pockets

[+] Stubbies are Australian shorts with and elastic waist, no tie cord and no side pockets

a smudgy flock of sheep-like clouds. They were still white but held the promise of upcoming storms and the healing monsoon in late December or early January.

'This is a good country!' he thought to himself.

He wasn't afraid to make a buck. He held the mail contract for Leichhardt and the north eastern part of the Northern Territory. The longest mail run in the world. His Ford F 250 four wheel drive was ready for the next run. He took half a load of mail and the rest was reserved for his door to door business. The women in the North West were always glad to buy clothes and other trinkets. At this rate he'd have enough to buy his own road train in another three years.

For an unmarried man, his was a good business. He was fond of women and he called in on many of them. During the day some women stayed at home while their men were out trying to tame this big land. He never touched women who weren't married and was quick to spot a potential victim. He wasn't choosy: once, or many times, would do him!

His investment was secure with Rhonda. She had been born in the 'Curry and wasn't happy anywhere else. Their parents were dead, or missing, and all she had was her big brother and the two kids. Her marriage to Charley Rider had been a disaster. She hated Boulia, where he worked, and the sex maniac from the road gang who Charley was willing to share her with. Now she was back home looking after the boarding house and Billy and Joe.

Bluey had a XXXX[*] and two rollies[+] before he went in for breakfast at 7 o'clock. He liked to roll his own thick and do the job with one hand.

After breakfast he went down to his truck. This was his baby. A dark blue Ford with a big bull bar and winch. He had two spotlights on the bar and another two wide angle lights on the front bumper. The bar was strong enough to throw a bullock. Inside, the driver's seat had a lamb's wool seat cover. There was a small fridge behind the other seat against the back wall of the cabin, inside the sleeping compartment. On the tray at the back were two compartments. The back one opened to the rear and was for the land mail. The front compartment was lined with carpet and had a door on each side. The right hand side was for clothes and hats while the left hand side was for electrical goods. Under the false bottom there was room for fifty flagons of wine to sell on the missions to the abos.

'See ya Rhonda! Boys!' he yelled. He gunned the powerful 354 cubic inch V8 and listened to the engine purr. The mailman listened carefully and then smiled again. It was right in tune. He switched the air-conditioner on and selected second gear. As the clutch engaged the beast moved forward like a tiger. Bluey loved his truck more than he loved anything else in the world, apart from himself.

A digital clock on the dash above the cassette player showed 7:45. He pushed in a Slim Dusty tape and sang along …'I like

---

[*] XXXX is a brand of beer, popular in Queensland.

[+] 'Rollies' are roll your own cigarettes.

Australian women and I like Australian grog, but I do not like Australian men to call me greasy wog. I'm a new Australian bushman …' Bluey nodded his head in anticipation. The mail train was due in Kajabbi at 1:30 pm. He would have two hours in Quamby with Jackie. She was a real tigress. Old Jock could hardly crack a fat any more and she loved it wherever she could get it. The mailman usually had to wait until he was on the way home. Jock was always home on Monday. Today, however, the old guy was not there. He had gone to a cattle sale in Julia Creek last Saturday and wouldn't be back till tomorrow morning.

As Bluey looked out of the window he enjoyed the beef road. This bitumen road from the 'Curry up to Normanton made life much easier. He could get to Gregory in three hours instead of six…, more time in Quamby and perhaps some time at the Burke and Wills as well!

The country was pretty dry but even this early in the season there was a sign of real good rain coming.

Later that afternoon Bluey pulled into the station at Kajabbi. It was called a station even though it didn't have all the regular features. A shed beside the line and one siding. The trains that came here loaded livestock and goods; there were no passenger trains. Over the line from the shed there were some yards and a cattle ramp. These days only a few drovers brought cattle over from the Territory and down the Gulf rivers. There were no ranges to cross on the way here. In fact, there were no real hills from Quamby to the other side of Turn Off Lagoon.

The little hill at Quamby was a perfect setting for the minuscule township. A pub, a post office and three houses made up the hamlet, just a wayside stop on the beef road. The river curved around the hill and was crossed by the road next to the back sheep paddock. To the west of the bridge was a pretty little water hole.

Bluey quickly snapped back to attention as Sambo, the old black caretaker, said, 'Still dreaming about Quamby, mate? You'll never get the mail away if you do that. You're already an hour late as it is. One day your dick will get you into a lot of trouble!'

'I'll be right, Sam! I'm too clever for any of the blokes up here. Where's the mail?'

'In here mate, there are seventeen bags today.'

'Great, put them in the back of the truck!' Bluey wouldn't work when there was a black fellah to do it for him. Sambo was twice the mailman's age and much less robust but there was no help for the old caretaker.

'Put them in order, Sam, or I'll kick you hard when I get back. Where's the list?'

Sambo gave Bluey the list and he read it quickly: 2 Gregory Downs, 1 Augustus Downs, 1 Brookdale, 1 Escott, 5 Leichhardt, 2 Lawn Hill, 1 Westmoreland, 1 Woollogarang and 3 Borrolloola. Bluey would drop all of the bags off in the next few days. He climbed out of the cabin and watched the older man puff and pant in the hot sun as he lugged the mail bags from the shed to his truck. When the work was done Bluey would sell Sambo a flagon of wine for $30.

The wine cost $8 and he mixed it 50-50 with water. He had to be careful when he watered down the wine. There was one idiot back in '76 who was selling watered down wine. He was too greedy. He sold one of the boongs a flagon for $35. The problem was that it didn't get the fellah drunk.

He complained to the police sergeant, 'This fellah, he bin gib me plagon for $35, but I bin not get drunk!'

The crook got ten years at Stewart Creek jail in Townsville. Bluey wasn't too greedy, he would always let the boongs get drunk for their money.

Sambo was sweating heavily by now, 'I bin done now, Mr. Walters!'

'Good boy, Sambo. You wanna drink now?'

'Yes, boss.'

'Thirty five dollars!'

'OK, boss.'

The poor boongs weren't allowed in pubs up here. They didn't know how much money a flagon should cost them. It was great for any business man out here in the bush who would deal with them.

Bluey remembered a story he had heard from Normanton. The publican up there used to sell mentholated spirits and orange juice out the back door to the boongs. They paid $10 a bottle. He sold it in 1 pint plastic bottles. The orange juice cost him $11.20 for a gallon and the metho 69 cents a pint in Isa. He made the trip south every second weekend and made about 500 bucks between times. The police sergeant eventually warned him off. He sold the pub and brought another one at Burleigh Heads. He was a millionaire now!

The mailman headed back to the beef road. It was longer that way than going straight to Nardoo but the bitumen meant he could save time and money. There was also less likelihood of hitting a big pot hole and breaking his flagons. Bluey loved the hamburgers at the Burke and Wills roadhouse at Three Ways as well. The lady there loved her husband and he had no chances with her but she often bought trinkets from him to resell in her shop.

The bitumen at last! It was much easier driving on this road than on the gravel. He could go faster and relax a bit more. Like all people who spent a lot of time on the road Bluey was able to lock his concentration on the road and then dream about other things…

He had always wanted to own Lawn Hill Station which included Turn Off Lagoon. This station was the jewel of North West Queensland. He had only been there once but still had a clear picture in his mind. The long straight road west from Gregory and then the hill which was guarded by the homestead. Down the bottom were a yard and some workshops. The three road trains were kept there. The big right hand bend around the yard and the tight nick back to the left up the hill. The great homestead set back from the road and the offices and houses for the station men around.

The big boss wouldn't have to ride a horse. He would take the 'chopper' everywhere. Of course there would be a manager to run the station. In fact he wouldn't just own Lawn Hill; he would own Riversleigh, Punjaub and Bowthorn as well. His would be the great empire of the north west.

Bluey also thought about the Lawn Hill gorges. All five of them towering majestic over the plains. He would make these into a world renowned tourist resort and conference centre.

Prominently in all his dreams was a magnificent woman. This time she looked uncannily like the woman who lived over the road from the police station. She was perfect in every way; always submissive and constantly ready to satisfy his voracious sexual appetite.

She didn't mind if he had any outside affairs but was always fiercely loyal to him.

He was hovering about fifty feet above the heads of a big mob of cattle. They were near the twelve mile yards. Some powerful steers snorted at the other 'chopper' buzzing around like an angry bee. The cattle were stubborn but the big bird didn't let up. The crew on the ground waited near the mouth of a hessian funnel. They were hard men, two gulf white men and seven abos. The cattle would soon be mustered and branded. His cattle would always be trucked to Isa and then sold in the markets. They would be much sought after beasts.

He would clear an area to the west of the homestead hill. They would build a big race track and rodeo ground. His rodeo would be famous and his picnic races would be more prestigious than those at Birdsville.

Bluey became expansive in his dreams. He would drive around the homestead in a Rolls Royce. His office and home would be carefully air-conditioned. Humidity and temperature would remain constant all year. There would be a penthouse suite reserved in the best of the three hotels at the gorge. He would fish for barramundi every weekend. Perhaps he ought to reserve one of the gorges for his exclusive use…

There was the Julia Creek road appearing out of the scrub on the right. Slow down gently. He wouldn't need to fill up at the Burke and Wills. His long range tanks took him about 800 miles. Petrol in the 'Curry was about 20 cents a gallon cheaper.

Indicator on now, gently bleed off the speed. Squeeze the brakes, back into second and ease right into the roadhouse area. He pulled in to the southern entrance. He slipped past the bowsers and then over to the parking area. This was his favorite roadhouse. There wasn't another like it in the entire world. The whole area was covered with gravel and there were three pumps. To the south of the pumps was a corrugated iron shed. Moving northwards one came to the diner. It was an L-shaped building, one section going east-west containing the kitchens and the serving area. This joined a small dining room on the north-south leg and then there was another room devoted to souvenirs. The area enclosed by the L was concreted and covered with a roof; it was also screened to keep out the flies and mozzies. Moving east away from the road was a camping area with space for 12 vans and room for tents. The northern side of the camping area was lined with a concrete ablution block. The generator hut was about 2000 feet away to the south east and could only be heard faintly if the wind came from that direction. There was a dam about 1 mile to the north and another one on the other side of the road.

The roadhouse belonged to Cowan Downs station. It was run by the owner's nephew, Geordie Swan and his wife Anita. When

Anita saw Bluey pull up she said to her husband, 'Geordie, here's that horrible man again. I'm going into the kitchen until he leaves.'

Bluey walked in with his best salesman smile. The light in his eye faded when he couldn't see Anita. He ordered his hamburgers: two with bacon and eggs. He munched them silently and forlornly out on the verandah and after relieving himself he drove on.

Out onto the road, turn right and then 200 feet on turn to the left and head for Dornoch via Nardoo along the bitumen. This was the last long tarred stretch on his mail run. He would look forward to coming back to this section of road for the next three days. This was a straight piece of road raised about 15 feet above the surrounding plain. There were scooped out dams every 200 feet on each side of the read. These holes had been excavated to provide the gravel foundation for the road. There were puddles in most of the dams from the recent storms. Each hole contained the skeletons of bullocks. After the wet these holes were full of water but by the end of the winter they had dried out. The cattle came to drink the last of the water and got bogged in the mud.

Fortunately Bluey had his windows up. The Ford sped by the recent carcasses of some beasts without their smell invading the sanctity of his cabin. There was no time for dreaming now. The road went towards the west so he was driving right into the setting sun. He now regretted the extra hour spent behind the Quamby pub. There wasn't a good place to pull over on this stretch of road. He could get a bed when he pulled into the Dornoch pub after dark.

Bluey woke up in a sweat. The sheets were wet and the smell lingered in the air. He always slept alone. Up here it was too hot to share a bed. He got rid of or left any women before he slept. Last night he had some fun with Rose, the grader driver's daughter. He sent her back to her own bed as soon as he was satisfied.

This morning he felt tired. He had a pain behind his eyes, his tongue felt furry and too large for his mouth. Beer was cool and refreshing when it went down but it always left him stale in the morning. Bluey had two beers and a cigarette for breakfast then he set out for Leichhardt.

The rich blue of the sky dominated the landscape. The dull red hue of the earth complemented the azure and together with the green of the scrub made a perfect picture.

Bluey chugged along the red gravel road, keeping to the crest. Behind the Ford was a large rooster tail of dust. In this country you could see the cars before you could hear them. An air-conditioner was essential. The pressure inside the cab was always greater than outside because of the forced air. In the old days you always got dust everywhere. In your hair, on your tongue, up your nose…

His Ford didn't have to struggle; its powerful V8 muscled along the road. The clearance was fantastic and its force unstoppable. Bluey had never used the impressive winch which snuggled into the bumper bar. $750 was a small price to pay for the insurance it gave!

The trees were green here as the road ran along the Gregory River. The heat was oppressive out in the sun but in the well watered shade it was cool enough for the cattle to browse and enough feed to keep them content.

'Ah, Leichhardt! Jewel of the north!' Bluey sighed to himself. This was one town he loved. He spent at least two or three days here in every fourteen. Or course when the rivers were up he stayed in the 'Curry. One day, perhaps, he would live here and run Escott…, along with Lawn Hill. The worst thing about dreams was that a man had to think hard. The Lawn Hill dream was lovely and the Escott fantasy bliss, but a man would get a headache trying to run them both. Better to stop that dream and go over the sales plan for the day.

Leichhardt was an established town. Back in the white fellah dreamtime, Burke and Wills came through this country. Later, still in that dreamtime, Ludwig Leichhardt passed through the region.

When real time had begun, at the end of the last century, hard men had come into the rich country of the Gulf Rivers. These men had come in with cattle and had built up the great stations of the area.

The Nicholson River flowed east from the Territory. Further south, the Gregory river flowed east then swung north in a lazy curve. The second river met the first and together they flowed north into the Gulf. The last twenty miles of the plain was mangroves and then the salt pans. In places the real land went right out to meet the water. Before the Gregory met the Nicholson, a small river called Beames Brook fed across to the Wills river. The Gregory flowed all year and so did the brook. Between the Nicholson and the Wills there was a 10 mile wide black soil plain running north south for about forty miles. This plain choked off into the mangrove swamps of the coast. The Burke River ran into the Gulf another five miles to the east.

There was an ironstone ridge running along the edge of the plain, about 15 feet above the level of the plain. The Wills river cut through the ridge in a narrow and well defined gorge. At the northern edge of the ridge the Wills tumbled over a 10 foot falls and ran into a tidal estuary.

The town of Leichhardt was planted on the western bank of the little gorge. There were plenty of trees including a massive grove of mangoes running along the bank of the river.

The early cattle men had established a meat works along the ridge to the north of where the town would soon be. After the river had tumbled over the falls it swung westwards along the ridge face before swinging north again. The river was tidal and salt below the falls; it was the home of old man croc! The meat works had been on the ridge to the east of the bend and docks had been driven into the bank on the bend. In the early days river steamers had come and taken the beef to Townsville or Darwin. The town sprang up between the meat works and the gorge.

Leichhardt was, built on a large T. The road from Dornoch ran northwards up the slope and onto the ridge. Another road ran east-west from the docks to cross the T. This junction was about three quarters of a mile from the gorge. It was a bitumen road and it ran from the docks to the river. Because it spanned the gorge, the Wills Bridge was passable all year round. The road continued east after the bridge but it soon became gravel.

*

The southern road was bitumen for about three miles running down off the ridge to the airstrip. This was an all-weather strip and the town's proud boast was that it was the best in the entire Gulf.

Huddled around the T was the lattice of roads which made up the township. The most pleasant sight in the town was the pub, on the left at the junction, coming up from the south. This imposing old stone edifice was grandly known as 'The Burke Arms' and called 'the watering hole', or just 'the pub', by the locals.

The town also had an aberration that Bluey wanted to forget. In the middle twenties some missionaries had come to Leichhardt. In those days all the young aboriginal girls were considered fair game. The station men often had more than one girl and some were as young as twelve. VD was rampant among the blacks. The men of the tribes often came into the stations to find work as stockmen and the women and children gravitated towards the towns and homesteads.

The missionaries came to work among these fringe dwellers. They started a home for young girls who were, in the language of the day, 'in moral danger'. The young man and his wife worked hard but were ostracized by the other whites. The Protector of Aborigines finally persuaded them to move over the river. They founded the mission now known as Boomallooba. Over the years 'the mission', as it was called, had grown to a community of about one-thousand souls.

This backwater of civilization had been on the bank of the Wills River. The Leichhardt people complained when the 'Abos' had taken their fresh water so they were moved to the next river. The boong kids had to come the five and a half miles along the road to go the school. Some soft headed government official had put a hospital at the mission so now there were two hospitals.

There was one very good thing about this place: it kept the boongs out of sight of the real people. In every other northern town the coons seemed to own everything. You were always seeing them around the place sniffing petrol or drinking grog.

Bluey's big blue Ford sped past the road leading to the airstrip. It had been traveling for three hours now. Bluey would be in Leichhardt at 10:30 at this rate. Just an average trip. Tuesday morning and all of the afternoon to sell his wares. He could take MasterCard, Bankcard and Visa, this certainly did improve his sales. He was also hoping to seduce that brown haired bird today. She lived near the cop shop. Second on the right, in town, and then to the left on the second corner. Straight across the road from the police watch house and near their barracks.

He couldn't understand how anyone could live that close, but he supposed that her husband had to be close to his work.

Bluey had no real friends in the town. He didn't live there but had some business arrangements with some of the townsfolk. Some of the men hated him. They were the ones whose wives had succumbed to his charms and opened their legs to him as well as their purses.

The salesman drove up the slight rise onto the ironstone ridge. The glare had been intense for the last few miles on the treeless black soil flat. The yellow of the grass made it worse. His Polaroids cut down on its effulgence but he still felt tight around the forehead and temples. Better book into a room at the hotel and have a shower first. No worries about the water here, the river flowed all year.

A store was just before the pub, on the left. It had a gravel parking lot and was set back about 30 feet from the road. It was only about four years old but was much better than its predecessor. The old corrugated iron shed had been over the road from the pub and about 300 feet to the east. That place had three large freezers and the kitchen table which acted as the counter.

This store had a wide verandah facing east towards the road. There were glass doors in the middle of the balcony leading inside to a regular air-conditioned supermarket. The shop even had a check out! Unheard of in the Gulf, until recently. One bored looking girl chewed gum while customers walked up and down the aisles looking for food, clothes and stationery.

Ronnie Lawler ran this store and the one up the road for the boongs.

Bluey gave Ronnie four boxes of cheap watches and trinkets then happily accepted the check showing a 500 percent mark-up on his cost price. These were delivered direct, by air, from a mail order house in Sydney to Cloncurry. It was much easier to sell these items to the store than to flog them off door to door. Clothes, however, had to be sold by the direct method along with any electrical items. The bigger items made a better profit when relieved of the burden of a middleman.

Ronnie asked Bluey, 'What about the packages for the other store?' He wanted to buy some flagons and sell them out of the back door of his other store in Boomallooba.

The deal was soon settled. Bluey kept some back to sell himself. He didn't want to compete with the pub and make any enemies there. All the sales would be out of town. They would meet down at the other store later in the day.

The mailman felt much better after he had showered and eaten. He had discarded his work clothes and was now a suave business executive. He was dressed for the climate and to suit his style. A bright cool floral shirt hanging out at the waist of some cool white slacks. His regular elastic sided boots were on with a view to ready distal exposure. He began his regular round.

It was not long before our tallyman warmed to his task. The flippant banter, the pleasant cajoling, the rustle of bills and the clack of the press over the plastic money. Twice Bluey offered extra services to women who were bored and frustrated by the tedium of their existence. Twice the women were satisfied and whispered their hopes for his speedy return.

The best was saved for last. He didn't attack this new conquest from the west but came down from the north. The big blue machine gently eased off the road to the northern end of the government high set house. Bluey's professional eye quickly sized up the situation. There was a barbed wire fence around the yard. The gate and the house faced south giving the living area the coolest aspect. The posts underneath had been closed by slatting and the laundry was to the north. The back steps went outside the laundry up to the back door. There were some old established trees in the back yard and a garden border around the slats. The flowers in this garden showed all the signs of succumbing to the harshness of this great land.

From the front, facing the house, there was a tilta-door to the right and a slatted door to allow access when the car entry was closed. The area underneath was concreted. A verandah guarded the front of the house and some stairs went up from the slatted door to this porch.

When Bluey reached the top of the stairs he saw a front door directly ahead and to his left large glass sliding doors. There were windows to two bedrooms to the right. He could faintly hear the wheezing complaints of the air-conditioner as it struggled violently against the November sun. He knocked, stepped back and adjusted his face. His jaded, cynical look was replaced by one of eager but fragile hope.

The door was opened by the brunette he had imagined. She had long well groomed hair, was about 5 feet 6 inches tall and slim. Her body was covered by a light cotton shift. He could tell she wasn't wearing a bra and he could see the outline of her high cut cotton briefs through her dress. He could also smell cheap wine; a good sign!

'Hi, my name is Bluey Walters. I run a small neighborhood business, from time to time in Leichhardt. I visit here once a fortnight and sell clothes and other items…My but you do look lovely. I have just the right thing for you in the van. Something that will show your beauty at its best. All the young men will be after you when you wear it!'

As Bluey was dressing himself after his shower, he heard the woman sobbing in the bedroom. Her name was B Collins but he still didn't know what the 'B' stood for. She was married to the cop sergeant and obviously a Catholic. She had spent $275 on the clothes that he had shown her and had paid by MasterCard. Her husband seemed to enjoy his work judging by all the photos around the place.

As he let himself out he began to wonder about Catholics. They didn't seem to enjoy life. This one was obviously lonely and needed some comfort. She had been reluctant at first but, he had persuaded her. She was like a tigress in bed but then afterwards had looked away. He could feel her shame, so he showered and quickly left.

Why weren't these Catholics realists? They felt guilty when they sinned. It wasn't really sin anyway! Just enjoyment! He despised her for her spinelessness. Why couldn't she just admit that it was good fun? Anyway he would come back later. What did they say? You don't have to look at the mantelpiece when you stoke the fire. The fire stoking certainly was fun and with married women you didn't have any responsibilities. She might feel guilty this time but it would be easier for her the next time. A bit of perseverance on his part and she would become a regular pleasant interlude. He definitely didn't lack any confidence!

The big blue Ford puttered its way back to the pub. He always boasted to his mates that this car was quite stubborn; it would never go past a pub without stopping and having a rest first.

Our red bearded man climbed up onto the bar stool. The bar was dark and cool inside the thick stone walls. Many years ago the stones had been brought here by a sailing ship as ballast. They were very thick and insulated the bar room well. It was 18 feet by 12 feet with the longer axis running east west, parallel to the road outside. There was a door in the north from the entrance and another one in the eastern wall from the lobby. The bar came out from the eastern wall and ran for about 12 feet before it did a bend towards the south where it met the back wall. There was a cool room behind the bar which also had a door to the kitchen out the back. Behind the back wall the bar continued into the ladies' lounge.

Bluey ordered himself a pint of XXXX. He wouldn't be driving any more today but would have to get a good start tomorrow for his drive west.

The publican was a small, dark man; probably a dago and his wife was quite fat. You had to nail a wog's feet to the floor before you hugged her other wise she would slip out the top. The couple ran around and shared jokes with the customers. Antonio and Maria had a reputation, locally, for great food and comfortable rooms. They had even entertained honeymooners upstairs.

Antonio was telling a story. Bluey listened absent-mindedly as he filtered the cool refreshing liquid gold through his moustaches.

'Lasta month. There wasa these a two city slickers coma to my pub. They havea biga trucka and a lotsa guns. They wearing moleskins anda Akubra hatsa. They wanna shoota buffalo.

'I tella them thisa no placa buffaloes. You musta go to Territory. They laugha at me.'

'We finda some here!'

'They go outa in the biga truck with the bedsa in the back. Onea week later they coma back. They alla dirty and wanna shower and gooda roomsa. After they hava their tucker they tella me abouta their hunting.

'We seea this biga buffalo! She a huga! Bigger than we ever dreama! We stalka the buffalo for foura daysa before we shoot him. It wasa bit scary but we brava. We shoota the buffalo, we spenda the tima catcha fish then we go homa.

'They geta in the biga trucka and drive away. I donna even know their car number or addressa. I jusa know they come Melbun.

'Nexta weeka Jacka Watson from Escott coma my bar. He mighty mada. He swearing plenty and drinka whisky. I aska, "What'sa wronga Jacka?" He startsa curse again.

'"Some guys shota my best Brahmin bulla! I killa them! He costa me two hunnert thousand dollarsa." Hesa really mad."

The guys at the bar laughed. All bearded men from the stations or road gangs.

'Them city slickers sure got no brains!'

The A.C.A.I.Q.

It was a typical November day in Brisbane. The mercury was hovering around the hundred degree mark. Clouds were building up over Cunningham's Gap in the South West. There was the promise of another tropical thunderstorm in the afternoon. It was only eleven o'clock and the sky was still clear overhead.

One man in a blue business suit swore impatiently at a red traffic light. He sat comfortably in his Ford LTD, shielded from the heat by his automatic air-conditioning.

The crowds of pre-Christmas shoppers surged up and down the streets of the city. They were flirting with summer colds as they moved into the shops chilled to 70 degrees and out into the heat again.

Over the river at the 'Gabba a crowd was slowly building. It was the third day of the Test Match. The West Indies were three for 45 in their second inning. Australia declared at six for 365 at tea the day before with a lead of 273 runs.

At the top of the Terrace, the Gazebo hotel staunchly defied the heat. It was a cool 72 degrees inside as the huge air-conditioning units gulped in the hot air and wrestled it down to the inside temperature. Outside a middle-aged woman sat on one of the benches overlooking the park. She was overweight and puffing heavily. It was a long walk up the hill, too much for her without a break! The woman cursed her alcoholic husband who forced her into this overnight job in town. She was a cleaner in the Public Service and finished work at nine o'clock. It had taken her two hours to get up this far but soon she would be home. After a hot cup of tea, she would try to rest in her overheated home.

Inside the hotel the guests were comfortable; they were not troubled by the heat. In one of the conference rooms behind the reception area there was silence. The delegates began their conference an hour earlier and were pausing for morning tea; 'smoko' as it is generally called in Queensland. 'Morning tea' was, perhaps, a misnomer. 'Smoko' was correct; a well-lubricated smoko! The attendees were enjoying the chilled selection of tropical fruits, wines and beers.

On the door was a plaque: Monthly Meeting of the Advisory Council for Aborigines and Islanders in Queensland.

The A.C.A.I.Q. was fully funded by the Federal Government. They sought to exert some influence on Aboriginal affairs in Queensland through this body. The socialist politicians in Canberra thought that the money was well spent. This body's goal was, however, more sinister. They longed to declare a white-free homeland in the mineral rich Gulf of Carpentaria. The members of the council had already given themselves the names of government leaders. As international diplomats these ministers visited Moscow and Libya to arrange contracts for uranium once the homeland was declared.

Andrew MacDonald paused and smiled to himself. He was President Elect of 'Murur'. The name they had chosen for the new nation was appropriate. This was the name given to the package taken by warriors when they were going on a vengeance raid. This nation would be the beginning of their vengeance on the 'murdergie', white man.

It was funny that Andrew hated white man. He had blonde hair, blue eyes and needed to use UV cream when he went into the sun. He was 5 feet 11 inches tall had a long narrow face and his hair was clipped and immaculately groomed. His legs were short compared to the rest of his body and quite fat. He had an interesting story: his maternal grandmother was a quarter cast aborigine from Coonabarabran.

The president had grown up in Sydney living in Bellevue Hill with his orthodontist father and solicitor mother. He had gone to Scots College and was the third of three sons. His brothers were both duxes of the school and were now Queens Councils in Sydney. He had done poorly when he was at school and wanted to leave when he was fifteen. His mother sent him to her mother for a holiday. She intended to shock him into some responsibility.

Andrew found himself a cause as well as lots of nice young girls. He returned to Sydney and eventually became a lawyer and aboriginal activist.

The meeting was called to order. Andrew insisted that everything was done to order; his order! He scanned the people in front of him. Billy Ah Chee, sitting on Andrew's right at the round table, was the Vic President and Minister for Finance. He was a short man, 5 feet 1 inch tall and weighed 7 stone after a thunderstorm, dripping wet. He was of mixed Chinese and Aboriginal descent. His Chinese forbears had come to North Queensland to look for gold. His skin was the color of copper and his hair was long enough to be permed into thick curls. He was mercurial in nature with a very quick temper. Billy was also a charismatic speaker and good at negotiations. He had recently returned from Moscow having made proposed agreements for uranium and other minerals in Murur. Billy was finding it hard to keep quiet and wait for his turn to report.

Archie Riversleigh was on Andrews left. He was the Treasurer. He was responsible for the A.C.A.I.Q.'s ten million dollar annual budget. They had money from the government, from foreign sources, from the sale of alcohol in aboriginal communities and the importation of drugs. He was the remains of a once powerful man. Archie played rugby league for Queensland some years ago. This man was a full-blooded aborigine from Kowanyama up in the Cape. He was 6 feet 2 inches tall and his 17 stone included a large beer belly. He had large shoulders and his hands were like bunches of bananas. His long hair was straight black and hung down in dank strands. His legs were long and on the thin side like most full-bloods. The treasurer had helped to paint the bank up in Georgetown so he was well qualified for his job.

Nigel Jackson sat opposite Andrew. He was the Special Minister for State. Nigel was 5 feet 9 inches tall and weighed 11 stone. He was neither imposing in size nor personality. He was medium brown in color and had spent two years in the Australian Army before he was discharged for smoking marijuana. Mr Jackson was in charge of a profitable business in North Queensland smuggling drugs, alcohol, rare animals and plant seeds. The many square miles of tropical rainforest were ideal areas for growing pot.

Raymond Walden was the Minister for Resources. He was responsible for coordinating the sale of the natural resources belonging to Murur. Ray was a mixture of races. His mother was half Afghan and half Chinese. His pedigree was more diverse on his father's side. Ray's grandfather was a Japanese pearl diver and his grandmother was half aboriginal and half Irish. He was 5 feet 7 inches tall and weighed 10 stone. There was evidence of his Chinese and Japanese ancestry in his eyes while his skin color was mid brown. He had done well in school but had left Quilpie, where he lived with his aboriginal grandmother, to work on a cattle station. The cattle slump had forced him out of his career as a ringer and back to school. Ray went to Queensland University and then Harvard where he did a Masters degree in Political Science. He then returned to Brisbane after spending two years in Moscow. Ray at twenty seven was a promising politician but he had a weakness for alcohol.

Charles Lawson, the Foreign Minister, made up the group at the table. He came from Adelaide. He was 6 feet tall and weighed a trim 12 stone. Charles was about five o'clock, in the common way of stating color. He had just returned from Cuba where they had discussed the equipping and training of the Murur Armed Forces.

'How was Moscow, Billy?' Raymond asked.

Andrew quickly stepped in, 'Ray, you must address all your remarks to the chair! Don't talk out of order... Now we will ask our Foreign Minister to make his report.'

'We had a good time in Cuba. As you know I went with three of our young men. They spent the two weeks with a Cuban Army regiment.'

'We must get them to give us a report later on!' interrupted Andrew.

'Fidel was very nice to us. He said that we should get as much area as we could for our land. He also suggested that we control as much water as we can.'

'That's a good idea, Charlie! I wonder how far we should go.' Andrew mused.

Billy had been waiting for his chance, 'Mr Chairman!'

'Yes Billy?'

'The people in Moscow thought that we should go for all the uranium areas in the north.'

'I don't think that we could get Darwin or any of the cities on the main north south line.' Nigel chipped in.

Andrew quickly took control again, 'There would be more money for us in uranium. We would do well to let the white guys keep the cities. It would be hard for them to keep their economies going. If we can get the minerals then we will control the wealth.'

Ray coughed.

'Yes, Ray?'

'Mr President. I think that we can ruin the channel country and the areas south of there if we can control the water. The monsoon rains usually fall as far south as the Selwyn Ranges. The great inland rivers flow south from there. If we can dam the Diamantina, the Georgina and the Thompson then we could sell the water!'

'That's a good idea! I think we should get as far south as the Tropic of Capricorn.' Andrew replied.

'We could get the Barcoo as well, then.' Ray added.

Andrew reasserted his authority; 'Is there anyone who wants to try and define our boundaries? ... Yes Charles?'

'Let's say everything north of the Tropic as well as everywhere else we have land rights.'

Andrew knew his history well, 'We can't have a divided nation! Countries divided into two sections usually end up as two countries. Look at Pakistan…'

Billy interrupted, 'Come on Andrew, that's a lot of bull! We can use our divided land to negotiate for more territory. What about Hitler, he joined up his country.'

Andrew was angry now. It hurt him to have anybody mock his ideas. He had charisma, he had charm, he was appealing, but he was arrogant and couldn't accept the second place.

'Billy, you have no right to speak out of place. I will ignore your outburst. If you won't accept party discipline you can leave your job now! There are many people with qualifications like yours who can do your job!'

Billy kept his cool. The position of Minister for Finance was better than the dole or settlement work in the north of Queensland.

Archie cleared his throat discreetly, 'Mr President, I have heard that OVG have made some good finds up in the Gulf.'

'What do you mean, Archie?' Andrew was interested.

'Well, I hear that they have been drilling for oil up near the Nicholson River.' Archie continued.

'What is the verdict?' Andrew was eager to hear.

'They have found a good supply of oil. It is not like Arab oil but it's better than Bass straight.' Archie was happy. He had made the best contribution today.

Andrew decided to shelve the other discussions for a while. They would work for a short term advantage.

'I wonder if there are any sacred sites in that area? We should get someone up there to talk to the local tribal elders. If we can find some good areas for land rights we should get a lot of money out of the oil. It would be good for our cause… We will have to get someone on a plane this afternoon.'

Ray was very eager to get away. He enjoyed the wide open spaces and the bush. He was also Minister for Resources.

'Excuse me, Mr President…'

'Yes, Ray?'

'That's good country up there. Rains every year, plenty of water. I'm Minister for Resources. Can I go up and see the local elders?'

'Well … Ray, we can't really let you go up there. You've got a real problem.'

'I'll be right.'

'You know what happens when you drink. If you get too much pressure, then anything could happen.'

'I've got over that problem now. I know all about these things. Send me!'

'Okay, Ray. I'll send you. You have a good chance to prove yourself. Do you know anyone in Mt Isa? There are a lot of people up there with relatives in the Gulf. I expect you'll have to go up to Leichhardt, that's the big place up there. The old tribal people live on the mission station near the township. But remember, don't drink!'

'Rightio, boss!'

The meeting continued but Ray had stopped listening. He was looking forward to catching the plane that afternoon.

A Press Conference

Vivian Swan sucked in his breath and drank a glass of cold water. He was dressed in a tailored blue, pin striped suit with a white shirt and a red spotted tie. His dark hair was carefully cut and groomed. His hair dresser had begun to despair of hiding the growing bald patch on his crown. He was a thin man with a dark, five o'clock shadow face. Many afternoons were punctuated by the sound of a strop and the slap of a brush. Viv was a conservative man and had a high regard for his own masculinity. He imagined that the people who knew that he used the cut throat razor admired his ruggedness.

His nervousness was understandable. Viv was the high flyer of the cabinet. At thirty four years a man shouldn't even be a minister, let alone Minister for Police! On top of all that he was Deputy Premier and heir apparent. It was not widely known but his aging boss, Wolfgang Hammerstein, had cancer. Viv recently found this out and was beginning to feel the pressure of succession.

Every episode before the public had to show his authority and integrity. He was not going to stumble this close to the coveted prize! He could expect to be Premier soon and then after ten years or so a carefully choreographed move to Canberra and immortality.

The main problem on Viv's mind was Jock Williams. He was ready to accept the Premiership 20 years ago when Wolfgang pipped him at the post then. Jock was waiting for Viv to stumble so that he could steal the crown.

There were four men in the office. It was tastefully decorated in reds and yellows. A large window looked out over the Brisbane River and its beautiful south bank. Viv could sit and watch the spectacular fountain from his window at night. The office was high enough to see over the freeway. It was one floor below the premier's penthouse. He had luxurious motel style accommodation next to his office and three floors below was the parliamentary gym.

The Police Minister sat behind a Jarrah desk with his three minders sitting in the comfortable red leather armchairs. The colors had been carefully chosen to remind the Deputy Premier of his Carpentaria electorate and homeland in the eastern Gulf. His minders were all well over 6 feet tall and towered over Viv's 5 feet 7 inches but this gave him an air of executive authority.

'What's this conference about, Rick?'

His senior minder answered, 'Just the regular weekly news conference. With the boss away you're acting premier and need to reassure the people of a wise hand at the wheel.'

'Good, let's go!' Viv did a great job of hiding his apprehension.

The four men walked out of the office and straight into a lift. The executive lift remained at the floor on which the top man was, at any time. It went silently and swiftly down to the press rooms seven floors below. This parliamentary building had a scrupulously controlled climate. The windows were all tinted to reduce the glare. These privileged men had to be able to dress for England, with impunity, in the Brisbane heat.

The press room was large and comfortable. There was a long table with seven chairs between the table and the window. In front of this were carefully spaced lounge chairs with plenty of space for camera crews. The regular gaggle of political journalists were here and their camera crews were waiting with barely disguised boredom. At this time of the year nothing ever happened. They were all waiting for the traditional cabinet meeting at Tangalooma and then the Christmas recess.

Viv's eyes flicked over the assembled roundsmen. He corrected his thoughts; roundspersons! There was only one worthy of notice: Ted Stewart, the old bloodhound. Viv searched through his mind wondering why he was here.

Ted was a big man. At 6 feet 5 inches tall he easily dominated the gallery. He wasn't only tall but tipped the scale at 17 stone. He carried his forty two years as easily as his blond locks. His chest was just beginning to slip.

This man was feared throughout the country by those who knew him. He was the nations leading investigative journalist. He worked for the top rating 'Today Under Review' current affairs program at 6:30 on Channel Thirteen. He was usually onto something big and very few people came out smelling nice when he was finished with them.

Viv composed himself as he sat. He was outwardly calm and relaxed but, in reality, his mind was racing.

The regular banal questions began. The acting premier fielded them with ease. His confidence started to soar.

Old Jock slipped into the back row with a smug look. He seemed like a waiting vulture, eager to feed on an abandoned carcass.

'Mr. Acting Premier, what do you intend to do in order to minimize this year's road toll?'

'We have cancelled all leave and intend to have the largest police presence ever seen on Queensland roads!'

'Yes, but what about the ongoing situation?'

'We have that well in hand!'

'Surely the roads contribute to the carnage. They are the worst in the country!'

'You know that's a lie, Jason!'

Another one of the hacks took up the cudgels.

'Can you do anything about speed and other disregard for the road rules?'

'We have a plan to combat that…'

'What about…?'

'Let me complete my answer! We plan to bring in a system whereby every car in the state has a small radio transmitter with a unique signature.'

'Blah, blah, blah...' The meeting droned on but there was anticipation in the air. They were all going through the motions, no one really wanted a big story to spoil the Christmas break. Each person was waiting for Ted to speak up. Something big was in the air. Perhaps someone would find fame in the next few weeks.

Ted cleared his throat, 'Excuse me, Mr. Acting Premier.'

'Yes, Mr. Stewart?'

'There has been a disgraceful history of violence to Aborigines in police custody in this state.'

Viv breathed a sigh of relief. His record was good in this matter.

'In the last six months eight Aborigines have died in jails in this country. In every case the circumstances were suspicious.'

'We have only had one Aboriginal death in our jails in the last two years. All the other deaths were interstate.'

'I have heard that there was a cover up in that case!'

'The man died in tragic circumstances. He was known to the police as an aggressive alcoholic. He regularly drank after his Saturday game of rugby league and bashed any woman he could find.'

'He was killed for that?'

'This man suffered a broken neck during his game. He was found drunk that night and put in jail. Later that night he had a fight with another man and died as a result of his earlier injury.'

'That sounds like a cover up!'

'There was a coronial inquiry. Andrew MacDonald, an Aboriginal lawyer, assisted and he was satisfied!'

Ted changed his tack, ‘We have evidence to show that Aborigines are still beaten in Queensland jails. I also have evidence that a directive from your office has sanctioned this approach to justice.’

‘Show me the directive!’

‘It says, I quote, “When Aborigines are put in jail, great care must be taken to show that they are not marked. We don’t want any Aborigines found dead in our jails.”’

‘Yes, I sent that directive. Its meaning is plain. No one is to be beaten in our jails especially Aborigines.’

‘We have heard that the real meaning is this: “Beat them up but don’t mark them.”’

‘I will quote from memory another paragraph in that same report, “No police officer will be disciplined for assaulting any prisoner. He will immediately be discharged and pursued to the full extent of the law.”’

‘Some say that means; “Do it; but don’t get found out.” They say your office is notorious for saying one thing and doing another.

‘Fortunately, Mr. Stewart, justice is not determined by the abstruse insinuations of your sordid mind! You are trying to whip up a story out of nothing. I refuse to become a victim of your squalid attempts to create a journalistic award for yourself. We have a policy of no police violence and I insist that this be kept. No police officer will be allowed to get away with any assault. If you can point to any incident we will call a royal commission and every guilty party will be punished without mercy.’

‘Thank you Mr. Acting Premier!’

The questions continued. Viv noticed that Jock walked out looking disappointed. He felt triumphant. Defeating Ted Stewart was a real feather in his cap.

When the five men were back in the office Viv tried to cover his tracks carefully.

'Rick, send a special message to every police station in the state. It has to be read and acknowledged by every officer, even the cadets.'

'Ready, Viv, what do you want it to say?'

'Every police officer suspected of assaulting prisoners will be suspended until the incident is fully investigated. If there is a case to be answered the officer will be charged and prosecuted to the full extent of the Law.'

'What about a special paragraph about murder?'

'Any prisoners found dead in jail will result in an immediate investigation. Police officers whose actions contribute to the death of prisoners will be found guilty of premeditated murder. An amendment is being made to the Crimes Act to include this eventuality.'

The letter was drafted and then sent to the legal section to be checked and validated.

Viv sent his men to their own quarters and then slipped down for his regular exercise in the parliamentary gym.

Ted Stewart smiled to himself after Viv had left. He threw out his second cigarette pack for the day and opened his third. After that exchange Andrew MacDonald, his intended victim, would now be lulled into a false sense of security.

The Sergeant

While Bluey was stirring in the Gregory Hotel imagining his time in Leichhardt, another man was already getting up from his bed. He had a slight headache and the taste of stale beer and tobacco in his mouth. He sucked in his raspy breath and hacked out a deep, painful cough. This man spat his thick, dark yellow phlegm into the sink in the bathroom.

His bedroom was untidy, but that didn't bother him. Even though heavy blinds were pulled down, they were too weak to overcome the strong tropical sun even at this early hour. The room was too bright for more sleep.

The bathroom was just across the hall and easily accessible from the bedroom. He spat again and then lit up the first of at least fifty cigarettes for the day. He inhaled deeply blew out the smoke and inhaled again, savoring the rejuvenating drug. Soon he began to feel his nerves calm down. He limped painfully on his left knee and cursed the storm season. Every wet he felt the agony of low atmospheric pressure but plenty of grog eased his pain and anaesthetized his soul.

Ernie Collins, police sergeant and lord of Leichhardt, didn't have much time for reflection! He pulled out a can of XXXX and drank greedily. Then he took his second cigarette and began to feel human again. After a while he limped back down the hall and into the bedroom. It had one high long window above the double bed and another full window facing on to the verandah. They had a regulation Department of Works dressing table opposite the full window and the other wall was covered by and open, built in wardrobe. One of its doors was broken. The bed, under the long window, was starting to sag. Ernie stretched his sore back and rubbed his inflamed liver.

His wife was snoring gently on the bed in an alcohol induced sleep. He fondly remembered their first meeting eleven years ago. She was only sixteen but looked twenty one. He smiled with pleasure as he though of her delicate naked body… Then her pregnancy and abortion that he forced her to have. She couldn't have any kids after that. She hadn't been the same since.

Bernice still loved frilly little nighties. He sighed and looked at her now: a small nylon shift twisted up around her waist, pink knickers and one breast hanging out. There was no top sheet and the bottom one was crumpled. Ernie often wondered how he fit his 6 feet 7 inch frame around her on the bed.

The sergeant showered. He looked down at his scrawny body. His arms had lost their firmness and so had his legs. His belly didn't hang out though!

He lathered himself up well and then stayed under the cool water of his shower for about twenty minutes. The refreshing coolness helped to take some of the tiredness out of his body. When the temperature only dropped to 85 degrees at night, it was hard to sleep well. He was looking forward to the rain when the heat would ease for a time and so would the pain in his knee.

Ernie toweled himself down, and was already sweating when he pulled on his clothes. Regulation Queensland tropical police uniform. He always wore the blue with pride. His big boots were polished carefully. Ernie had his second beer and his third cigarette before he cleaned his teeth.

He was ready to leave. He didn't worry about disturbing Bernice. It was only 6:30 and she could do with the sleep. The sergeant loved her in his own way but didn't show it very well. He thought back to his own parents. The days at the old Charleville pub were great with Bill and Elsie but that all ended when he was eleven. She shot through with a salesman to Brisbane and they took him along. The salesman cleared out before long but Bill had divorced Elsie by then. Bill wouldn't see him again because he had gone with Elsie. The family after that was rubbish. Marriage to Andy Beckett who died six months later and then a series of de factos. He was big by then and playing first grade rugby league so he left home and met Bernice.

Pity they couldn't have any children but he would never leave her. He was a bit worried about all the wine she had been drinking lately. It did help to numb her loneliness, though.

Ernie slipped down the steps and over the road to the police station. It was a long low building and air conditioned. Thank goodness for the police union! He walked past the watchouse cells and into the main office.

Angie Johnny was in there already cooking; breakfast for the inmates. Ernie drank some coffee and ate three eggs on toast with the drunks before he took Angie down to the last cell. It was shielded from the other cells and normally reserved for females. No one was in there this morning.

Angie was a slight, pretty Aboriginal girl. She had been Ernie's lover for about two years now. At eighteen she had a promising career ahead of her. Not many Aborigines were employed by the Queensland Public Service Board. The sergeant had taken her under his wing.

Somewhere in his Catholic part there was a dull recollection of the penguins telling him that adultery was mortal sin. He didn't care about that now! Nuns and priests and their rules were just a bad memory.

Ernie did not feel any guilt or any sense of wrongdoing about his affairs. He loved Bernice and would never do anything to hurt her; but the fire had gone out of their marriage. He was always gentle with her but never satisfied now. The sergeant prided himself on being a great lover.

As a great sexual athlete; once or twice a week, with little fire, was not enough for him!

There was no real love in his extra relationships. The girls were just boongs. Not good for much but spreading their legs. His physical needs were met and they wouldn't want anything more from him. After all everybody knew that the black women were hungry for white men at any price. This particular girl was one to treat carefully, however. She was the grand daughter of Jumbo Seven Emus. He was the closest thing that the coons had to a chief up there. Jumbo had considerable influence with the Department of Boongs and could get a policeman transferred. Angie was sensible, she took the pill because she wanted to move down to the Isa and didn't want to get pregnant and spoil her life. Anyway, it was true that boongs were mad about sex and would do anything to get it.

They only had till 7:30 to have breakfast and sex, so they didn't waste any time. Ernie knew that she enjoyed it and he was satisfied. At thirty eight he could still give a woman, any woman, all that she could take.

When the two detectives arrived for their duty at 7:30 Angie had just begun to clean up the breakfast.

The rules had been bent a bit to allow her to have this second, part time job. There was an emergency last year when old Ida had died and, anyway, Angie needed the money.

The police station was entered through the main shop front room, or charge room. It had a counter behind which the duty officer sat or stood, in front there were chairs and a space for anyone who had to wait. To the right as one came in there was a corridor leading to the cells, the sergeant's office was off this corridor. To the left was a door leading to the lunch room and the officers' desks. The complex was air conditioned, except for the cells.

This cell block consisted of two rooms, one large and divided into four holding pens. Each had two sets of bunks, a wash basin and a toilet. The smaller room had one similar pen for women and a kitchen-washroom. The single cell was invisible from the other bay.

Every prisoner in the larger block could be seen by all the other prisoners. This was to keep violence down to a minimum. In this part of the world the prisoners were usually drunks who were let out the next morning. The prisoners were always persuaded to wash the floor and clean up any mess before they went home.

Bill Ransley and Ossie Schaub reported to Ernie in his office. He was reading the latest police journal and drinking a cup of brewed coffee. An inevitable cigarette was suspended from the corner of his mouth. Bill was solid with black hair and brown eyes. He was a plodder who would always have the hack postings. Ossie was balding and already running to fat. Both were over 6 feet tall as regulations stipulated a minimum height and weight. The men were correctly dressed with their belts and gun holsters polished. Ernie had no complaints about their attire.

'Better get out and do some running, Ossie!'

'Yes, sarge.'

'The new regulations say all police officers must have a good level of fitness, you know.'

'I've been trying to lose weight but I can't. In this climate you gotta drink lotsa beer, it's so hot.'

'Yeah, I know.'

'You're not too fit yourself!'

'I've got an injury! When the inspector comes up from Isa I'll send you out to the border to patrol for a week.'

'I'll lose plenty of weight out there, anyway. What if I get bogged?'

Those bludgers never come up in the summer so you don't have to worry about that.'

Ernie gave Ossie the station keys and went out to his police car.

The police further south had Falcons or Commodores but up here they had Toyotas. Those slick city machines wouldn't last long in this country! Ernie's Toyota was a short wheelbase, petrol engined hardtop. There were extra fuel tanks and it could go about 800 miles without a fill. It was grey in color and had a blue police light on the top. The back section was caged so that he could carry any troublemakers back to the can.

First visit today was Eddie Jack, the Aboriginal police sergeant on the mission. Ernie had overall responsibility for the whole area but they had their own police force out at the mission. Eddie was the sergeant and had been in that position for about six years. His four constables were regularly changing. They gave anyone, who could stay sober, the job until he got drunk.

Eddie did a good job out there but Ernie felt he had to go out there about once a week to fly the flag. There were some things over which the Aboriginal police had no jurisdiction. The whites who went there without permission had to be dealt with by Ernie.

Sergeant Collins' Toyota started easily. The seat and steering wheel were hot as was the air outside. The sergeant turned on the air conditioner and turned the fan up to 'high'. He left the door open until the cold air began to blast out of the vents. Another gift from the police union. Long patrols in this country would be impossible without cool air. It wasn't long ago when the police had to get out there in hot cars and before that they patrolled on horse back or camels.

Police cars were always parked to the south of the station. Ernie's had the eastern spot and got the morning sun but it was in shade from about nine o'clock on.

He eased out onto the north-south road and turned left. Past the station, slow down for the intersection. He passed his own house and saw Bernice hanging out the washing. He tooted the horn and she waved. Up to the nurse's quarters on the right and then the bitumen road. Ernie stopped and looked both ways. His trained eyes swept the scene to see if there was anything wrong.

An ironstone ridge dropped away quickly in front of him to the river. He eased out onto the bitumen road and turning right and began to head east. He pulled down the shade. The sun was still low enough to trouble him. Out here in the west the sunrise was later but in December and January it didn't get dark till nine o'clock at least.

A borehead was on his right now, spilling out hot smelly water to run down towards the river. It was heavily encrusted with lime and nitrates. In the first thirty years of the century the river didn't flow all year. When the beef works were here they needed extra water and so a bore was sunk. There was plenty of fresh water now. The bore was about as useless as tits on a bull.

A mango grove was on both sides of this road along the river bank. There were some boong kids trying to get the remains of the mangoes. Greedy blighters they were. They wouldn't wait for them to ripen in August but got them 'uncooked'. Some of them got quite bad burns around their mouths. No brains though, they would do it again next year.

The season for mangoes was over now so they would only find some old ones right at the top of the tree. Some years the flying foxes came and you couldn't sleep for the noise.

Ernie was on the bridge now. It had been rebuilt two years ago. The old wooden one was unsafe. The new one was concrete but it had no sides. In the last two years three drunks had driven their cars over the side. One had drowned but it didn't count because his skin was as dark as the night on which it had happened.

Ernie's Toyota bumped off the bridge and the bitumen and onto the gravel. The council didn't bother to continue the bitumen down to the mission.

Immediately a billowing red cloud of dust sprung up behind Ernie. He was unconcerned in his climate-controlled cocoon. Almost five miles and he reached the mission. Three long streets parallel to the river and two more short ones to the south of the main road. They weren't given any special names. The mission had grown away from the river. The best houses were close to the main road and to the west of the road that was farthest from the river.

The best houses, a row of twelve, were built with Federal Government money. They were the silver of aluminum and high set. The upper class coons lived here. The next row were low set and about fifteen years old. The next four rows were built by the missionaries. They had been built during the depression and were, for the time, outstanding; two rooms with a concrete floor. These houses were corrugated iron and painted many different colors. The paint was peeling and the houses were all drab. Towards the river, bunched in an untidy array, was a group of humpies. These were for new comers who had moved in from the territory.

North of the road was reserved for administration. There was a hospital, store and post office. The abo kids bussed every day to town for school. The Queensland education people had stuck with the original school even though there were one thousand people on the mission and only three hundred in the town. The white, government people lived on top of the ridge, behind the store.

The trees thickened and were more established towards the river. They had been planted much earlier. There was another gorge, about thirty feet deep, through which the Burke River ran all year.

The main road plunged over the edge of the gorge down a steep incline and over a crossing. There was water running under a culvert here, at this time of the year. This road climbed back up and mounted the other side of the gorge.

Ernie pulled up to the left on the lip of the gorge. A local jailhouse was here. Eddie lived over the road from the hospital but Ernie met him in his small office behind the Post Office.

Eddie was sitting in his office waiting for his visitor. Wearing his Queensland police blues. He had a light blue shirt with dark blue trousers and polished boots. His blue gaberdine jacket was hanging on the rack behind him next to his grey felt hat.

As he walked in Ernie fought his impulse to gag. Eddie was clean but the sergeant didn't like his smell. Here in the office it was almost overpowering. It was small bare room with cheap lino on the floor. There was a table serving as a desk and two chairs. There wasn't even a fan in here and even though the room had two windows the heat was oppressive. These police didn't do paperwork that was the responsibility of the government employees who had better offices in the air conditioned portion of the Post Office complex.

'Let's go outside and sit under one of the trees, Eddie.'

'Sure, Mr Collins.'

The abos always called the whites Mr or Mrs. It was a good subservient habit they had picked up over the years.

Eddie was glad to get out of there as well. He hated the indoors. At his own home he slept on the verandah when it was wet and by a fire on the ground all the other times.

'Any problems here?'

'We got one real bad fellah.'

'Who's that?'

'That fellah name Norman King.'

'Oh, him!'

'He bin selling cooking vanilla to them young fellah. They get plenty drunk!'

'What do you want us to do with him?'

'We get rid of him, dreckly. You fellah make sure he no come back. He gotta get on the plane.'

'He's going to be banished is he?'

'Yeah!'

The men continued to talk as the sat in the cool shade of another big mango tree. There was a bench built around the trunk for times like this.

*

Norman was a bit of a renegade. He had caused a lot of trouble; at one stage he was accused of raping a girl but nothing could be proved. Someone gave her a good hiding and she went to Mt. Isa.

The local aboriginal council had a lot of power on the reserve. They had declared the area 'dry'. No one was meant to bring any alcohol onto the place. They also had the right to refuse entry to anyone. The government employees, who helped with administration, had access but could be transferred if the council complained. Banishment, temporary or permanent, was available for any who would not accept the local rules. The area between the Burke and Wills rivers, from the coast to the junction of the rivers, was tribal land. There was also a strip of land five miles wide on the other side of the Burke which was included. It was good, well watered country and the Aboriginal Council ran cattle between the rivers.

Ernie would be happy to see the back of Norman King. He was more trouble than he was worth. In fact it would be best for everybody if someone put him in a wooden overcoat.

The two sergeants chatted together for about thirty minutes before Ernie returned to his vehicle and headed back to his jurisdiction.

His grey Toyota was about half full of petrol. Ernie pulled up outside the pub, next to the bowsers. This was a good sideline for the pub. There was no other place within 50 miles where petrol could be bought. In fact the next bowsers were at the Dornoch hotel. The stations all had their own fuel. Antonio Luchese made a good deal of money out of his monopoly. He charged at least 20 cents more a gallon than they did in Isa. He price was usually a cent or two less than Dornoch, however.

Maria came out of the pub, 'Fill her up, Capitano?'

'Yeah!'

Ernie slipped inside for an 'orange juice'. He wasn't officially allowed to drink alcohol while on duty but everybody knew a man couldn't get through the day without a little drink every now and then.

When the tank was full and the glass empty he signed the docket and pulled out for his patrol.

A quick call in at home to see Bernice was essential. Ernie would be away for one or maybe two nights before he got back. He gave Bernice a quick kiss.

'Got enough money, love?'

'Well, I can use the credit card. I might try and buy a new dress for the Christmas party.'

'Okay, here's twenty dollars for milk and food.'

'Thanks.'

'See ya termorrer or the next day.'

'Bye.'

The sergeant checked his watch as he pulled westwards towards the main road. It was 9:30. Good time!

The Toyota swung off the main north-south road about 30 minutes before the big blue Ford purred past that junction.

The main road ran parallel to the Gregory River and about a mile to the east. The road to the west cut away about 15 miles south of Leichhardt. This road crossed the Gregory just below the point where it joined the Nicholson.

There was another road running between the main road and the river. It was called the Punjaub road. Ernie had heard about this track a few times and had always wanted to try it out. It ran along the river bank, between the flood channels and wended its way through the thick river scrub.

This road was cool and fresh. It was in shade all the way. The river trees were all tall and majestic. The sergeant didn't know the names of any of them. Heavy undergrowth grew luxuriantly.

Everyone said that this was a good road to drive. It had been one of the best in the shire. The boss from Southwell had used this road when he was on the council. He needed good access to town in those days. It soon became obvious that the road hadn't been used for about 15 years.

Ernie slowed down and growled along in second gear. He was in no particular hurry. He didn't have to squint against the glare. The color green was good for the eyes. Much better than yellow or red. This was the country that one dreamt about. Living in a place like this you wouldn't get any wrinkles around your eyes.

Suddenly a track cut in from the side. The road began to look more used. There wasn't any growth between the tire grooves.

Ernie jammed on the brakes and bought his vehicle to a sudden halt. He pulled the car off the road and into the undergrowth. He had sniffed the scent of a problem. He pulled out his revolver and slipped along the track.

The sergeant appreciated the shade even though the heat seemed to squeeze his chest. He doubled over and kept his eyes peeled for snakes. Soon he heard voices and the track opened into a clearing. The side road had obviously been bulldozed while ahead of him was an open area. There were enough trees left standing to make the field invisible from the air.

There was a large crop of marijuana. Nestled away at the edge of the plantation was an iron shed. The roof was covered with shade cloth to camouflage of from any planes which might fly over.

Ernie marveled to himself. This place must belong to some locals. It was on a high bit of land that didn't get flooded. He had spotted this Island from the air during the big '76 flood. It was about a mile long and 100 yards wide. The spot in front of him was about 20 yards wide and 200 yards long. There was an irrigation system to pump in any water needed during the dry.

The sergeant nosed forward carefully. It took him 10 minutes to cover the 150 feet to the shed. He was concerned that he might meet an angry man with a machine gun.

He listened carefully near one of the windows. He could hear the sound of snoring. Quickly he jumped in the door and lifted his revolver. He laughed out loud. There was Ritchie Arnold sound asleep on a bed. Behind him in the shed was a large mound of dried dope.

He laughed again and said, 'Who's the dope!'

'Wha…! Oh damn! Sergeant!'

Ritchie rubbed his eyes and swore loudly to himself. Paul Arnold, his brother, poked out from behind one of the piles.

'Oh, damn'

The brothers were like a set of book ends. Both were over six feet tall with wide shoulders and thick necks. Both were wearing green king gee shorts and blue singlets. Paul's had a large tear through which his belly fought to hang free.

Ritchie was nineteen and his brother was seventeen. They were the half caste sons of Ambrose Da Silva, owner of Covent Garden, a big station along the eastern bank of the river. It had been owned by the Cholmondely family for about eighty years and named after some place in their native England. The last of the line had a daughter who married Da Silva.

This was a man with no scruples. He gave his wife three children but also managed to father quite a few others. His housekeeper, Noreen Arnold, had mothered these two boys.

They were both well muscled but local legend attributed them with an IQ of 10 between them. Some even said they took it in turns to have the whole of it to themselves but you could never tell which had it. Both men lived at the twenty mile outstation, just beside this island, on the river bank.

It looked like they were trying to earn some extra money.

'What you guys growing here, then?'

'We got some grass, sergeant.' Paul replied.

Both boys were scared. Ernie was known to be rough with abos. They thought that he might shoot them so they made no sudden moves.

'You know that you've broken the law?'

'Yeah!'

'This could cost you ten years at Stewart Creek!'

'Maybe we do something for you?'

'Your dad would kick you right off the station if he found out!'

'Sarge, I'll do anything! Doan tell the ol' man!'

'This crop has to be destroyed, first.'

'Sure thing, Sarge. Anything you say!'

'I want you to get some Round Up and spray all the marijuana outside.'

'Yeah, yeah!' Paul was still talking even though he was the younger.

Ernie noticed that Ritchie had wet his pants. Perhaps he had some kangaroos loose in the top paddock, like everyone said.

'You sold any of this stuff yet?'

'No, we doan know how!'

Ernie believed that after this conversation.

'Okay, get rid of the stuff in here and knock down the shed.'

'Dreckly, Sergeant.'

'How much dope is stored in here, then?'

'I reckon about a ton.'

'Load it on the truck and chuck it in the river.'

'Okay!'

The two boys got their battered Toyota out and quickly loaded the marijuana. They drove the load over to the river and threw it into the deep, flowing water.

'What you want now, Sarge?'

'Go home and come into town next week. I want to see ya. By that time all the grass here has to be sprayed. Don't let it happen again!'

'No!'

The whole episode took two hours. It was now one o'clock.

Ernie watched the two boys drive back to the east on their rough and ready track. They growled their way over the bed of the dry second channel. In the wet the water would be roaring down there as well.

The main road led over the bridge and away to the west for about half a mile before it cut down to the south.

This bridge was in a sad state of disrepair. There were two large tree trunks laid across the river and flat planks had been bolted to them. During the wet it would be well submerged. About half the planks were missing.

Our policeman edged his car down to the place where road met bridge. He stopped and looked at the place where the grass had been thrown. There was no trace of it. In front of him the bank had been washed away leaving a gaping hole to cross first.

The scene looked peaceful and harmless. Large trees hung over the bank and on the other side there was a nice open area to the left of the road. Ernie slipped into first gear and then selected low range four wheel drive. He eased out the clutch and blithely drove over the bridge unaware of the danger.

Anyone watching would have seen the back wheels slide dangerously on the logs but manage to grab the planks before they plunged down. Four times he should have gone over and four times his luck held.

When the big man was safe on the other side he got out of his vehicle and prepared his dinner.

He set some lines with beef bait and then made his fire. He boiled the billy and checked his lines. Two had lost their bait, the third had a long neck turtle and the last one had a sleepy cod.

This turtle was quickly decapitated and thrown on the coals. It was left to stew in its own juices while the fisherman filleted the cod and cooked the fillets in an old army dixie. A handful of tea leaves in the billy completed his preparation. There was a loaf of bread in his tucker bag. He cut off three slices and then made a fish sandwich. The turtle shell had cracked so he pulled it off the fire. He threw the bottom of the shell away and then ate the few choice morsels from among the guts. A cup of tea complemented his meal and then he stretched out on the bank for a siesta.

At three o'clock Ernie got up and drove on. The westward track soon pulled out of the trees and onto the open plain. He had to squint again but the road was better here.

Soon the route headed back south again and past Punjaub. Time for a quick chat. He hadn't bought any mail but the folk at the homestead were always glad to see a friendly face.

This day's patrol came to an end at 6:30. He was staying overnight at Southwell Downs. The station house was very large and high set. It had wide verandahs and about 15 rooms inside. The house had been filled in underneath. The boong stockmen lived there along with the domestic staff. There were a few families with the stockmen as well. This was a regular port of call for our patrolman. Someone dropped in here once a fortnight. Ernie came every four weeks.

He had another interest here as well. Noreen Peter was at the mission when he first arrived. She had cleaned at the police station.

She was a very thin girl with large boobs. Her skin was very dark about ten o'clock or more he guessed. At 5 feet 2 inches she was just right for a man like the sergeant.

Without these diversions this job would become quite tedious. These girls also helped him in his marriage with Bernice.

After tea the policeman retired to his room at the back of the homestead. The room overlooked an inevitable waterhole. There was a window looking out onto the verandah and next to it a door. The patio was fully screened to keep out the mozzies and bugs.

Noreen slipped in and Ernie wasted no time in talking. Later he lay on his back and smoked while she slept. His testicles were feeling quite sore.

'Twice in one day is a bit much for me at my age. I must plan my time better in future!'

In time he slept.

While he slept a shadowy figure slipped out of the bed and down the back stairs. The tall, snoring man didn't even stir and slumbered unaware.

The next morning he stirred in bed and then coughed his deep hacking cough. He sucked deeply on his cigarette and felt his sense of wellbeing return. A second cigarette allowed him to return to normal.

He shaved and showered then walked onto the verandah and allowed his eyes to enjoy the scenery. This was one of the most beautiful places he had ever seen. This homestead was on a ridge overlooking a majestic gorge. The head of the gorge was guarded by a waterfall and at the tail there was a large billabong. The river cut away to north over another set of falls. The Gregory River flowed all year round and the delightful chatter of falling water was the constant companion of the homestead folks. To the east was a small depression just five feet above the river level. This was like a lost valley. Rich in rainforest foliage with ferns and ancient palms.

This was the middle gorge in a series of five. All barramundi havens and carefully kept away from the tourist agenda.

The Barbers at Southwell had a truly exquisite paradise. Ernie remembered the priestly intonations about heaven and he knew that this would be the main mansion in any after life.

The busy policeman took one last lingering look before he reluctantly tore his eyes away. He lit another cancer stick and headed for the large kitchen.

Noreen was inside cooking breakfast for the upstairs folks. All the stockmen ate downstairs. There was a choice of fresh fruit, bacon and eggs or good old steak. What was the use of living in cattle country if you didn't eat beef? The station butcher slaughtered one beast each week and the fillets cut out from under the ribs were always sent upstairs.

Ernie chose beef, toast and eggs which were then washed down with a XXXX. Another fag completed his meal.

There was no police business here today. Two months earlier he had caught some cattle duffers but there had been no trouble since then.

He stood again and wondered at the wisdom of the early cattle men. All the homestead sites had been chosen carefully and positioned with the care of a chess grand master placing his pawns. He had never seen a homestead flooded in this country of yearly bankers. At Southwell they wouldn't get wet even if the entire Gulf was under water but they were still next to the river.

The sergeant regretfully nosed his Toyota out from under the shade tree and set out on the rest of his patrol. The gray vehicle ran smoothly throughout the day. He called in at Lawn Hill, Bowthorn and Turn Off Lagoon before he headed back down to Dornoch for a counter lunch.

After lunch the trip included Nardoo and Augustus, in the east, before he turned back towards the mission.

As he drove his thirst increased. At this time of day driving was hard work. He was heading towards the west and the setting tropical sun was directly ahead to blind him. The wallabies came out at dusk and the cattle chose this time to wander over the road. Red dust made everything much harder to see. The patrolman pulled over and lit his billy fire. He still had six cans in his Esky. They were chilled and inviting. He drank two cans, had another cigarette and then chewed the rest of his bread. He pulled out his swag and lay back. The mozzies were droning away so he threw some cattle dung on the fire as night closed in. This was the life; completely at peace. He rigged a mosquito net and decided to sleep. There were four more cans for the next day. Anyway, even the healthiest man only needed a smoke and a tinny for breakfast!

Ernie woke feeling stiff the next morning, he wasn't exactly cold. The mercury had plummeted down from 110 degrees to 90 degrees overnight. He was lying on his swag in his boxer shorts. Once again his daily ritual began another day. His deep hacking cough, thick yellowy brown spittle and a cigarette to ease the pain.

The sergeant strolled over to the river and dived in. He was secure in the safety of the falls further down the stream. No crocs had ever been known to scale them. A quick dip helped him to feel human again. He had another smoke and then drank his four cans quickly.

Later that day he climbed out of the Burke crossing and drove through the mission. He smoked and sang to himself until he reached the police station. The boss was back! He walked into the building to make sure that everything was correct. Roger Smallbone was in charge. Good fellah, Roger; a bit inclined to go by the book.

At last he walked over the road and into his home.

Bernice looked up guiltily. She was drinking wine and had a nearly empty flagon. When she saw her husband she began to cry.

'I didn't mean to, Ernie!'

'You didn't mean to what?'

'That horrible man! He came in here and I didn't want to but he made me!'

'Made you what?'

'He seduced me!'

'Here? In my house? In my bed?'

'Yes.'

'Who?'

'I don't know his name! He comes in a blue truck and sells things.'

'I know who you mean!'

Ernie gave his wife a double dose of Valium tablets to calm her down. He was very angry. Not with the woman. She was dumb.

The man who came in and ploughed with his heifer. Must have raped her!

This time he would get his revenge! He had heard from Eddie Jack that someone was selling grog to the boongs. All the evidence pointed to this man.

The policeman drank the rest of the wine while Bernice staggered off to bed and slept. He drank another four cans until his temper became controlled. All the time he drank he smoked as well.

'I've missed that swine by about 24 hours. When he gets here next Tuesday he will regret his actions.'

All day Ernie stewed at his desk in the station. He confided in no one. Somehow he would get that man. She was his wife! His sacred and inviolable property!

Self pity welled up within him.

'Why me? What have I done to deserve this? My own wife raped in my own home!'

As the day wore on his anger lost its heat. He had developed a cold vengeful attitude. He controlled himself and came out of his office determined to destroy this man. A criminal like that did not deserve the protection of the law.

When the day was ended his anger was buried deep within his heart. He had resumed his normal, relaxed exterior. It wouldn't do to telegraph his punches.

Ernie walked around to the pub. He still had to limp at the end of the day but the walk would do him good.

He ordered a counter tea. The talk got around to preservatives.

'Everything had preservatives in it today.' Ernie remarked to Antonio.

'Yeah, it's in alla my food.'

'They reckon, in America, that there's so much preservatives in everything that even bodies have a shelf life of up to a month before they rot.'

'That's specially true of the boongsa. They eat alla biscuits and cana food now.'

The conversation drifted on.

A Happy Family

The next morning began early for Roger Smallbone. He clicked off his alarm at 5:00 am and rolled out of the bed. He wasn't tired as he always got out of bed this early in the morning. Roger didn't cough or reach for a cigarette. This tall, lithe man stretched his body to rid himself of the last of his sleep. He walked quickly through to the kitchen taking care not to disturb his wife or his sons.

Their lounge room formed a U shape when combined with the open kitchen. The Smallbones used a large chest freezer to separate the kitchen from the rest of the room. This acted like a servery. The kitchen was square, 7 feet by 7 feet. A window faced north and below that were the back steps. There were cupboards and a single sink below the window and along the eastern wall. In the corner of that wall was the stove. The southern wall which divided this room from the hall was covered by the fridge and the freezer.

Roger walked past the side door, flicked on the light and slipped between the freezer and the cupboards. He took some orange juice from the fridge and a glass from the drainer near the sink. He poured half a glass of juice and then filled it with water. Roger drained the juice and smacked his lips.

Next he moved back into the lounge room, switching off the kitchen light and turning on the lounge light near the front door.

Their house was not impressive. It was small and set about three feet off the ground. It was rectangular in shape with the short side facing the road. The house sat east-west. Its entrance was shrouded by a front verandah which had been enclosed with mosquito screening. A door into the house was in the middle of the front with a window on each side. Steps led up to the southern side of the front patio.

To the outside observer there was a landing and steps to the north and along the front and southern side were neat gardens. There were two medium sized Poinciana trees situated halfway between the road and the house.

Steps on the north led to the outside toilet and laundry to the north and east of the home. There was also a carport in which a battered commodore rested peacefully.

A verandah kept the western end of the house slightly cooler than otherwise during the long hot afternoons.

Roger, and his wife Cathy, installed an air conditioner in one of the front windows. Once inside the door, the U shaped room faced the visitor. The kitchen on the left and before it was a table and chairs where the family ate. On the right was the lounge filled with a battered, old, government issue lounge suite.

There was a corridor directly ahead with a bathroom and bedroom on the left and another bedroom on the right. The passageway ended with the door to the master bedroom.

Roger eased himself comfortably onto the couch and commenced his daily devotions. He was a devout Christian and this had been part of his routine for many years.

By 6:30 his devotions were over and the tall blond haired man stretched himself again. He did fifty pushups and fifty situps and then ducked through the side door. At 6 feet 3 inches tall he was just too big for the 6 foot doors.

Still fit and healthy, though he had stopped playing rugby union three years ago when he was twenty four, he skipped easily for half an hour.

He went back inside and showered himself. His shorts were wringing wet when he dropped them outside the shower. Roger vigorously toweled himself dry and then wrapped his towel around his waist. His sons, Paul, a rowdy four year old, and Matthew, still unsteady at two, were waiting for him in the passage way.

Three firm friends walked to the dining room. Matthew was very wet but Roger didn't bother to change his nappy. The father put his younger son in the high chair while his brother sat at the table. They both took their bowls of Kellogg's cornflakes and began to ease their hunger of the night.

While his sons ate the big man slipped back into the bedroom. He stopped and thanked God as he feasted his eyes on his lovely wife. He adored her with all his energy. She was sleeping serenely with her red hair spread over the pillow. Her skin was still milk white, even though she had spent some years in the tropics, so unlike his own deep brown, tanned skin.

He dressed in his blue police uniform and brushed her lips with his before he gently woke her. In spite of the fact that they had been married for more than five years his first love had not yet subsided.

Roger wondered again how he had managed to win her heart. She was eighteen and a university student; he was twenty and a policeman. His ambition had always been to follow his father into the Queensland police force. They met at a Christian camp at Burleigh Heads and married two years later.

Cathy completed her honor's degree at St Lucia and had won the university medal in computer science. The newly graduated woman joyfully accepted her child born soon after and energetically embraced motherhood.

This lovely woman slept well. She had no vices so did not wake up unrefreshed. Quickly she slipped out of bed and grabbed her cotton brunch coat, no need for slippers in this climate. Her pretty red hair was tousled and knotted slightly where she had been lying on it. She ran a brush through her hair and the delicate red curls bobbed gently around her face.

A mirage of beauty she was 5 feet 7 inches tall. She had a very pretty face and bright blue eyes. Her magnetic personality seemed to glow around her.

'Hello, darling.' She stretched, 'Mmm…, even though it's hot I had a lovely sleep. Have you fed the boys?'

'Sure have, my love. Come for brekky.'

The husband and wife walked through to the front of the house. Their two sons had eaten their food by now and the older had given the younger a Magna Doodle to play with. Their baby pealed out a gleeful chuckle as he erased the lines with a quick slide of the button.

Both boys had their father's blond hair and their mother's wavy curls. Their eyes were blue as they should be when both parents have azure eyes. Cathy used to joke about the boys eyes, 'Well, they're both blue, couldn't have been the milkman.'

Both parents were going to eat paw paws, grown on the trees out the back. Cathy took two from the fridge and sliced them in half. She scraped the seeds into a bucket by the stove, devoted to compost.

After breakfast the family sat around the table and read the Bible. They then prayed. This family devotion time had been a tradition in both their families.

Roger kissed his wife and then the boys got a peck. He walked out of the side door and jumped the fence. Fences were important in Leichhardt where, periodically, cattle strayed into the town. They had no respect for gardens or ornamental trees. He walked over the road, away from the rising sun, and entered the police station.

Cathy sat and read from her latest novel while she waited for the jug to boil. Her husband didn't drink tea or coffee, but she liked her morning cup of International Roast. She pondered on her day. Since coming to the north she had been doing a correspondence course from Moore Theological College in Sydney. Exams were coming up in a couple of weeks and she would need to study. That would have to wait till later! This morning she would take the boys down to the mission. There was preschool group there who met in a house called Meerara. It was a project for disadvantaged children that was funded by the Federal Government.

At about ten o'clock that morning Cathy climbed into their old blue Commodore. It had been a good car, an SLE, but was getting old now. Many kilometers of bush driving were beginning to leave their mark

She strapped her two boys into their car seats in the back. The engine coughed into life and then she waited for the cabin to cool down. While she waited, she selected a tape and slipped it into the player. The voice of Jim Reeves flowed out of the speakers and caressed her ears, 'The chimes of time ring out their news another day is through, Some one slipped and fell, was that someone you...'

Cathy sang along as she backed the car out onto the road. Its engine purred contentedly while she shut the gate. She slipped the gear lever into drive and headed north to the highway. At the main road she swung around to the right and drove away to the east.

The morning went quickly. There were five ladies in the group with Cathy. She didn't know four of them but the fifth was Sylvia.

Sylvia was not a young mother. Rodwell was her sixth child and the first she had brought to preschool. She was quite large, like most of the Aboriginal women who had borne children. It was almost inevitable that the slim young girls became much larger when they grew older. Rodwell was smaller than Paul and he was much less active. Of the eight children in this group her boys were the only really active ones.

These children would often fall asleep when they were put down or play listlessly. The undernourishment of the Aboriginal children was a disgrace. It was difficult to know who to blame, but certainly not the mothers. Each one cared for her children and would often do without for their sake. Fresh vegetables were hard to get up here in the Gulf. The store manager flew up a DC 3 load every second Monday from the Isa. Prices were high and the more needy people couldn't afford them. This fruit didn't ever get out to the mission and only the more acceptable blacks were allowed into the town store.

Each mother brought along something to eat, at these meetings. Today everyone was sharing.

There was a lovely big damper, butter and golden syrup. One of the others had bought some wallaby meat while another had some goanna. Cathy brought along two dozen oranges and a big bunch of bananas. This was one way she could help the kids without offending anybody's dignity.

Their meal was washed down with a big billy of bush tea. Strong and left brewing for some time it certainly coated your insides. The tea was usually drunk without milk but plenty of sugar. It was customary to use enamel cups which left one with blisters on the lips if care wasn't taken.

Sylvia cooked some damper on the open coals of the fire she had set when they all arrived. It was amazing how hard her hands were! She could almost pick up the glowing coals and had no trouble lifting the damper and turning it over.

All the kids enjoyed their fruit. They happily came back for more until it was all gone.

Young Matthew began to show signs of tiredness. He needed to get home for his sleep soon. Cathy wrestled him to the ground and changed his wet nappy. She called to Paul and told him to go to the toilet before they went home.

She strapped both boys into their car seats and gave Matthew his Care Bear. Paul had decided, last month, that he didn't really need to have a special friend to cuddle. He sneaked out of bed at night and grabbed the old teddy just in case, though!

There was an old battered hospital just to the north of the road. It had been built by the missionaries. For thirty years it was staffed by a delightful old sister who had been on call twenty four hours, seven days a week. The government had taken over the hospital recently. The new nurse was called Adele Andrews. She was 5 feet 3 inches tall and weighed 11 stone. Angry dark brown eyes dominated her face which was haloed by unruly black hair. This bundle of female energy was a feminist who had burnt her bra even before she needed to wear one. Her mother was unmarried and a man hater too.

Adele became angry at the thought of women not working in an outside job. Being a domestic engineer was an anathema to her and her kind.

One of the church leaders had been quite sick of late and had been admitted to the hospital. Dear saintly Charlie Norman was the spiritual head of the church. The missionaries started a church back in their days and then had, wisely, left its running to the local people. Charlie was one of the young men trained in those days and he was truly their success story. He was starting to age now and his body was continually wracked by pain.

This poor man was treated very badly by the hospital staff. Often people who were not really sympathetic to the needs of the original inhabitants took these jobs.

Both boys fell asleep almost straight away. Cathy wanted to visit the nice old man so she parked her car in the shade of one of the mango trees and left the boys. She undid their seat belts carefully and the back doors were opened.

Old Charlie was asleep when she went into the hospital. He looked shrunken and very sick. A ragged cough wracked his body and he twitched a few times but he did not wake up. Sadly Cathy slipped away leaving some oranges hidden away on the bedside table.

As she walked out of the door, Adele was waiting.

'Hello, Sister Andrews, how are you?'

'Ms. Smallbone, is it?'

'No, Mrs, but everybody calls me Cathy.'

'Cathy, is it?'

'Yes, that's what I said!'

'I've heard that you are a university graduate. Is that true?'

'Yes, but that's not really important, is it?'

'It is to me.'

'Good, but it isn't worthwhile to talk about what happened then. It seems like another lifetime.'

'I have heard that you studied computer science!'

'Yes, I found it very interesting.' Cathy enjoyed studying computer science. She had a real flair for software development and had produced a useful program for predicting the state of the money market for her honor's year.

'Well, what are you doing here, then?'

'I've come to visit old Charlie in the hospital.'

'Not here, stupid! Here in Leichhardt, there aren't any computers up here!'

'Well, I've come here because my husband works here.'

'That's not a good reason. It's women like you who give us all a bad name.'

'I don't understand what you mean?'

'Look, women are meant to be free. It is a gross insult for a man to force his wife to stay at home. Women should be out in the work place shaping the world of tomorrow.'

'Well, I believe that I should stay with my husband that is my first duty.'

'He's just a stupid cop! What a waste!'

'I love my husband, and I don't think that is fair. He is a good policeman and intelligent as well.'

'That's not really the point! You go to church don't you?'

'Yes, I do. That shouldn't change anything though.'

'It does! The church has always tried to subjugate women. They are always consigned to the menial tasks.'

'I don't agree. Christianity gives women real dignity. We are treated with real concern and respect. Historically, it was Christianity which emancipated women.'

'Well, then why aren't you a leader or a minister if you've got so many brains?'

'I'm not trained in that field.'

'It doesn't matter, in any company the brightest should float to the top, especially the women.'

'Well the Bible requires that the church leaders and teachers be men.'

'See what I mean, inferior status! You should rebel and seek to rule.'

'I believe in the Bible and for most of my life I have tried to live by its guidance. I can't just change what I don't like.'

'You should change the things that subjugate women. It must be wrong if it disallows us the top jobs.'

'I'm a programmer by training. I have done some big programs in PASCAL.'

'So?'

'Well, if I want to use that language I have to follow all the rules. There is a defined protocol in the language. If I don't program according to all the rules I won't have bug free programs. Christianity is just the same. The protocol has been defined and so we must live according to it.'

'Yeah, but if you don't like that language you can choose another one!'

'That's the point! I wouldn't be using PASCAL any more. If I don't abide by the guidelines of the Bible I won't be a Christian any more.'

'Well you shouldn't be a Christian then; being a woman is more important!'

'I can reach my ideal as a woman by following the Bible. God was the one who inspired all the scriptures and he made me so he must know what is best for me. We always get the best out of something if we use…'

'Come on, I don't believe all that crap!'

'As I was saying: when something is made, it is made for a purpose. We don't use a watch to drive a toy truck because that is wasting it. The same is true for people. If we follow the designer's instructions we will have the best life.'

'Sounds like you've been brain washed to me! You ought to give all that bull away and assert yourself.'

'The complete answer to Christianity lies in Jesus Christ. All our attitudes must be determined in the light of what he has done. He died, even though he wasn't a sinner, but because I was a sinner, in order to free me from God's anger.'

'Don't talk to me like that! I've never been to church in my life. I wasn't even christened. Anyway I think that all the priests are poofters otherwise why don't they have anything to do with women!'

'I want to obey Jesus; he gave me the gift of salvation. Now I belong to his family. When I'm a member of the family of God, I have a responsibility to live in a way which does not dishonor my father.'

'Shut up! You stupid woman! How could you get an honor's degree and be so stupid! I'll give you some books to read that will change your mind.'

'I don't need to get anything more. I am perfectly happy just the way I am! After all, Jesus said, "I am the way and the truth and the life; no one comes to the Father but through me" Why don't you read the Gospel of John and find out why the Lord Jesus is God.'

Adele swore at Cathy and stalked off.

Cathy returned to her car. She had been praying for an opportunity to tell Adele about Jesus Christ and now she had her chance. As she traveled home Cathy gave thanks to God for the occasion.

When they arrived home, the boys were gently carried to their beds. Both were tired and did not wake up. There was still some washing to do and it was easier when they slept.

There was an old twin tub washing machine in the laundry. It wasn't one of the clothes' eaters; it tumbled both ways. Just to be safe Cathy always put the clothes in an old pillow case.

The policeman's wife was reading in the lounge room and the boys were on the verandah playing with their Lego. The air conditioner was pumping cold air onto the room making it pleasant inside. Suddenly she heard the boys shouting and jumping up and down.

'Daddy, daddy!' They called out in unison.

Roger walked in through the door and hung his hat on the rack on his right. He had Matthew in his arms and Paul hugging his leg. Both boys had been bathed and fed. They always waited up until their father came home. He read them a story and they prevailed upon him for a second. Reluctantly he agreed. After the second story they went through to bed. They said their prayers and climbed onto the beds. The cool air hadn't really affected the bed rooms but they were on the east so they weren't too hot.

After he had clicked the light off the tired, hungry man walked back to his wife. He gave her a cuddle and a kiss.

Cathy had the tea served so they sat down to eat.

It was beef and salad. The meat was fillet steak but still a bit chewy. They had potatoes with lettuce, capsicum, cucumber and tomato.

Roger seemed tense. Cathy asked him what his problem was.

'It is so hard to work with Ernie! He wants to bend the rules all the time. I don't want to break the rules myself but sometimes he insists.'

'Oh, that must be hard. Remember, though, that you have been put there for a purpose.'

'Yeah!' He let out a deep sigh. 'I am trying to be gracious. He hates the aborigines as well. I've even seen him bash one guy.'

'That's bad!'

'I should report him but I would ruin my own career as well. Ernie tells me a cop who dobs is in for a hard time. I don't want to spoil his life but I have to live with my own conscience.'

'You'll have to have a long talk with him.'

'I tried to today but he's even more difficult to talk to now. He seems to be sitting on something. He's as nervous as a cat and ready to jump on anyone. He really tore poor Bill Ransley apart this afternoon. Bill had a flat tire near Beames Brook this afternoon. When the unfortunate guy got back, he had dust everywhere. Ernie swore at him and gave him an extra night shift for not keeping his uniform tidy.'

'Oh dear, we must really pray for him.'

Roger smiled, 'That's a good idea. Enough of my problems. How was your day?'

'Well I got a chance to witness to Adele Andrews today.'

'The dragon lady?'

'That's not nice. She isn't a dragon.'

'Martin Stone, the DAIA representative out at the mission, calls her macho woman. Her mouth would crack Ayers Rock!'

'Well, she was a bit nasty but at least she listened.'

They finished their meal, washed the dishes together and walked to the lounge. Roger began to read a book on Systematic Theology while Cathy read her novel.

They were in bed by 9:30.

The Diplomat

Ray Walden stretched out in the lounge at Brisbane airport. He smiled to himself: knowing that he cut a fine figure of a man. Any person with his high position in life should have the powerful presence he now displayed. The Minister for Resources, Assistant Deputy President and Commander in Chief of the Murur Secret Service chose to sit in the economy lounge. He smiled to himself again; the extra titles would be added to his name soon after he returned from the north with remarkable success. Already he could hear President MacDonald's commendation being read with due pomp and ceremony.

In here the temperature was a meticulously controlled 70 degrees. The blue seats were comfortable without being ostentatious. Our future potentate sat among the ordinary people. His epitaph, at the end of an outstanding life, would include the words: '… though great he never lost the common touch.' His people would always love him! And he would love them too!

An announcement sounded over the public address system: 'Australian Airlines flight twenty six, for Mount Isa is now boarding from gate three.' Ray's heavy, gold Seiko watch showed exactly 9:49. The flight would be on time.

This secret agent stood and mingled with the crowd. His regular 5 feet 7 inches was increased by an impressive two and a half inches due to his Cuban heels. He wore faded but expensive Levi's with a large, buffalo horn embossed leather belt. His calf length boots were worked carefully into delicate patterns and polished highly. His jeans were tucked in to show the excellence of his footwear. Ray's light blue cotton shirt was gaudily embroidered and only the bottom two buttons were done up. A few scraggly hairs valiantly struggled to demonstrate the virility of his chest. He wore a custom made Akubra hat pulled down low over his eyes. It was black and decorated with a plaited blue band and a bright red feather from the wing of an Eastern Rosella.

When the slow moving line headed through the door, a blast of the morning heat caused him to break stride momentarily. Even under the colorful canvas walkway it was at least 100 degrees. Ray manfully strode on, spurred on by the fact that in future years the press men would have to brave the heat to photograph his famed visage.

A delightful young hostess welcomed him aboard. Ray showed her his boarding pass and gave her the condescending smile of the seasoned wayfarer. He was directed to one of the larger seats at the front. It was good for a man to have a feel for the people but he must travel with the correct amount of dignity. First class was the only way for a leader of the people to travel; especially if he wasn't paying for it himself!

The oligarch settled comfortably into his chair and stretched out his legs. He slipped his hat down over his eyes and relaxed with the casual indifference of a hardened voyager.

Later on he removed his hat and lay it on the vacant seat next to him. In future years this seat would be reserved for one of his trusted aides but now fortune left it empty.

The flight lasted two hours, during that time our ex ringer[*] ate his meal with gusto and drank his coffee. As he looked around, he noticed all the senior executives in this section lubricated the flight with spirits. A sense of his own importance began to control his mind. His boss' stern injunction was quickly relegated to the nether regions of his consciousness.

Ray's preference was for XXXX or a rough red but to keep up with the company Ray ordered scotch on the rocks. This order was repeated twice. When the plane taxied up to the terminal at Mount Isa, he was sustained with false courage.

The terminal was small. Just one big room, really. There were a departure lounge, a bar, and a souvenir shop. The walls, away from the airstrip were decorated with copper artifacts to remind one of the foundation of this city.

Over to the left was a baggage pick up area and then outside was a bus to town. His new, blue airport bag was easy to see as was his empty calf skin attaché case. Ray's bag contained spare clothes

---

[*] 'Ringer' is an Australian name for a cowboy or stockman.

and toilet articles. He had no papers to carry, but it wasn't a good idea to advertise that fact.

There weren't any taxis outside after our secret agent collected his bags. He decided to travel incognito and catch a bus.

It was hotter here than in Brisbane but once he was seated in the bus the heat was comfortably held at bay. The driver backed out from under the awning and turned the bus around. They drove down the side road and through the white gates. A Toyota, towing a caravan, sped past before they eased out onto the road and turned right.

Twenty minutes later Mr Walden strode into the plush lobby of the Valencia Hotel. This was only two years old and definitely five star. The premier hotel in Mount Isa boasted luxury that would impress even the wealthiest American tourist.

The foyer was cool and shady. It was wide and carpeted with a deep, soft pile. Inside the sliding glass entrance doors and to the left was an informal dining room. Many business deals were clinched within its embrace. To the right was a door leading to the Copper City bar, favorite of the Northern yuppies. Straight ahead was a gilded staircase leading to the elegant suites.

Ray stood for a moment and enjoyed the scene. He picked up his bags and headed for the reception desk to the left of the stairs. He glanced over to right and spied a gift shop. His American Express card began to burn a hole in his pocket. The card was a gift from the Australian taxpayer funded through the A.C.A.I.Q. Ray reasserted his self discipline and he headed for the registration desk. An officious looking man was sitting at a desk through a door behind. He looked up and frowned. The ambassador gave the bell a brisk tap.

The hotel employee looked towards him, 'What do you want, choco?'

Ray swallowed his anger. This man would soon lose his job over such rudeness. The manager would certainly apologize.
'I want to book into one of the executive suites please!' He was showing remarkable restraint.

'Sorry, we don't let boongs into the hotel. It would spoil our reputation.'

'Do you realize who I am?'

'Yes! Just some stupid abo who's had too much turps. You look like you just stepped off the set of some third rate western.'

'I am an official representative of the Australian Government. I hold a very important position on one of the high priority committees.'

'Every boong has tickets on himself! Look carefully at my lips. I will tell you what to do … get lost!'

'I demand to see the manager!'

'Hey, Charlie, get this idiot out of here before he gets the desk dirty.'

A large man, who looked like he could punch out a sumo wrestler, walked over and placed a firm hand on Ray's shoulder.

'Get out of here, you myall Aborigine! This place is civilized!'

Ray knew when he was beaten. He picked up his bag and walked out the door. Where is the Post Office? I'll ring Andrew

MacDonald straight away. The police will be forced to arrest those men.

As he stood outside the hotel the ambassador fought hard to control his tears of anger. His bag was heavy and his smart leather brief case seemed, somehow, incongruous. He decided to book his bags in for the flight to Leichhardt. Then he could go and try to find some friends to stay with.

In the old days he had been in this town a few times as a ringer. Once they had brought cattle down through the Yelvertoft dip to the rail head in Isa from the Territory.

Senator Walden would be welcomed by his many friends in this great town. Well, maybe he wasn't a Senator yet, Secretary Walden would be better!

It was getting towards 1: 30 pm; his bags were booked in and he was free to walk the streets. There were very few people walking anywhere now even along the main ridge. There was another Aborigine staggering towards him from the direction of the police station. This would soon stop; when they had the dignity of being citizens in their own country. It was so hard to be treated as outcasts by people who had only recently come to this ancient land.

Ray's eyes brightened with recognition. The shambling gait belonged to Archie Jerry. Good old Arch; one of his mates from Quilpie. They grew up together and even shared their first sexual encounter with the same girl one night when they were still at school.

Even though our esteemed statesman was an alcoholic he refused to admit it to himself. When he had been so rudely rejected, his anger had quickly turned to self pity. In this state of mind he hungered for the bottle. He fought strongly to suppress this urge and was at the point where one small event could tip the balance. He knew in his heart that this could lead to a binge. MacDonald's words still stung in his ears. Would one episode of ignorance jeopardize the whole project?

As Archie neared his old friend recognition slowly came to him.

'Ray! What for youfla bin here?'

'I came to do some work for the Aboriginal Council.'

'Youfla good fellah. Come and work for us to make ebrythink good.'

'Well, we'll get a lot of good if I'm successful now.'

'Them white fellah, they gib you nuffink. Youfla come with me. Dreckly we hab good drink. I bin get big plagon.'

Ray's resolve began to melt. That longing deep inside him started to well up. There was a magnet inside him pulling him towards the bottle. A couple of good drinks would certainly deaden the pain of his rejection. The recent prejudice had opened up some nearly healed wounds deep within his soul.

Ray's work with the council gave him a sense of dignity he hadn't known before. Growing up as an Aborigine in an outback Queensland town made him feel dirty and useless. He had left school at fourteen feeling that he was only good for menial work. He chewed the dust behind some big mobs before the cattle slump came.

Ray met Jamie Dickson, a bush pastor who taught him to believe in himself. His years studying at Saint Lucia were so far removed from Quilpie that he began to forget. After he met Doctor Jamrichson and went to Harvard to get his Masters, Ray felt like a gifted and worthwhile man. His time in Moscow hardened his resolve to fight for his people and to find his sense of personal dignity.

Here, in the street in Mount Isa, he was just a stupid black boong. No one had called him 'choco' since before he began cattle work. Hatred welled up but self pity took over. The man with a mission whose life must be worthy of his high office was gone. Thoughts of the bottle and its release fought their way to the front of his mind. After all, Archie was a real mate. It wouldn't be right for a man like him to divorce himself from his past!

'Where d'ya get the flagon, mate?'

'Down at the Digger's Rest.'

'Let's go back!'

Two old friends walked back up the hill again. Ray's card began to burn a hole in his pocket.

The publican questioned his credit card, at first.

'Steal this from someone, boong? Perhaps you sold your lubra to a tourist!'

'It's a genuine card! Ring the office!'

'All right, don't get your lap-lap in a knot.'

Ten minutes later the two men came out. They walked over the crest of the hill and down to the river bed. Sometimes this was a raging torrent but now it was dry. It was cool and shady under the bridge. The case had been hard to carry but when they sat together and viewed the six flagons of claret they knew it was worth it!

The pain of the brutal reminders in the afternoon slowly dissolved in the rich red liquid. His terrible feelings of dirtiness and worthlessness were no longer pressing heavily on Ray's heart. A vague loss of contact with his extremities had also broken the shackles that bound him as a child. A person who is an outcast in his own land from his earliest years did not have the same anger as one whose dignity was stolen from him! The staff at the Valencia had treated him like dirt and he felt totally unimpressed with his own person. Years of hard work and praise had taught him to respect himself and beat the bottle. Now the slender thread that maintained his balance had been snapped. His sense of equanimity was now restored; although artificially. As dusk began to embrace the land with darkness our two comrades were fast approaching that state known in the vernacular as paralytic. They were both sprawled carelessly on the rough gravel. The barest elements of some dimly remembered songs stirred their vocal chords. Seven empty flagons lay randomly beside the men. Ray's ostentatious Akubra was now a battered bushman's slouch hat. Its proud feather was crushed in the dust.

The deep growl of a well tuned four wheel drive struggled through his stupor. Rough voices fought their way into Ray's consciousness.

'Look mate, two more stupid boongs. These black mothers have no sense!'

'Better chuck them in the back. Uncle Wolfgang will pay for a night in the midnight motel.'

*

Next morning Ray woke on a hard bed. The springs were pressing against his scant clothing. At some time the mattress had disintegrated due to contact with second trip alcohol. These cells were there for coons and they didn't need mattresses anyway. It was well known among the police that a brain preserved in alcohol felt no pain.

He fought hard to remain still. The pain inside his head was indescribable. A loud voice invaded his private hell, adding to his burden.

'Come on Niggers, breakfast time. The rooms in this motel must be vacated by nine o'clock or an extra day's rent will be charged.'

Our hero groaned from his prone position. Breakfast was a watery gruel. It fought viciously with the acidic remains of his previous ingestions.

By nine o'clock the bedraggled remains of a once proud government official staggered out into the blazing tropical sun. The clouds with their hint of rain promised exhausting humidity as well. His clothes were creased and stained and even the gloss of his boots was badly scuffed.

Archie and Ray went to the AIM hostel in town where Ray was able to clean up. A shower and shave restored his sense of well being, somewhat, his headache was eased with codeine. He desperately tried to organize his thoughts. This one slip could easily have jeopardized the whole mission. Fortunately he was still able to continue. His clothes were not good enough now for an august personage. The smell of vomit and urine caught in the back of his throat.

The two old friends parted company at the hostel. In borrowed clothes, our man with a mission returned to the main part of town. He replenished his wardrobe and by the time he was ready to fly on he was restored to his former splendor.

This gifted University graduate had now imposed his will upon the memories of prejudice and hatred. His self discipline had resumed its authority. Never again would he allow himself such a disgraceful display of self pity, reducing him to the squalor of the gutter.

His head boomed with a hangover but his face showed no sign of this when he caught a cab. They were not all as prejudiced as those he had met yesterday.

There would be no drinks today!

Ray's head was again full of plans while he sat in a rattling old DC 3 as it groaned its way north.

Whose Rights?

'I punch you, you wil' ol' black fellah!'

'No, I punch you first you myall aborigine.'

This group of boys squabbled good naturedly among themselves. The higher pitched tones of the girls were more sinister. Adam Angel groaned inwardly: surely they weren't building up to one of those hideous fights. He heard about the last fight between two girls. It happened about three years before he came to the school. The blood letting had been over some boy. One girl came with a knife and a horrendous fight erupted. Furniture was flung wildly aside and their clothes torn off.

A foolish teacher, who tried to intervene, early in the fight, was slashed. He managed to get the knife but lost the use of his right hand for his troubles. Finally the battered, bleeding girls collapsed in exhaustion and were carted off by the police to their own territory.

Adam's piping voice struggled to master the cacophony. His meager frame looked somewhat ridiculous as he sought to dominate the group. Some of the boys towered over him and all the girls were taller than he was. Fortunately these Aborigines were well cowed before he got to them. They settled down under the authority of his whiteness.

'Sit down and I'll call the roll.'

This was useless; he knew that they were all there. A cursory glance told him that all the seats were occupied. This tradition was meant to settle the class and help to improve the small man's estimate of himself. They all sat quietly for this. Mrs. Macleod, that gigantic woman who taught first grade, had battered them into the habit of total silence during roll call.

Adam was a small effeminate man. At thirty one he was prematurely bald and called 'Ol' Bally', among other things, by the students. At five feet one inch tall, with his boots on, he weighed eight stone. He was, however, a paid up member of the Labor party and knew his rights well. No one would dare to cross him. While a student he lived with Roland Smythe, who was now the president of the Queensland Union movement. They had come to realize that their aspirations were not compatible with their relationship and had parted as the best of friends.

His eyes tenderly surveyed the boys and the faint beginnings of desire stirred within him. He imagined the pleasure of the hard sweaty flesh parting beneath him. A sigh escaped from his lips. They were all interested in girls! That American psychologist was right! Blacks were evolutionarily retarded. These people didn't appreciate the higher delights of homosexuality. That was the crowning glory of civilization. We should all slide into oblivion enjoying only men! No one should have to associate himself with that ugly, hairy slit that was hidden between a woman's legs. With good reason! He shuddered as he remembered seeing what looked to be a cavernous hole between his mother's legs waiting to take him back. She used to lie with her legs spread on the bed after her clients had gone. Certainly men were better! He had normal sexual desires but at this moment was doing his doctorate in Sociology. That was why he was here. He had sworn himself to temporary celibacy but would certainly have fallen if the boys had responded favorably to his suggestions.

'Ronnie Douglas!'

'Here!'

'Roderick Eric!'

They didn't bother answering him now. They knew that his eyes would scan the class. He was an object of derision among them all. So ready to fight for his rights but so unable to do anything about it!

'William Gangala!'

'Boy Mars!'

'Andy Rickard!'

'Norman Rumble!'

'Jack Sambo!'

'Rickie Tango!'

Now for the girls!

'Noreen Billy!'

'Grace Daylight!'

'Bethel Diamond!'

'Marita Johnny!'

'Angela Jupiter!'

'June Mercury!'

'Erica Needham!'

'Suzanne Pluto!'

'Sylvia Snake Oil!'

'Winnie Yelham!'

'Wanda Yulurie!'

The first stroke of the cross had been precisely placed, from the bottom left to the top right, in the squares. This book was an official document and could be tendered as evidence in a court of law. The names were all written down the left of the page, girls first and then boys. There was a large grid of squares, two for each day. The top of each column had an elongated square in which the principal's secretary carefully wrote the date in Queensland regulation script. The columns and rows all had to be added for days and half days absent. At the end of the term the rolls had to be balanced. There was hell to pay if they didn't!

The children were between fourteen and seventeen years of age. They were the high school class. There were no white kids among this class; they all had been sent away for a more refined education.

Mr. Angel taught, among other things, Peace Studies. This was his favorite subject. Today was going to be a special day. They were having an excursion! The Council at Boomallooba was meeting today and his class was to observe. Next week they would be able to have their own council here in the school.

It wasn't long before all the class was seated in the Toyota Coaster bus belonging to the school. It had been a gift from some Government trying to buy off their conscience, troubled by wrongs to Aborigines in previous years.

No one volunteered to sit next to Adam in the front seats.

The school was situated on the main east-west road. It was bitumen here but soon became gravel; at the far corner of the property, in fact. The pub rose out of the ground about 500 yards to the east.

Adam turned the key, the engine whirred, groaned, coughed and then sprang to life. He eased in the clutch and the bus moved forward before it jumped up onto the bitumen. They rolled smoothly eastwards towards their destination.

As the bus neared the intersection beside the pub Adam had to jam on his brakes hard. A grey Toyota swung out in front of him. He sounded his horn angrily and the other car pulled up.

A sob of fear escaped his lips. The 6 feet 7 inch frame of the police sergeant unwound itself from behind the wheel. This man signaled to him to pull over.

The entire portion of his body between his ribs and knees turned to water. His guts gurgled within him.

The sergeant limped over, placed his hat on the top of the bus and leaned on the driver's window. Those cold grey eyes bored right into Adam's soul.

'Hey fag, whatcha blowing at me for? Got a problem?'

Our little teacher knew his rights but was totally overawed by the size and cold hatred of the man beside him.

'S … s … sorry sir!'

'That's better! No one interferes with my authority in my town! Do you understand?'

'Yes sir.' Adam swallowed hard and fought to suck in some air. Suddenly it seemed to be so breathlessly hot.

Ernie looked at the students inside and laughed humorlessly, 'Touch any of those boys, poof, and I'll make you into a girl!'

A spasm of horror shook Adam's tiny frame. That second mouth of his mother's seemed to laugh mockingly at him from between her legs. That picture was forever burned within his brain.

Ernie spat on the ground and returned to his vehicle. He drove away in a cloud of dust as he dropped his clutch too quickly for the dirt beside the road.

Adam was wet all over with perspiration. His new floral shirt clung dankly to his back, its earlier charm all gone. He shook angrily and wept to himself in frustration.

The children in the bus laughed mockingly at him. He continued his drive towards the mission. A strong resolution came over him. Adam would not be pushed around by anyone, or see it happen to another. It was essential to be assertive. Beside that; he had a right to his own personal space and to his own preferences!

Later that morning the group sat at the back of the corrugated iron hall in the center of the township. It was rectangular; about 15 feet by 20 feet and the roof rose from 7 feet to a 12 feet peak. The floor was roughly concreted and had a door in the middle of each wall. There were two large corrugated iron shutters one on each of the long walls. These were held open by poles.

Half of the hall was furnished with rough wooden benches. They were arranged in six rows with an aisle in the centre. Being backless made them even more uncomfortable.

There was a large wooden table near the door at the other end. This door was bolted shut and had been like that as long as anyone could remember. There were four chairs behind the table and in each chair sat a man.

At the left of the table, looking from the hall, sat Andy Johnny. He had snow white hair and the dark skin of a full blooded Aborigine. This man was big in every way. His chair was set back from the table and his enormous belly rested on his thighs. He was respected by the people and had a reputation for being a fair and wise councilor.

Next to Andy was Jimmy Douglas. His pale yellow skin contrasted with the darkness of the others. His face was thin with high cheekbones. Sparse stubble struggled to conquer his chin and upper lip. This man had been an outstanding stockman in earlier years. His small thin frame stuck to the back of the wildest brumby like a limpet. In later years he had educated himself and was now articulate and literate in English. It was his job to draught official communications. His experience in station management was also invaluable.

The grand old man of the community sat next: Jumbo Seven Emus. He was of regal bearing, tall and straight and still, at about seventy years of age, carried no extra fat. He had been born in the bush and trained as a song man in the traditional lore of the Budalanga tribe. Considered to be ignorant, by the whites at Seven Emus station where he worked briefly in his twenties, he was really a very educated man. Without any written help he contained in his mind all the legends and complex relationships of his tribe. He was the last of his kind and longed to teach all his tribal wisdom to the youngsters.

Adam recognized Jumbo as the stupid old fool who came to the school on Tuesdays and Thursdays. He was amazed to see the old fool accorded so much respect by his own people. Surely they should know better!

Last, but not least, was Roswell Sambo. He was young, and to the little school teacher, highly desirable. This man was well known in the town. He sprang from the bush four years ago and was totally myall. The man was still clad, or unclad, in the traditional manner. He had lived, with his clan, undetected by the station people, up in the Nicholson gorges. His arrival in town was prompted by sickness in the family. There were said to be others up in the gorges. Roswell had brought a large group to the mission with him. His ridiculous name had been given to him by some Government official with a sick sense of humor.

To the left of the main table was a smaller table behind which sat Martin Stone of the Department of Aboriginal and Islander Affairs. His job was to liaise between the Government and the duly constituted local authority.

Eddie Jack was also in attendance. He sat on the opposite side to Martin in a high backed wooden chair; relic from some station office.

The children were quiet and attentive in the presence of these august personages.

Business was transacted at a leisurely pace, matching the temperament of the leaders. The penning of pigs was passed into local law. This was prompted by the goring of a child the weekend before. It became compulsory for all visitors to have the unanimous approval of the council.

As the morning progressed, people from the camp wandered in and soon the hall was crowded.

Suddenly, there was a sound of violent oaths and a struggle outside the door. Every neck craned to see, although no one left their seats out of respect for the council. The scuffle at the door ended as a group of mission police escorted an angry young man into the hall, none too gently.

The new arrival was Norman King. He was a case study by himself. He was the product of an unholy alliance between a Jesuit priest and his full blooded Aboriginal housekeeper. The ecclesiastic was cruel and hounded the poor woman to her death soon after this miscreant sprang from her womb.

The boy had grown up as the property of the Jesuits over on the Barrier Reef coast. He had been forced to work hard from a tender age. The first priest was replaced by another one, in due course. The new father had different tastes and the young boy was forced to keep him happy.

The brutalized young boy soon became an angry teenager. It was not long before this priest was forced to wear a wooden overcoat. As a minor he was further ill treated by other sections of the church. At eighteen he left his childhood prison and began to wander the outback. He felt that his blackness had caused his pain and, hence, he hated Aborigines.

This evil bird had, at last, roosted in our fair town. Immediately his trouble making tendencies were displayed. He had beaten and cruelly treated half a dozen women. His latest escapade was to bring ten large bottles of vanilla into the camp and sell them to the children. Angry people were often alcoholics themselves; it an ideal anesthetic for the soul.

His latest escapade had its conclusion in the council meeting today. The charges were read, evidence was given and all the proceedings were kept legal under the watchful eye of Mr. Stone.

Finally it was time for the verdict.

Jumbo cleared his throat, ‘Norman you hab cause big trouble! You bin gibbin all our ladies hard time! You bin drink ebil drink! You banish for all time prom Boomallooba and prom Leichhardt!’

Martin Stone added, ‘This is within the authority of the council. It is passed into local law.’

The angry man was ushered out to the battered utility with its cage. He would stay in the big town until a plane came to take him elsewhere.

Adam Angel was angry. This morning his rights were severely violated. As a physical coward he had shied away from the defense of his rights. Here were a new man and a new cause. He knew the rights of every Australian.

A shrill voice piped up, ‘No! You can’t do that! Every Australian is allowed to live where ever he chooses!’

Martin Stone growled, ‘Shut up, you fool! This is quite legal!’

‘I’ll get the television crews up here! This man has been treated badly because of his race!’

Jumbo stood. Everyone else sat in stunned silence.

'Eddie, get 'Ol' Bally' off the mission!'

Adam was carried, kicking and screaming, from the hall. He was placed in a dilapidated old Kingswood for the journey back to town.

Jumbo cleared his throat, 'Long time ago, we make agreement with Govmin. Missionary school close down and we send kids to school down road. Big boss promise, we doan like teacher we get rid of him! This man want our boys to be like women for him.'

Martin knew that there was no recourse. A telex would have to be drafted and sent before noon. Ernie would be told that Adam Angel must join Norman on the plane.

The children were given the rest of the day off. Someone could come down and collect the bus later on.

A Bushman

Next evening an old man sat next to a fire in the village. The sky was clear by now and the trees looked like giant old scarecrows. They were looking forward to the coming wet when they could recover from the depredation of the locusts earlier in the year. Around the man an aimless crowd of people ebbed and flowed in confusion. He was at peace with himself. As he sat in the dust he worked hard. Earlier that day he had selected a sapling with care and now he was straightening it. The green wood was pliable in the heat of the fire and soon it would be a perfectly balanced killing machine. His years of bush experience were more valuable than a university degree. He would be able to balance the spear by eye. When he was finished, it would fly straight and true. He would not have to waste time testing and retesting his equipment.

His hands and feet were hardened by this kind of work. The hot wood did not burn them as he pushed and pulled at the shaft. A small handful of sand was all the protection he needed. Sometimes he used his mouth to gain extra leverage for the job.

This man was no ordinary man. To the people in Leichhardt, perhaps, he was an object of derision. Taking time off to go walkabout was scorned by the murdergy; the white ghosts.

His mind contained the archives of his tribal knowledge. He knew every waterhole and tucker plant in an area ten times the size of the largest station. This man could observe a flock of emus feeding on a plain. His experience would tell him where they would run if frightened. He could then leave a man in a tree while he scared the big birds. They would run under the chosen tree. The emus would not be randomly chosen from the flock. Before they began, these majestic hunters would choose the bird they wanted.

Many times the old hunter had surveyed a mob of wallabies and decided that he should wait. In another two weeks they would be fatter. A mark would then be upon the selected animal, as surely as the white man earmarked his cattle.

Later that evening our man laughed with pleasure, the spear shaft was ready. His skilled senses knew that it would fly true. This was not a flimsy shaft to be sold to the tourist. The sapling had been two inches in diameter. A man's back would break if hit by this spear. A clean hit would bring down a big kangaroo.

The spear blade was ready to be attached now. This head began its life as a large knife. Its blade was taken from its handle and shaped; wicked barbs were filed into it and both sides were sharp. Its makers in Sheffield, England would not be eager to acknowledge its manufacture now.

Before darkness stole over the camp the spear was complete. The blade had been skillfully joined by gum and the large leg tendon of a previous kill.

The old man then removed his clothing and changed into his lap lap. He went down to the river bed and by the light of an old lamp he painted himself. His body soon showed the precise markings of the Jabiru dreaming. Other old men had painted themselves too. Some younger men and boys waited patiently. Soon all their markings were complete as well. It was time to begin dancing.

Jumbo Seven Emus straightened himself up. He did this easily. His eyes scanned the group. They were all painted distinctively. Some, like him, were of the Jabiru dreaming. Others were Dingo or Brolga, there were also Bush Turkey and Wedge tail Eagles. In the tribe each animal had its own cultic subgroup. The ties of dreaming were more complex than those of blood. In his mind Jumbo knew all the rules of kinship and dreaming. He spoke his own male language fluently. This language inflected at the end of each word. As a child he had spoken a woman's language which had inflected at the beginning of each word. During his initiation he had spoken a third language which inflected in the middle. If he had been white his vast knowledge would have been worthy of great praise. Being a wild blackfellah meant that he was thought to be stupid.

During the Japanese war an American bomber crashed up in the Gulf. One airman had survived as a starved wreck. The others had died after their food ran out. Jumbo could easily have grown fat in that country!

The Americans mocked him and treated him with derision. But he found their wrecked plane! Tonight this story would be related at the corroboree.

The old man put his tall hat, made from human hair, on his head. He was the song man and a tribal leader. This role rested easily on his wise shoulders. The burden of his knowledge weighed him down. There was so much to teach and so few willing to learn. The sons of proud hunters had become dependent fringe dwellers. The younger men carried large bellies and fawned at the edge of the towns waiting for hand outs. There was, however, some hope, for the very young men seemed willing to learn. They would never know the land as he did. Jumbo was born by the side of a creek and did not sleep under a roof for his first twenty three years. The land belonged to him but he was its lover. He would tend the country with care because he respected it.

This old chief knew all the Dreamtime stories. Every rock, hill or billabong had been placed in the dreamtime. He knew why it had been placed and who it belonged to. The young men did not belong to the land as he did. Some of them were yellah fellahs and did not belong to the country at all. His true people accepted the yellah fellah with the patience of those who had adapted themselves to this land over many thousands of years.

When the dance was over Jumbo returned to his own camp fire. His voice was still strong even though he had sung and clapped boomerangs for two and a half hours. His three wives were waiting.

Rachel was old and large. There was a comfortable familiarity between them gained from shared years of hardships. When the winter winds blew her bulk shielded him from its icy fingertips at night. She was a great grandmother and also a wise old woman. Her mind contained many secrets and skills that would take a girl a lifetime to learn. She had been born out in the west somewhere and was chosen by her father to be Jumbo's wife. Her knowledge of language was as great as his, her mind as keen.

Nina was not as large and only middle aged. As a second wife she was not as important but was still enjoyed by the grand old man. His third wife was only young. She was the delight of his old age. Lurlyn revived his virility when they married. Already they had two young sons.

Jumbo took his family, his three wives and all his younger children, into the bush whenever he could. He wanted his youngsters to obtain that innate bush sense which came from a childhood in the wild.

Next morning the family rose early. They ate the remains of last night's beef and damper. Rachel made some strong billy tea. They wanted to walk the five miles out to Bannock Burn before the day got really hot.

Bannock Burn was a pretty billabong by the side of the Burke River. There were plenty of trees and some fat fish still swam in the little lake this late in the season. It was surrounded by a rim of boggy drying mud. Being near the river, the lagoon was sustained by the water table. It was like a large boomerang bending away from the river and about 200 yards to the west. It was the remains of an old river channel.

Our family group set up camp under the shade of a large river gum. The old man carried his spears, woomera and some boomerangs. There were six young boys, including his two youngest sons. This morning they would sit while he taught them of their heritage. Their school teacher would complain about their absence from school, again! Those fellahs could never teach these boys what they really should know.

The day passed peacefully for the family group. Nina pulled out a feast of fish. Rachel went with some of the girls and found some lilies, a miracle this late in the year. The seeds would be ground and tonight they would have real damper. She had also found a sugar bag, the nest of the wild stingless bees, and some 'Chinese apples'.

Jumbo decided that it was his turn to contribute. He yawned and stretched out the stiffness from his afternoon nap. He carefully selected his new spear and his old, tested woomera. This man only needed one spear to provide food for his family.

Before he went he got the fire sticks from Nina. Both had been cut from a custard apple tree. This type of tree had been introduced by the white man but the sticks still did the age old job. One was about 18 inches long and the other just a little shorter. The long stick was sharpened on one end while the other had a groove in the middle.

Jumbo sat with his legs crossed. He put the shorter stick on the ground. Carefully he took a pinch of sand and placed it in the groove. He placed the long stick between his horny hands and lowered its sharpened end into the groove. He rubbed the stick rapidly between his hands. Soon there was a glowing ember in the groove.

The old man took a handful of dry grass, dropped the ember into the grass and held it up to the breeze. Gently he blew into the grass to help the breeze. Soon the grass sprang alight and it was not long before the family had a fire to cook its evening meal.

The day had now passed its hottest time. There was a mob of wallabies feeding in the grass over the water.

Already the old hunter had sensed the breeze and knew which way to go. He walked with patience and care, keeping among the trees. The grass was long and the animals he hunted could not see around while they bent down to feed. He moved while they fed and stood still while any one looked up. The wallabies were unaware of the deadly game they were playing.

Along the edge of the water, the trees were thicker and offered more cover. The old man stayed between the trees and watched the animals for about fifteen minutes. Carefully he chose his target. He selected a buck that was big but not the dominant male.

The blunt end of his spear was placed in the woomera and an age old drama began. The weight of his worries left his shoulders now; he was immersed in total concentration. This job could be done quickly and easily with a rifle but would not offer the same satisfaction.

Like the silent shadows of his ghostly ancestors he approached his quarry. He moved while the animals bent to feed and always kept some cover between himself and his prey. His boys watched in amazement as he stalked his quarry. Their minds were filled with the stories of great hunts.

At last there was no cover left. His chosen wallaby continued to feed unaware of its fate. Twenty five yards away the silent hunter measured the distance. He scanned the ground between them. His right arm lifted above his head, spear at the ready. Quickly he dropped his arm as the wallaby lifted its head. A quivering nose sensed the air but there was no hint of danger.

Jumbo exhaled slowly when its head had dropped down again. He tensed for a spring. He lifted his arm again. Suddenly he rushed towards his target, one…, two…, three silent steps. The startled animal turned to flee but already the deadly killer was in the air. Our hunter's aim was true. The force of the blow knocked the wallaby to the ground, its back broken.

The boys cheered and raced over to carry the kill. The old man removed his spear and hung the evening meal around his own neck.

His family ate well, on wallaby, that night. Its head was left in the coals as they slept. It would make a nice cooked breakfast, along with their fish, next morning.

Jumbo's family returned home after their breakfast. They had a bogey (swim) in the river and were shining clean.

As Jumbo trudged down the dusty street, towards his home, his eyes registered delight. Cathy Smallbone was visiting the camp. She was a delightful woman who really seemed to care. The old man regularly attended church and said that he was saved. This did not nullify his position as song man to the tribe.

Cathy was very fond of the old man. He was honest, straight forward and without malice. He was a wise and worthy leader for the tribe. She remembered hearing of how he had worked for the police. His reference from the sergeant was legendary:

To whom it may concern,
Jumbo Seven Emus is one of nature's Gentlemen,
Anyone who does him a favor does me a favor.
Yours faithfully,
Signature
Reginald Pickwither, (Police Sergeant)

'How are you, this morning, old fellah?'

'I'm good, Mrs. Smallbone.'

'Call me Cathy, please.'

'I bin hunting yesterday. I bin get him wallaby with this fellah spear, Cathy!'

'You must take us out hunting some time. Roger would really enjoy that, so would the boys.'

'You take 'em little fellah piccaninny in the bush, soon they forget they white fellah!'

'That's a chance we'll have to take.'

The old man enjoyed that, he laughed uproariously. They parted company soon after. Cathy hoped they would make good his promise before the month was out.

Fighting Prejudice

Ray climbed out of the DC 3 at the Leichhardt airstrip. His headache was just starting to dull. Codeine was controlling his pain.

It was a hot day and he was sweating through his cotton shirt. The crispness had already gone even though it had been new earlier in the day. He was tired and wanted to rest.

The airstrip was a barren place. It was fenced off from the rest of the flat plain. There was one runway: east-west. It was made of gravel and had been raised above the rest of the land. The residents of Leichhardt boasted that this was the best all weather strip in the Gulf. The strip was exactly one mile long with a grassy verge of black soil all around.

Towards the north were a graveled apron and a corrugated iron shed. Behind the shed were two outhouses. The strip itself was 50 yards wide. All the planes landed from the east and came towards the main road. They turned around to take off again.

This DC 3 came four times a week. It landed here going each way on its twice weekly trip from Cairns to Mt. Isa and back again.

Planes were always met by the old Toyota truck which belonged to Ronnie Lawler, the store owner.

Billy Ah Fat drove the truck and did the deliveries. He always picked up the airmail. He dropped the first load up at the Post Office in town and then went out to the mission. Air mail only came to the town from Mt Isa. This was different to the land mail brought in by Bluey Walters.

The sun was beginning to burn into Ray's back now. His new hat kept his head out of the sun but he had lost the habit of finding shade to stand in. There were quite a few items of air freight being unloaded. The hostess smiled sweetly when he entered the plane but now she was in the plane ignoring him.

The worst part of the flight had been his visit to the toilet. Its window was covered with an opaque, white piece of paper. It felt like a coffin when he closed the closet door. His stomach had rebelled violently. The bitter after taste had to be chased away with a drink of lemonade.

Ray looked around; there were no buses or taxis here. In fact the only vehicle was a battered old truck. He felt slightly light headed and longed to sit down.

At last, the truck was loaded and the plane doors were closed. The engines coughed into life and dust blew everywhere. Ray backed away and quickly grabbed his hat. The DC 3 turned around and headed off to claw its way into the air before it headed back towards its base.

'Wanna lift, fellah?' Billy smiled through his almost toothless mouth.

'Isn't there a bus or anything?'

'Yeah mate, this is the bus! You gunna walk or come with me?'

Ray picked up his bags and threw them in the back. He wearily climbed into the seat beside Billy. It was hot from the sun. The inside was tattered and covered with dust. Already his new clothes were muddy from the mixture of dust and sweat. He wished that the trip was official so that he could be more comfortable.

The town was on a slight rise ahead. They drove up a dusty road. It certainly was a battered old place. This flat was a typical, treeless black soil plain. A ridge had that reddish tinge of ironstone. The bitumen of the road was not the best, when they bumped onto it.

Our undercover man's experienced eye knew they were going north along the road. He spent enough time mustering cattle to tell his direction straight away. The country was good up here. This big flat must be very valuable land. But, this wasn't his reason for being here!

Yesterday's alcohol surged in his blood and its residue churned in his stomach. He felt like being sick again. His headache was just under control. This type of job would have to stop soon. All those years of study, the rewards must come soon. Why should he have to be treated this badly? If that grinning idiot, Billy Ah Fat, only knew who he was! He would really get respect from these people. After all he was ensuring their viability as a nation.

Some of this lovely country would have to be ruined but the money would compensate for that.

Houses were scattered along the road. Mostly they were old weatherboard places badly needing painting. Back on the right behind the first row were some newer, Department of Works houses. There was a new store on the right and the pub beyond that.

'Where d'ya wanna go, mate?'

Ray thought for a minute. What's going on now? He had been dreaming for a minute. He fought for his concentration.

'I want to go to the hotel in town.'

'Look mate, they woan take yer in there!'

'They have to, I've got enough money!'

'I got to go to the Post Office. I getcha after.'

'No need to worry, just drop me at the pub. Then I'll be right. I'll need transport later in the day; perhaps you can help me then.'

'I'll get you, dreckly!'

As the beaten truck pulled up at the main intersection in town Ray opened the door, 'How much do I owe you?'

'Nutten, mate!'

'Sure?'

'Yeah!'

Ray climbed out of the truck and grabbed his two bags from the back. He fought hard against the self pity which welled up within him. He had not been in this town before but it had a harsh, familiar look.

The pub brooded, dark and stony in front of him. It had a long shady verandah. Some of the rooms upstairs were air conditioned. Perhaps he could get one of those. 'Must hurry in out of the sun!'

It was certainly much cooler in the shade. This was typical of any country pub, but unique in other ways. It was an old stone building. That would keep out a lot of the heat. He did not know where they could have got the rocks from. There was no way that he would have known what kind of rocks they were either.

On the verandah there was a long shady bench. Ray sat for a moment and caught his breath. The memory of his reception in Mt. Isa was still raw and fresh. He decided to sit for a while longer. Next time all the arrangements would have to be made in advance.

He searched his memory. Who was the local representative of the Department of Aboriginal and Islander Affairs? As an employee of the Government he was entitled to stay in this pub. The name suddenly popped into his head: Martin Stone. He hadn't ever met the guy but it was a good time for him to find out who Ray Walden was. If they didn't let him stay here, he would get the Government man to use his influence.

The hotel had a large bar but as he walked along there was another door first. This door had a wooden frame with glass inserts. A name was etched into the glass: The Burke Arms. Above the next door was a plaque, A. Luchese Licensee.

He felt a bit happier; sounded like a dago in there! Surely he would be kinder to him. He must have experienced prejudice before. They hated wogs up here in North Queensland as well.

The door pulled open outwards. It was well oiled and swung easily. Inside it was much cooler again. There was passageway running through to a flight of stairs at the back. On the right was a door to the bar. On the left was a window to the office. A sign above the window said, 'Reception'. There was a table set into the wall inside the window. Just at the opening there was a small bell. Ray struck the bell which responded with a sharp 'Ding'.

A man looked up from the desk with a smile. The cheerful face quickly disappeared and was replaced by anger.

'We donna like nigger in the hotel. Get lost! Bastanio!'

'What do you mean?' Ray's anger returned but this time he was prepared. 'I am an employee of the Government! I am entitled to stay here! It is in all the awards!'

'You a boong, mate! Stay with the coons downa the road. They gotta some place you staya down there.'

'Where is the man from DAIA? I'm going to see him. He will ensure that I can stay here like any other Government employee is entitled to.'

'He'sa down the road too.'

'Why aren't I allowed to stay here?'

'You gotta black skin!'

'What's wrong with black skin?'

'Maybe the blacka rub off onto the furniture. Or worsa still somebody else!'

'How do I get down to see the Government man? You certainly are an ignorant man.'

'You may be lucky, Billy Ah Fat driva down there soon.'

Ray left his bags in the hall and angrily stalked out. He pushed the door hard and stepped through. Heat hit him like a hammer. He staggered again in its blast.

Billy Ah Fat's face leered at him through the truck window.

'What I say? Youflah needa lift?'

Ray didn't answer his question. He just angrily walked around to the truck door. He jerked it open and climbed inside.

Billy eased in the clutch and the truck rolled forward. He swung around in a U turn and headed back towards the east.

Ray was angry with Billy because he had been right. Beside that he was an idiot! He kept blabbing away about all manner of trivialities.

The visitor wanted to be left in peace. His self esteem had already been crushed in Mt. Isa. This time, however, he was going to win! He knew that he was a worthwhile person and that his life mattered. These people, of small consequence, would soon be driven out. This hotel would, perhaps, become a special monument to his own work.

The young man had to make these positive assertions to himself. When he was studying, he had learnt to be positive. Right now all his training was being used.

He kept on top of the situation. He would certainly not do any drinking this time. As a great leader of his people he must not crumble under the pressure. Even though that dumb dago in the pub didn't recognize his greatness, his own people would be sure to. They would, apart from dumb Billy, recognize his charisma.

After what seemed to be an uncomfortable eternity, the car ground to a halt. Ray shook himself out of his meditation and took stock of his surroundings.

'That fellah you gotta see, him work ober there! He gib you place to stay.' Billy said in a way that annoyed Ray. His unintelligent, smiling face seemed to be mocking him in some way.

Ray saw a big shady tree and some bolted together buildings. Typical Department of Works rubbish. He went to the building indicated by Billy.

The main office was closed and air conditioned. He wasn't in the mood to carefully examine his surroundings. The verandah was comfortable, because of the shade, and there was a window opening onto it. It seemed to be where the Post Offices business was conducted. There were three people lined up. All were black and raggedly dressed. There was quite a pretty girl inside. She had light yellow skin and was small and delicate.

Next to the window was a door. The future leader opened the door and stepped inside. It was cold in here and Ray shivered as his hot body reacted to the blast of the air conditioner.

Inside there was a desk on the right and some chairs on the left. A girl sat behind the desk. She was much darker in color and much bigger than the girl he first saw.

'What for you come in here?' The girl demanded.

'My name is Ray Walden! I am from the Advisory Council for Aboriginal and Islander Affairs. I would like to the Department Representative.'

'Them Govmin fellah not gib job to colored fellah. You lying!'

The first girl came over from the window. 'Angie don't be so rude!' She seemed to be much more articulate. 'What do you really want?'

'I would like to speak to your boss. What's his name?'

'You want to see Martin Stone?'

'If that's his name, yes!'

'Who shall I tell him is calling?'

'Tell him Ray Walden is here to see him. He should know my name!'

The girl walked over to a door behind the chairs and knocked before she went in. Ray breathed a sigh of relief. At last someone knew what they were doing.

It wasn't long before a nondescript man came out of the office. There was nothing remarkable about him at all. Average height with the makings of a beer belly striving against his belt.

'Ray Walden?' The average voice came out of the average face quite unremarkably. Good man to have working for you. At least you could be sure that he wouldn't take over the top job!

'Yes that's me! I'd like to talk to you!'

Martin had hurriedly looked up the Government Directory to find out who he was. Rachel told him that someone from the Advisory Council was here. It might hurt his career if he was rude to this man. All these coons seemed to be coming out of the woodwork these days. A few years ago and the Department of Boong Affairs was all white, now they seemed to be dragging lots of chocolate drops out of the hat. The council he represented was pretty important. They had a white lawyer, who called himself an Abo, in charge. These guys could do a lot of damage to his career.

'Angie, get us both some coffee please! You had better brew up a pot I think. Use the proper milk as well.' Martin called over to his office girl. He turned to Ray, 'I hope you want some coffee with me.'

'Thanks, I'm thirsty and I would love a hot drink.'

Ray was being careful, too. He was not here in an official capacity. This man could be a good friend or he could make life very difficult.

The two men walked into a quiet office and sat down. It was quite a large office with a desk and comfortable chair. There was also a low table and six easy chairs. Martin led his visitor over to the easy chairs and sat opposite him. Ray's back was to the door but he didn't mind. Already the power of his position was beginning to assert itself.

'What can I do for you?'

'Well, I'm actually here in an unofficial capacity. I'm making a visit to this community on behalf of the Advisory Council. We want it to be a quiet affair. The Council feels that a quick surprise visit is sometimes best. We can see the people as they normally are: without any special preparations being made. I'm calling on you out of courtesy!'

'Thank you for dropping in. Have any arrangements been made for your accommodation?'

'I wanted to stay in the hotel in town.'

'That's a good idea!' Martin breathed and inward sigh of relief. When people stayed in the official guest quarters they stayed with him. He would have to work and pretend to care about the people. This boong would probably expect him to like Mother Theresa or something. If he stayed in town at least he would be out of the way.

'There is a slight problem!'

'What's that?'

‘They won’t let me stay there! The hotel manager told me that Aborigines are not allowed to stay there.’

‘Would you like me to make an official protest?’

‘Yes! That would be a good idea.’

The men continued talking on other matters. Neither was really interested but protocol required that they discuss the local situation. Soon the coffee was brought in and Ray drank his greedily. He was thankful that the pot had been brought in and he could have a second cup. Coffee was one of his American habits and a good one too! He didn’t enjoy the instant stuff as much and was glad that Martin Stone had taken this trouble.

After a while the two men decided to go on a short drive. Ray thought it would be a good idea to see the place and get his bearings. They walked out on to the verandah. In front of the window was the usual line of bored spectators. This Post Office had a special service; the girl inside would read letters to those who could not do so for themselves. She sometimes took the time to write letters as well.

A quick glance gave the visitor a good idea of the place. He walked to the southern edge of the verandah. To his south ran the main road. It was gravel and all the houses showed signs of dust on their level surfaces.

To his right was the Aboriginal hospital. It was run by a sister and some nurses. The Flying Doctor probably came every couple of weeks for a clinic.

On his left was the store. It was a very large building. The high roof gave lots of room for storage during the wet season when this place was completely isolated, apart from a suspect airstrip.

There were houses on the other side of the road. In the west were new, high set places while in the east were old corrugated iron sheds. There was a river in the east. Along the edge of the river were humpies. These were shelters built of corrugated iron and Masonite. There were people who actually lived in such squalor.

Martin walked over to a new Toyota four wheel drive. It had air conditioning and cloth seats. This was a government issue vehicle for senior appointees in the North West.

The two men sat quietly as the car began to cool down. They were planning to have a drive around the community.

Martin enjoyed starting his scenic tours by driving down to the crossing. This usually managed to engender a sense of outrage before the tour began. The river cut through quite a channel here. The gorge was about forty feet deep with a river running through its base.

A road dipped straight down and then up the other side. In the bed of the stream, at this time of the year, was a chuckling little brook. The creek ran over a battered crossing. The flow was minimal, just now but it was enough to wet the road for about ten feet, at its lowest point.

Ray and Martin men gazed at the crossing in silence. Ray remembered the nice bridge over the river near Leichhardt and felt a sense of outrage.

Abruptly Martin spun the wheel and the car swung around towards the west. They soon headed south and in half an hour the trip was complete.

Some of the features which stood out in Ray's mind were these:

Every home had an outside dunny*. There were no sewerage or septic systems here. Pans were emptied three times a week and taken to a pit in the south. The pit was about a mile south of the village next to the tip. It was an open pit and its gentle aroma caressed the village when the wind blew the right way.

Martin explained the local government regulations. He told him of Jumbo Seven Emus and his role. Then he described the situation from the previous day.

Ray was saddened to hear about the propensity for evil in Norman King. He heard that Norman was staying in town waiting for his papers to be finalized. When the administrative work was complete he would have to fly down to Isa. He would be leaving early the next week.

As the two men talked Ray casually mentioned that he would like to see old Jumbo.

'I'll arrange that as soon as I can. The old fellah spent the night in the bush last night. I suppose he'll be back today. Let's go and get you into the hotel and then I'll make the arrangements.'

'That's a good idea. I think I'd like to have a nap this afternoon. Perhaps we can see each other later today.'

'Good idea. I'll pick you up at about four thirty.'

'Great!'

The new car gently carried the men back to town. It wasn't long before they were parked outside the hotel.

---

* 'Dunny' is the Australian name for an outside bathroom with a bucket emptied on a regular basis.

'Just you wait here, Ray. I think I'd better talk to Antonio myself.'

Martin left the engine running so that the car would stay cool, at the tax payers' expense. Ray helped himself to a can of coke from the Esky in the back. He eased himself down into the seat and waited, indifferent to the scorching heat outside.

The government man returned in about fifteen minutes.

'Everything is OK now. You have been given a room. The locals will object if you use the bar, so don't do that. You can get a drink out the back. Tony always serves Aborigines from the kitchen. You will be allowed to use the dining room. I've got an air conditioned room with an en-suite, for you. The Government is paying so have a good time.'

Ray mumbled his thanks. He was greatly relieved but very angry. It was disgusting that a man like him should have to bear such shame. Some of his ancestors probably owned this land when there were no white men here at all. Now he was like a leper in his own home.

The temptation to take a stiff drink was strong. It was funny how it seemed to come to him here. All those years of study had been free from this pressing urge. Even in Moscow the desire had not been this strong. He had always been treated well.

Now that he was back in his own country Ray had been made to feel unclean and somehow incomplete. He was treated as an outcast. Just because I'm black doesn't mean I'm any less human. I have feelings too, you know!

The urge to have a drink was almost irresistible. Its smooth embrace would soon begin to ease his pain. The future leader fought back strongly. I am a man of dignity! I don't need to escape from reality! In real life I am worthwhile! In real life I am outstanding!

As he talked to himself he pulled off his boots and then dropped his clothes on the floor. A warm shower helped to wash away the stiffness. Soon he felt relaxed. After a vigorous toweling Ray dressed in a pair of shorts and lay down on the bed. It was cool in here so he pulled up the cover and slept.

Pulling Some Strings

Bob George sat at his desk in the parliamentary offices. He was very comfortably catered for but his soul was restless. His heart was back in his Windorah electorate.

As a youngster he had ridden big mobs down the Georgina trail. He had mustered in the Gulf and Channel country and earned his money. Those years of hard work had eventually resulted in a big station of his own. The stockman had become a grazier and then a Member of Parliament. He usually enjoyed his job but found the paperwork onerous.

Now that he was the minister for Education the bureaucracy imposed upon his freedom. There were continued requests for special treatment. He had to negotiate with the Teachers' Union and attend many parties, official openings and prize giving ceremonies. Bob enjoyed the school visits! As minister he was free to declare a holiday whenever he visited an elementary or secondary educational establishment. The young scholars always enjoyed his proclamations and that gave him a warm feeling.

He remembered fondly all the firm young breasts he had pressed. As minister it was his job, often, to congratulate new office holders in the school. He always insisted on his privilege of pinning the badges on the jumpers or blouses of the girls.

He noticed a letter from Boomallooba on his desk. It caught his eye because he didn't usually deal with that settlement. There wasn't a school there.

Bob stood, a tall, gaunt man. His face was weather beaten. His tailored suit could not erase all the traces of his youth in the bush. He sat and picked up his pen. The pen looked like a baby's toy in his huge hands. He'd always had trouble getting a pen big enough for his hands. They were meant for throwing bulls and branding steers not holding this awkward instrument of communication.

He sighed to himself and jotted down the date and his monicker* on the top of the letter. He began to read. His secretary had highlighted the significant portions.

'We, the local council, have decided that a school teacher, Mr. Adam Angel, is no longer acceptable. It is our wish that he no longer teach at the Leichhardt School. It is also our wish that his removal be effected immediately. If you are unable to do this we will begin to negotiate with the Federal Government…

Bob knew that the last bit was an empty threat, in educational terms. This was a state responsibility and guaranteed in the

---

* Name

Constitution. However…; there was still the matter of Jurisdiction. The State and Federal Governments had argued over the rights of Aboriginals. Were these things within the sphere of influence of the State or Commonwealth? If it blew up, it would give the boys in Canberra some extra ammunition!

The name Adam Angel rang a bell in his mind. There was something about that name which set a flag in his memory. He eased his frame back into his chair and searched through his retrospection. He may have been a stockman and a farmer but the keenness of his intellect was legendary.

At last it struck. That stupid poofter! Slept his way to influence in the Labor Party. There was a scandal associated with him!

Roland Smythe, President of the Queensland Labor Party was reputed to be his boy friend. Roland of staunch Irish Catholic background. The leader of the old guard and opponent of Federal intervention in the Local Branch. The wounds from the big bun fight of about five years ago were just being healed. Roland's election to the presidency was the consummation of the reconciliation.

This man was now happily married with seven children. His wife: Ms Margaret Connell, former housewife and journalist/television compère extraordinaire. Roland would be destroyed!

'Get me Roland Smythe on the phone Sylvia, please.' Bob's voice sounded bored over the intercom.

The intercom buzzed on his desk after about fifteen minutes.

'Hello, Bob George here.'

'Oh Bob, its Roland Smythe. What do you want?'

'Mate, I've got a problem here. I'd like you to sort out the Teachers' Union.'

'It'll cost you some favors to get me to do something for you!'

'Listen to my proposition first, before you say too much!'

'Go ahead. Shoot.'

'You ever hear about a guy called Adam Angel?'

'Whatever you've heard it's a lie!'

'I'm not too sure about that! Anyway the problem concerns him.'

'What's the little fellah been up to now?'

'The Council of Boongs wants to kick him out of the school up there.'

'Can they do that?'

'Yeah, they got the power!'

'What did he do?'

'Seems he tried to buy into a fight he had no reason to get involved in.'

'Stupid little guy.' Roland was still quite fond of Adam, but a seat in the Senate would come soon if he kept his nose clean. Sometimes one had to make sacrifices for public life!

'I'm going to transfer him out next week!'

'What do you want me to do?'

'Get in touch with Jason Antonello and ask him not to cause any trouble.'

'OK I'll do that, but don't let it spoil his career will you.'

'No one wants to alienate the Aboriginal vote just now. The Labor Party is going flat out to get all the coons just now.'

'See ya later mate.'

Both men hung up at the same time.

Roland called out to his secretary, 'Get me Jason Antonello on the phone will ya, Dave.'

This new young man did a great job in the office. He also helped compensate for Adam's absence.

The Union was told that the case must be brought to a speedy conclusion. A few token noises should be made but the man would have to go next week at the latest. The representatives were to wait until the news reached them from the field before they knew about anything.

Sorry Mate!

Adam Angel cried with frustration and anger. He was teaching Peace Studies when the principal had come into the classroom. At first he felt annoyed. This was his favorite subject: the rape of the world by American Capitalism and the salvation offered by the benevolent friend of the oppressed in the Soviet Union. The Boss gave him the telegram.

Adam Angel, State School, Leichhardt.

You have been transferred to Palm Island State School, stop. Appointment to begin Mon 29 Nov, stop. Leave on first available plane, stop. You have one week to effect transfer, stop.

He didn't bother reading the sender's name. It had to be Cecil Hindley, the staffing inspector. It was so hard to be here away from all his contacts. This thing could be easily overturned! Just a quick call to Roland; that would get some industrial muscle on his side!

These isolated places were hard to live in. Adam had always been keen to get things done as quickly as possible. Here in the bush it seemed that you had to wait for everything. Every time he tried to communicate with the University it took him at least two weeks. He often wasted two or three months over something that should have taken him two days!

He felt like blaming his mother again. His older sister had become a medical doctor. Prostitute's daughter to doctor was quite a step! He had always been compared unfavorably with his sister. When he went to St. Lucia, he had to go on a Scholarship. His mother couldn't afford to send two students to the University. It seemed like his sister always got the best at his expense.

His PhD was his chance to show the family that he was just as good. This type of achievement would satisfy him. He would overcome his own feelings of worthlessness. To have to be only a teacher was about as bad as being a complete failure.

His father was a school teacher who became a radio personality. He overcame his failure! The trouble was that Dad was a drug addict. He had sent his church brought up wife out to sell her body after introducing her to drugs. The old guy was knifed in an argument over drugs. His mother only knew how to support herself one way.

Adam hated himself! A constant failure throughout his childhood. A failure in relative terms. His hard work had always led to disappointment. This new betrayal was enough to destroy him!

All his work would soon be wasted. He would have to start all over again.

Adam's squeaky voice was hoarse from his angry crying and cursing. His remorse and self pity had almost exhausted his meager frame.

He sat in stunned disbelief at his desk. He refused to teach any more. As he sat, the bitterness of his childhood welled up again and again. His hatred of his mother whirled around and around in his head. If only he had been somewhere else. If only his sister hadn't been so good!

As he sat he thought to himself. What am I doing here? I am a member of the Labor Party! I have plenty of friends who can help me! I will do something about my predicament!

His strength began to return as he began to think of his friends and the power he could wield. He would stop his remorse. It did no good to let self pity destroy oneself. There were still plenty of resources available.

The Angel got up and walked in to the Principal, 'Rick! I'm going to make a phone call! I've got enough clout to reverse this decision, and I will! I want to ring up my friends in the Union.'

'Look Adam, you haven't got a chance. This is an Aboriginal matter. The Union won't go against the blacks. Too much bad publicity!'

‘You’ll be surprised! I assure you, mate. I’m going to prove you wrong!’

Adam stalked out of the office. His pretty clothes were creased and wet. His temper tantrum left him drained. Inside, however, there were reserves of strength. He had the resolution of a man sure of his rights.

There was only one public phone in Leichhardt. It was in the Post Office. It would take him about fifteen or twenty minutes to walk down there. He went back into the office.

‘I want to use the school bus!’

‘No! This is not officially school business. I can’t allow you to do that, I’m sorry.’

‘You will be sorry! I’ll make trouble for you with the Union as well!’

The youngish man, with all the friends, had to walk. He was completely humiliated. His deep sobs wracked his whole body as he walked into the sun. It was a hot and humid day. The heat seemed like a huge burden pressing down on his shoulders.

This school building was shaped like a capital H. The administration was housed in the cross section while the classes were in the arms. Wide, screened verandahs surrounded the building. All the rooms were on the second floor and there was an open space underneath. It was cooler inside but as soon as Adam left its protection he began to sweat heavily.

The school was about half a mile west of the pub. The bitumen road increased the temperature for a walking man. His fashion shoes were great for an aspiring business executive but not for a long walk in this heat. The tar on the road was starting to melt. His thin cardboard soles offered no real protection from the scorching road. These soles weren't called cardboard and among his friends in Brisbane they were universally admired. He doubted their real value. His light weight nylon socks were not much help either.

It took him five minutes to reach the pub with his peculiar stiff legged gait. All his Brisbane friends thought that his walk was particularly attractive. It didn't get him far here!

The poor man was ready to faint when he reached Leichhardt's premier intersection. He staggered on to the verandah and then into the bar.

One of the incumbents cried out in mock alarm, 'Backs to the wall boys, there's a poofter in the house!'

This comment was greeted with howls of derisive laughter. Even this early in the morning the bar was well populated. Livers were given about fifteen years past maturity in this country. By then they were shot even thought the bodies struggled on.

'Tony don't give a drink to the fag!'

'We can't drink with him!'

'Maybe we will catch something!'

'Send him out back with the boongs!'

There was a loud chorus of protest. These 'virile' men felt threatened by the presence of a homosexual. What would their mates say when they knew about drinking with this thing?

Antonio shrugged his shoulders apologetically and pointed to the lounge at the back of the hotel. Adam limped through the door and ordered a cold chardonnay in the other room.

He didn't usually drink but this was an emergency. How could he maintain his attractive, stylish, thin figure if he abandoned himself to debauchery?

There was that man he'd tried to defend so recently. He couldn't even remember his name. He was drinking at the 'back' bar waiting for the next plane to Mount Isa. It would be here next Tuesday, after the weekend.

Adam was meant to go on that plane too but he would reverse that decision. There was no way that he was going to go on that plane!

After his drink Angel left the back bar and headed for the Post Office again. He hadn't even spoken to the man in the bar. It seemed funny that he should jeopardize his career for someone he didn't know. That wasn't important though! It was his responsibility to defend anyone against oppression.

As he waited on the back verandah steeling himself for the onslaught of the sun he saw the police truck. He immediately hid. Even though he had rights, that man seemed to overpower him in some way. He felt weak and afraid whenever he saw the man. Those steely, grey eyes flashed out of his memory and bored right into his soul again!

When the coast was clear, he finally ventured forth. His clothes were soaked from a combination of the heat, anger and fear. By now he would look a real mess. The curls which clung prettily to the sides of his dome now hung in dank ringlets. He was glad that he wasn't going to see any of his friends now. They would think of him as common and uncouth.

One block south and then turn to the left. There were no trees here; he could feel blisters beginning to form on his denuded pate. The sun was merciless. Another block towards the east and he reached the Post Office.

It was really an old house. There was a verandah at the front and halfway down each side; the section formed by the verandahs was the Post Office. Behind this was the postmistress's house.

There was a window on the right side. This was the business counter. As far as Adam knew, no customers actually entered the Post Office. The door was always locked. The clientele conducted their business through this widow. It was barred to prevent thieving blacks. Adam could see a hole in the window and a sill for money and other things to be passed. A bench was against the half wall at the edge of the verandah.

There was a phone box tucked away in the corner opposite the bench; the only phone in Leichhardt was inside this booth.

There were three people waiting in line at the window.

'Excuse me! I've got an emergency. Let me use the phone right away, please.'

Audrey had ruled the Postal Service here for thirty years. She was never troubled by any emergency. Even the seventy seven cyclone did not rearrange her priorities. There was no emergency big enough for a restructuring of her queue.

'Young man, if you want to use my phone, you will wait your turn!'

'But don't you understand! I can arrange to have you black banned.'

'I can arrange for you never to make another phone call from here!'

Adam ground his teeth in anger. He would have to wait. No one seemed to be sympathetic with this real emergency which threatened to destroy his life.

At last, it was his turn. He walked up to the window, 'I would like to make a call to Brisbane, please.'

'You'll have to pay beforehand.'

'This is official Department of Education business!'

'Do you have a voucher?'

'No! But I am on official business!'

'You can pay me and reclaim the cost!'

Adam knew that he was beaten. If things weren't so rushed, he would argue and make a stand. Right now he was not in a position to do that. He was witnessing the complete destruction of his life. He would soon be an absolute failure but no one cared.

In his childhood he had always admired people who had full wallets. It had been one of his ambitions to carry enough money at all times. It was hard to do that up here with the limited banking facilities but today he had some fifty and hundred dollar bills. He had already broken one fifty at the pub.

'How much do you want?'

'How long do you want to speak for?'

'I'll need to make some calls. I'm not sure how long for. They need to be person to person.'

'Give me fifty dollars. I'll give you any change afterwards. There will be a five dollar charge for opening up a line.'

Another sob wrenched its way through Adam's body. There seemed to be no one who cared. He pulled out the money and swore vengeance.

He walked down to the phone booth and picked up the hand piece. It was an old, black phone with no facilities for dialing. He wound the handle and waited.

'Yes, what do you want?'

'I would like to speak to Jason Antonello at the Queensland Teachers' Union.'

'What is the number?'

Adam pulled out his wallet and fumbled through his papers.

'Would you ring again when you have the number?'

There was already another line outside the window. Adam couldn't wait for another half an hour.

'I've got it here, it's a Brisbane number.' He read out the number and heard the phone ring away in the distance.

'Hello, Queensland Teachers' Union.'

'I have a person to person call to a Jason Antonello. Is he available?'

'I'll just buzz his office.'

Adam prayed to all the gods he had ever heard of, during this next intolerable delay.

'Hello, Jason Antonello here.'

'I have a call for you from Leichhardt. Just a minute, I'll connect you.'

A line clicked inside the ancient machinery.

'Jason!'

'Yes, speaking.'

Jason knew who was on the line but he did not make it known to his caller.

'It's Adam Angel here. I have a problem that requires immediate resolution.'

'What is the problem?'

'I have been transferred! The papers take effect immediately. I'm to go to Palm Island next week.'

'That should be really quite good for you. It's close to Cairns and you'd be likely to find more friends there.'

'I've got nearly a year's worth of research that will be wasted. I don't want to go! I've got enough clout in the party to get a strike at least!'

'Angel, baby! We have had a call from your friend Roland. He has said that there is to be no fuss on this issue.'

'Roland would never betray me!'

'The broader spectrum of the party needs consideration in this matter. There is a Federal election next year. Jack Winslow wouldn't want the party to go against the boongs. He's running on a platform of better race relations. We can't have a battle like this for the opposition to latch on to.'

'What do you mean? What about me?'

'Roland said that he was sorry you would be hurt. The party must take precedence over the individual. We have had enough trouble with Andrew MacDonald as it is. We don't want any more strife!'

'I want to stay here Jason! Can't you get something done? Maybe negotiations till the end of the year? It'll all blow over by then.'

'Adam, we can't do anything! The party machinery is against any action just now.'

'I'll make it up to you later.'

'I'll ring Roland, I think!'

Adam broke the connection and asked Audrey for another line. He knew Roland's number by heart and told it to her quickly. It was a private unlisted number and was to the phone on his desk.

The phone rang four times and then was answered.

'Smythe here, can I help you?'

'Ronnie, it's Adam I have to get some help. Please do something for me! God how I miss you.'

'Adam I've had a call from the Minister for Education. He has explained the situation. I can't allow him to jeopardize my standing in the party.'

'But, sweetheart, all our times together, don't they mean anything?'

'My power base is in the conservative, Catholic portion of the party. If they knew anything of our relationship I would be dumped straight away.'

'Ronnie! What about me?'

'I have the inside running for the top spot on the Senate ticket when old Barnes retires before the next election. If I alienate my power base I can kiss that goodbye. You can come to Canberra with me if you like.'

Adam realized, at last, that he was a beaten man. He was only a pawn in a very large game. He could easily be sacrificed for a win. It was time now for him to accept his transfer and then use these favors for the furtherance of his own career.

'OK, Roll I'll go along now. See if you can get me a party job later on. I'll complete my doctorate at Palm Island.'

The phone was disconnected. He held the hand set in disbelief. The tinny sound of Audrey's voice came through, 'That was some conversation, pansy. I think the whole fifty dollars better stay in my pocket. I know Roland's name and number and I can find out that he is whenever I want to!'

Adam slammed down the phone. He sat on the bench, emotionally wrung out and wept again. Before long he sadly got to his feet and walked back to the pub. His pretensions were gone. His self esteem was deflated. He had to re-evaluate his own standing. Even his most trusted friends had deserted him in his hour of greatest need.

Blind Love

Bluey woke up on his verandah bed. He always tried to sleep the night by himself. The morning was hot and held the promise of steamy pre monsoon incubation. His bed was well sheltered by the mango trees but, in spite of this, the early morning sun drove him from his bed. Many years on the roads taught him to rise at sparrow's fart. He enjoyed the relative cool of the early dawn.

He walked around the verandah and scanned the northern sky. Clouds were building up away in the distance. His eyes gauged their heaviness. A couple of storms would make his next trip hard. He thought that perhaps the storm season wouldn't start for another week.

The joy of love sung in his heart. He had not been with another woman since his time with Bernice. He still did not know that her husband sought his hide.

The hungry look in her eyes had touched some chord deep within him. His selfish lusting heart felt a hiccup. This lust was more meaningful than all the rest.

This extent of love troubled him vaguely. Bluey had lusted after many other married women. They were the ones who would not tie him down. He had even had a brief fling with his own sister. That subject was taboo between them now. She seemed to have grown out of sex, somehow. Stupid priests! They must have frightened every desire out of her loins.

Bluey was going to buy that girl a new dress. His professional eye assessed her size. For a moment his mind digressed. Selling dresses was good business. It was always an easy way of getting dresses off women. From there it was short step to removing their knickers.

That poor lady in Leichhardt. Perhaps she could be his regular northern distraction. In her later years, she could inhabit his town house in the north while Bluey strutted on his stations.

He showered. It was a long cool shower. With the wet so close there wasn't the same need to conserve water. It looked like a long, rich wet too! He carefully soaped his entire body with Imperial Leather soap and then stood in the cooling stream of water for twenty minutes.

Rhonda's voice floated into his dreams, 'Bluey, breakfast's ready.'

Now that was really important! Breakfast must come first, even before dreams of women, no matter how attractive!

Breakfast was already on the table when he went into the kitchen. The boarders ate in the dining room and not quite so well.

There was a large plate with steak, eggs and grilled tomatoes. In beef country it did a man good to eat the fruit of the bullock. A man size mug of strong sweet tea was next to his plate. Beer and cigarettes might do others for breakfast, but not Bluey!

Only the best steak was bought for his plate. He ate butterfly fillets, almost exclusively, for breakfast. A budding business tycoon must eat in keeping with his status. Dinner would be lighter while tea might come from a restaurant. In the bush his fare was simpler.

After breakfast our self declared Casanova completed his morning ablutions. He cleaned his teeth and gargled with green Ultra Fresh. It was a good idea to have a clean mouth; he didn't want to catch any diseases.

His tuneless whistle floated down the stairs and in the direction of his automotive friend. He imagined the blue Ford giving a fond smile as it saw him come around the corner. This was indeed a magnificent piece of machinery! Ford's engineers reached the pinnacle of their art when they created this chariot.

Its engine coughed to life as soon as it was asked. It began to purr smoothly. The goliath under the bonnet began its battle with the climate. Bluey went upstairs and drank another cup of tea. He was wearing a shirt today, in honor of his quest. The car would be a precisely controlled 70 degrees inside. His shirt would have to remain immaculate. Even the smallest amount of sweat would mar his self image on this important day.

Ah Bernice. You will soon be mine! Already the strings of your heart are bound tightly to mine. Fair siren of the north, soon you will have a dress worthy of your new station as my mistress.

The road to Mount Isa was different to the other roads, around here. To the North, South and East the roads were monotonously flat with few turns. This road, to the West, ran along the Selwyn range. There were hills and corners. It was much harder to drive. This road was still unfenced, however. More cattle seemed to die on the curved sections. They came onto the road at night but didn't get the same warning. The vehicles jumped out at them from the rocks. Cattle were usually stupid. They'd see the car and turn away. Its headlights would throw their shadow to the side. When the cow saw its shadow it would spook and turn back. Straight roads gave the drivers time to do something. Sometimes the driver would switch the lights off and pray.

Cattle were no problem in the day. They could see any cars and kept away from the road. Bluey could remember days in his old truck. It wasn't climate controlled. Whenever there was a carcass on the road he would examine it carefully, from a distance. If it was blown up everything was fine. If it had burst, he would wind up the window to avoid any smells.

Country and Western music blared out of the speakers in the doors and on the parcel shelf. John Williamson's singing was good but Bluey's accompaniment left a lot to be desired. His voice sounded something like an injured cow or maybe a band saw cutting metal.

The forlorn remains of Mary Kathleen floated past on the right. Once this town held the promise of prosperity, the old uranium mine was a monument to idealistic politicians. Our mailman sighed, wouldn't it be good if there was some idealism left. They were all pragmatic today prostituting their beliefs in an egomaniacal effort to retain power.

Soon the smudge of the big mine's smoke appeared on the horizon and Bluey knew that Mount Isa was close. The road began to wind more seriously and he stopped singing to concentrate on his driving.

Mt Isa's suburbs appeared as he came over the crest of a hill. This town had been spreading out to the east in recent years. Meanwhile the road continued towards the mines. Soon there was K Mart and the Y junction. Bluey's big blue truck swung to the left and up onto the ridge in the old part of town. He found a park and made his way over to a ladies wear shop.

His salesman's eye was always good. He knew his trade and was sure that he could pick the exact size. His mind tended towards electric blue. This dress would have shoulder pads and puffed short sleeves. It would have a wrap around look at the top with a plunging neck line. Its waist would be low and the skirt would be about knee length. He had never liked dresses that were too short. The longer ones always looked more elegant.

It took him about half an hour to find the exact dress. He fussed about while the assistant packed it in a box.

'Careful there, we don't want it crushed, do we?'

The poor girl thought to herself, 'Buzz off, you dirty old man! I know what I'm doing.' She only smiled meekly because the dragon lady, her boss, was watching with haughty disdain.

When the box was wrapped to Bluey's satisfaction, he braved the heat to return it to the Ford. He had put a blanket over the windscreen and door windows. It was still very hot inside. The box was carefully placed on the floor away from the driver's seat.

Time for dinner. Our intrepid lover had his regular watering hole up here on the ridge. They served a delicious counter lunch and the beer was cold. Some of his mates met there regularly and he tried to get over about once a fortnight.

Billy North and Rex Altridge were already in the bar when Bluey came in. Both men had been at school with Bluey in the 'Curry. They both worked in the mines now and made good money. The freedom of the road and being one's boss outweighed any of the advantages the security a regular job might bring as far as Bluey was concerned.

'Billy, Rex, howryagoin?'

'Good, mate! Sit down. Bartender give us another XXXX please.' Rex replied

These men were good at small talk. Not the cultivated small talk of the English vicar. This was a more basic kind; that of the miner with his mind on sex and beer. The comments about women were demeaning and the greatest insult was to be called a girl. Friends were casually called names descriptive of female genitalia and illegitimacy. They frequently used the copulatory adjective.

Their conversation was about wives with headaches. It seemed that men's minds sought new conquests once their marriage had been consummated. Forbidden fruit was always alluring. Stories of encounters were repeated. Many more imagined than real. The minds of men made most noises when they were empty. The more they talked about 'It' the less they seemed to be getting 'It'.

Before long their lubricated tongues were loose and the banter flowed easily. These friends were also devouring steak covered with mushrooms accompanied by chips and salad. Real man's food!

As their tales of sexual exploits deviated more and more from the truth they bored of the topic. The next best topic concerned the original inhabitants of Australia.

'Bloody boongs! They never do any work but get plenty of handouts. We white fellahs have to carry them all the time.'

'Yeah, every time we do something good they hang around and try to get land rights or something.'

'Half of them aren't coons anyway. Just half castes.'

'Yeah, the whole lot have an average of about half past five.'

'The midnights are the only ones who deserve any consideration.'

'At least they know something about the land!'

'Yeah, they still live in trees.'

'These fringe dwellers; never lived in the bush. Don't know the difference between kangaroo dung and bull's dung.'

'Pretending to be boongs but not doing a good job.'

'Hey guys, I heard a good joke recently.'

'What is it?'

'D'ya hear about the two Boongs on "That's Incredible"?

'No.'

'One was sober and the other had a job!'

'Ha, ha, ha, what a bewdy mate.'

'D'ya hear about the arse bandit in Leichhardt?'

'No.'

'Billy's wife knows the old hag in the Post Office up there. She used to be her mother's friend.'

'What about the fag?'

'He got kicked out. The boongs wanted to get rid of him.'

'Probably got tired of keeping their backs to the wall.'

A slight altercation started at the other end of the bar. A man of Italian descent was arguing with one of convict stock.

'Stupid Dago, you spilt my beer.'

The publican looked to be on the wisdom side of fifty but he quickly managed to put a stop to the row. Both men were summarily ejected.

'Nothing wrong with Dagoes!'

'Yeah mate. They seem to work hard enough.'

'Better than slopes!'

'You know there's three things I hate!'

'What's that mate?'

'Boongs, arse bandits and prejudice!'

'You're right there, prejudice is bad!'

'Yeah, but we don't need boongs and poofters either!'

'Never heard of a poofter boong, have you?'

'No, not as advanced in evolution! Still controlled by raw animal instincts.'

Not long after this Bluey had to leave. The two miners returned to their jobs as well. It wouldn't do to have too much grog. He had to drive back to the 'Curry. The pigs were out to get honest men, as well, these days.

Bluey's junket was successful. Soon his paramour would be endowed with his gift. He decided not to visit any women in 'Curry this weekend, it would be good to save himself for Bernice!

Yellah Fellah!

Ray Walden was feeling nervous. He was now ready for his meeting with the local tribal leader. This meeting would be the crowning achievement of his early career.

This old man would be sure to listen with respect. He was a respected man of the bush but surely he would bow to the greater wisdom of the sophisticated modern Aborigine.

He enjoyed himself in the hotel last night. Its dining room was like a tidy restaurant in a small town. The food was quite memorable. The pub owner, Tony, as far as he could remember, was a great cook. Some of Ray's battered confidence began to return. While the lady of the house served at the bar, he talked to Tony. Ray loved the food. One of the hotel staff asked, in the afternoon, what he wanted. The choice was easy, a big plate of spaghetti with some Bolognese sauce and garlic bread. Ray even chanced a bottle of wine.

His meal and the conversation helped to boost his flagging morale. He then went to his room and prepared his case.

Martin Stone came over during the afternoon. The public servant said that the old fellah, Jumbo, couldn't see him that day. Their meeting would have to wait till late the next afternoon. Ray didn't mind it gave him time to get his thoughts together.

Today was very pleasant. Martin drove him out to a waterhole somewhere and they lunched there. There was a nurse who came on the trip but he couldn't remember her name. After their meal someone suggested that they 'wet the lines' but this venture was unsuccessful.

Ray promised himself, when he was young ringer, that he would have a siesta every day. He sat behind the cattle in those days and now that he was making his way to the top he was often too busy.

This trip gave him the chance to do that. The day was almost unbearably hot outside but an air conditioner gave him the respite he needed. Ray stripped off all his clothes and covered himself with a light sheet.

Being unused to daytime sleep meant that, now, his head was a bit heavy. He lay on his bed and carefully planned his approach. He got up and showered under a cool refreshing jet. Ray was glad that there was plenty of water here, so that he didn't have to conserve water. He dressed carefully in conservative jeans and a quiet, checked western shirt. His calf length boots were too much of a status symbol to be discarded.

Martin returned at about the same time as he had come the day before. They took afternoon tea in the dining room. Tony seemed to be much more eager to help than he had been earlier. Perhaps he was intimidated by peer group pressure before. After all, he was a foreigner himself and only tolerated because he did such a good job in the pub.

As they drank their coffee and ate some savories, they talked.

'Traveled much, Ray?'

'Yeah mate, I've been to the States, Asia and Europe.'

'Did that come from Department business?'

'No, I traveled before I joined the Council. The Government only lets pollies travel; not the workers!'

'What about Queensland, been many places here?'

'I came from Quilpie and started out as a ringer.'

'Where did you work?'

'Mainly droving down the Diamantina and the Georgina. I've eaten lots of dust but I haven't seen too many Outback towns.'

'What about Isa?'

'Only time was on the way up. We got most of our cattle from the Tablelands up in the Territory. I've seen a lot of Camooweal.'

'Nothing to do there but drink and screw.'

'That's about right, mate. I hated that place!'

'How did you make the move from ringer to public servant?'

'Well..., that's a long story. I went back to school after a few years. I realized that I wouldn't get anywhere eating dust. I studied for a BA at St. Lucia and then did a Masters in the States.'

'Sounds impressive! I went to Queensland Uni myself. Great place they have there tucked up on a bend in the river.'

'Loved it myself! St. Lucia is a pretty spot.'

'What did you major in?'

'Government. What about you?'

'I studied statistics and history. A funny combination but it got me a good job with the D.A.I.A. My honor's was in history, early settlement in North West Q…'

'Look, why don't we get out there and try this old guy?' Ray's mind snapped back to his job.

'Jumbo?'

'Yeah…, if that's his name.'

'He'll not be ready to see you till a bit later. I thought that I'd prepare you a bit. These people are a bit different to the ones you'd know in the South west.'

'What do you mean by that?'

'It's hard to say… I was in Charleville for a while. The guys here are wilder or something… A lot of them have never been fringe dwellers.'

'That's the saddest part of Aboriginal history, so many leave their old ways but never make it into the mainstream of the society.'

'There are a lot of people who want to stop them from getting there.' Martin replied thoughtfully. He had almost unknowingly touched a raw nerve. There was pressure in the Outback to keep the boongs subservient. The Government was not much better; a bit of noise here and there and a few handouts. Keep them happy but don't do anything to alienate the real electorate.

'You're right there. We want to overcome the hatred and bitterness.'

'Look Ray, I think you'd better get out into the camp for a while before your meeting. Walk around a bit and talk to some people, maybe. Get a feel for the place and then you can have your meeting. Something like that would help you with your report.'

Ray and Martin left the dining room and walked out to their vehicle. The heat seemed to beat at them like a giant hammer as they left the cool embrace of the hotel.

The journey out to Boomallooba was uneventful. Both men were locked into their own thoughts. Both wondering how they could use the other to further their own aims.

Martin parked under a big tree near his office and said goodbye to Ray. His meeting was scheduled for 'before dark', that meant in about three hours.

Ray decided to take his time and see the place carefully. The drive he'd taken earlier had not given him a good feel for the place. He was going to walk now and see what life was like here. There were always stories coming through the press about conditions on the settlements in the north. Perhaps it would be a good time to check them, incognito. If he could unearth some genuine grievances that would add momentum to their budding campaign it would earn him some points back in Brissy. It would also help him to persuade Jumbo to help.

In spite of his pretence about not knowing the old man's name, Ray had it locked away permanently in his sharp mind. A bit of vagueness would often help when he talked to some people. On the other hand, it was always important to be precise about a man's name when you talked to him.

Ray stood on the verandah and looked towards the south. There was a gentle breeze blowing up from the black soil plains. It was pungent and malodorous. This breeze had picked the fumes of the septic on the way through. As he watched the people coming and going, he realized that most of them didn't even notice the smell. No wonder the health of the Aborigines was so poor. No precautions were taken to effectively dispose of sewerage. He wondered how seepage would affect the water table.

The store was on his left and the hospital on his right. He planned to visit the store first. Would the standards here be equal to those of stores in Brisbane or would it prove to be another source of disease?

Ray walked towards the east, a distance of about fifty yards. This store was a large building about one hundred and twenty feet by fifty feet. It was rectangular with a high roof. The long axis ran north-south. The southern wall and no windows and faced the road. There was a room added to the south western corner. An entrance was next to that room. That was good, at least. The gravel road seemed to generate clouds of dust and the wall would keep most of it out. The appended room also sheltered the main entrance.

A double door greeted Ray as he strode towards the entrance. Inside were three check outs with their tables. They were about six feet back from the entrance. It seemed as though they were more trusting here. There were no gates just a walkway each side. The walls were unlined but the shelves were well stocked. It was clean and open. The little room beside the entrance contained a large freezer unit. It was fully enclosed.

Some large chest freezers and also a fridge for drinks were within easy reach. There were the usual goods found in a supermarket. At the back, on the left as you walked into the store, was an office with windows looking into the store. The store manager and some administrative staff worked in there.

A door led off towards the north. Ray could see bulk storage through that door. The supermarket was not crowded and seemed to be unhurriedly moving towards the end of its daily trading. It was quite a good store compared with others he had known.

Behind the store was a large white building, surrounded by a hedge; a really imposing building. It was now the official guest house and residence. Any further visits Ray made would be official and he would have to stay there. Martin was the only occupant of that imposing edifice. He, as the manager, was the host of any official guests.

This home was the residence of the last missionary/manager before the Government took over. It had lovely river views from the upstairs drawing room and wide cool verandahs. The gardens had been immaculate but were now in a state of disrepair.

To the west of the residence was a series of Public Service buildings. All were of a light yellow color with dark brown trimmings. They were high set homes with car accommodation and a laundry underneath.

All these homes had green manicured lawns and gardens. Some had fruit and shade trees as well.

Ray walked past the gardens and houses. He could smell damp earth. All the lawns had been watered. An aboriginal gardener tended the gardens and also the 'white fellah' swimming pool nearby. The public servants lived in the genteel isolation of yesteryear.

To the east of the houses was a large workshop. It was mainly for mechanical purposes. There were vehicles belonging to the Government and others belonging to the Council which were maintained here. A tack room was located inside the complex and to the north was a horse paddock. The local Council ran cattle on the Aboriginal reserve. At this time of day, the shed was locked up. Outside were a grader and bulldozer which were used to maintain the roads and where necessary make new ones. There was also a large truck. It was an old World War Two, six wheel drive, blitz.

There was a chook* shed between the garage and the main road. It was an enclosure that was about half and acre in size. It had and eight feet cyclone netting fence which was heavy with passion fruit vine. Inside was a shed with about two hundred chooks. The rest of the yard was populated with citrus trees. They were growing well thanks to the fresh chook fertilizer. The whole yard was watered daily, it seemed, because large irrigation sprays were set permanently in the ground. There were plenty of free range eggs to be sold in the store.

This chicken run shared a common boundary with the hospital. Chooks seemed to pass freely over the fence and there was manure in the hospital yard as well.

Ray checked the files stored in his memory. It was a twenty bed hospital staffed by eight nurses. There were two on duty at all times. They worked a regular eight hour shift. The chief of staff

---

* Chicken

was the matron called Adele Andrews. She worked a regular nine to five shift, five days a week. The hospital was visited by the Flying Doctor, once a week, for his regular clinic. The doctor was also available for emergencies. There was a rough bush strip running north south to the west of the township.

This hospital, according to the map he'd seen, was an L shaped building. Its long axis ran east-west. The shorter one was at the eastern end and face north. Starting in the west there was a men's ward, men's showers and toilets. At least they didn't have a dunny! Next came the kitchen then the drug room. There were two rooms which acted as the surgery for the Doctor and outpatients. A nurse's station came after that. Women's facilities and a ward were at the end. In this wing were the labor ward and maternity facilities. There was a verandah running along the south side. It also ran along the eastern edge but had been enclosed.

The hospital looked out onto the road and was troubled by dust from the traffic. It was a very old wooden building. It looked as though the verandah needed frequent scrubbing. There were five steps leading up to the wards and the whole complex was set on timber stumps.

The chooks seemed to have found a second home here and some of them were roosting underneath. A large spotted dog lay in the cool as well; must belong to one of the ol' fellahs. It had been bitten by a goanna; one of its ears had the top cut off. This hospital was not good by city standards. Our People's Representative could imagine someone, down at the Department of Aboriginal and Islander Affairs, saying, 'Good enough for Boongs!' He swallowed back his anger and faced the village.

The sun was dropping away in the west but the heat had not gone out of the day yet. A newer part of the camp was in the west and an older part by the river. As one moved from the west to the east the buildings became more crowded. A first row of houses had ten brand new buildings. They were set back from the others. Each was high set. There were no large trees here; the land had been cleared recently. The homes were all the silver color of unpainted aluminum.

Ray saw that there was a well defined gravel road going south almost directly in front of the hospital. About fifty yards to the west there was another newly graded track. This seemed to service the newer houses.

The whole Settlement was based on a rectangular grid. In the north was the main road. There were three well defined roads running south, each about eight hundred yards long. An east-west road connected the three in the middle and another one connected their ends in the south. The new track snaked away from the southern road and met the main road in the west. There was another track running away to the south and from it another to the air strip in the west.

The easternmost of the streets ran along the river bank with some houses overlooking the gorge. The majority of dwellings here were humpies.

Our hopeful leader walked out to the track which serviced the newer houses. As, he walked down this track he examined them. They all had broken windows and looked uninhabited; the concrete slab under each showed signs of life. There was a family living in the space under each house. It occurred to Ray that this must be some sort of bureaucratic blunder. The buildings in the west would be too hot and the families had to live underneath. Each home had an open fire for cooking and the water came from the laundry there. Even these new homes had dunnies with pans.

There was a large water tank at the end of the middle cross street. Some small boys were playing on the steel ladder which serviced this reservoir.

Ray was making an effort to note all the details. He was very nervous; he was concerned about the meeting he had to attend. It was extremely important. His future could very well be riding on the outcome. He had never had much contact with the real bush Aborigines, the myalls, as they were sometimes called. His only experience had been with fringe dwellers and city blacks. He knew the American blacks better than he did these wild blackfellahs. Ray hoped that spending time this environment would give him some understanding. Maybe insight would fall upon him in some spectacular way!

He found walking uncomfortable and his feet were hurting. His boots looked nice but they weren't designed for walking. The narrow portion above the arch was great for stirrups but not for pedestrians. Cuban heels may stop the foot sliding forward and being caught but they also caused lower back pain. In the old days he became used to walking in his R M Williams elastic sided boots. They were all he had. Stockmen had to do quite a bit of walking. He became accustomed to sneakers at St. Lucia and needed more support now.

Boots, however, were essential for the well dressed politician. All the Council members wore boots. None of them did much walking any more. Official cars made life easier. They also made men soft.

The ambassador winced as a spasm of pain crossed his stomach. It seemed as though he had suffered from an irritable colon all his life. In recent years he had largely managed to avoid the stress that led to this condition. The pressure of his upcoming interview was enough to develop a relapse; it began with increased flatulence earlier today.

Ray checked his watch and estimated that it would take another hour till sunset. He would have to meet the old man then. He knew, from his previous trip, that he would have to meet Jumbo near the river at the far end of the camp. Our secret agent took care to avoid that corner until the time came. Already there was that reddish tinge that seemed to accompany sunset in this country. He was sure that his memories of this trip would have a red color to them. He reached the end of the track by now and turned towards the east. Any observer, who cared to, would have noticed that he was limping slightly by now.

There were two newer houses along the western edge of this first real road in the settlement. They did not differ in any aspect from the other new houses. On the other side of this road was a row of ten more houses. These were of the same aluminum material but were not high set. They were about three feet off the ground on stumps. Each one had a small shed outside and the essential dunny.

These people lived inside their houses and on the verandahs. None of the houses had any fly screens, but then the mosquitoes weren't too bad at this time of the year. There wasn't much water lying around so they did not breed. After the wet there would be millions of the beasts. They would be whining their way around everybody's heads. He would then see people slapping their bare legs as they tried to chase them away. Ray remembered, too, that the old black fellahs would escape mosquitoes by staying near a fire. They didn't miss anything, here in their land.

After Ray passed the cross roads he was amazed. He saw that under one of these low set houses there were beds and there were two fires near this house. He asked a kid who came by and was told that the Starlight family lived underneath that house. They had recently come in from the Territory and needed somewhere to live.

He reached the main road again and turned to the right. The next street contained twelve blocks on each side of the road. Each was fenced. This part of the camp was much older. Their fences often had runners growing on them and each yard was shaded by trees. Some stately old Poinciana stood out like vast skeletons silhouetted in the setting sun. There were also some large mango trees for shade and tucker.

One noticeable feature was the lack of grass cover. There were clumps in some places but most of the houses were surrounded by bare earth. The breeze, which had so assaulted Ray's senses, continued to blow. He was, by now, somewhat used to the smell, although it left a bad taste in his mouth.

There were crowds of people wandering aimlessly up and down the roads. Clouds of dust blew up and coated Ray's trousers His sweat left wet patches all over his shirt and they were now red mud.

This dust was dangerous. It contained millions of eggs. Every parasite in Australia must have eggs in this dust! There was so much feces left behind each tree that the risk of contamination was very high; even the cleanest of people would be lucky to escape. He had heard, from Martin, of an anthropologist who stayed here. The man brought his wife and child. They lived in a caravan and made a real effort to be clean. The child became lethargic and then sick. When tested she was found to be loaded up with hookworm, round and thread worms. The mother and daughter quickly returned to Brisbane.

That option was not available to the kids he could see now. They were, on the whole, pathetically thin but they had distended bellies. Some had legs so spindly that they seemed to walk with supernatural assistance.

All these houses were served by dunnies. They did not have the laundries behind, just a tap in the open. They were much smaller than the newer ones. Each was made of corrugated iron and would be unbearably hot at this time of the year. They all had two small rooms inside and not enough windows to ensure a good flow of air. At least, each one had a concrete floor.

Martin had told him of one guy, called 'The Gentleman' by everybody in the camp. He shared his home with his animals for many years. Some bleeding heart Christians had cleaned his house out. It had eighteen inches of very good dog and chicken night soil instead of a carpet.

The only closed door in the street was that of the village hall. It was on the right of the road and south of the cross street. Every house seemed to be the home of some chooks. They wandered in and out and jumped up on the windows. There were one or two,

Ray noticed, that was much cleaner than the others and did not have free animal access.

There was one yard with three huge black pigs wallowing in a mud bath near a dripping tap. One big sow lay beside the road with about a dozen piglets nearby.

The population was officially one thousand, three hundred and twenty six, at the last census, two years ago. Ray thought that at least thirteen hundred of them must be wandering up and down the roads tonight.

At the end of the street, in the bush, sat a group of men; they were passing a flagon of red wine to each other. Each one was past caring about the airborne menace in the dust.

One thing which horrified Ray was the number of children carrying old milk tins. There were no refrigerators in the houses. All the milk was powdered and came in tins. He walked close to one kid and smelled fuel. The children were sniffing petrol. Some seemed to be only five or six! Perhaps their inadequate diet had stunted their growth. Allowing for malnutrition they would definitely be no older than nine or ten.

Ray walked down the middle of the street. He checked his watch. Still another thirty minutes. He walked back up the street and passed the remains of an old generator house. It had been gutted by fire; as recently as five years earlier the power had come from here. The noise must have been terrible. Someone started the motor at eight am and switched it off and ten pm. There had been no power overnight.

The time for the meeting inched closer. His watch seemed to be stopped. Pains were ripping up and down his guts, playing a concerto on his intestines. His flatulence was almost non stop.

When he reached the head of the road, he turned right again. A further right turn had him on the riverside road heading south. The older folks seemed to live here. There were still crowds of people aimlessly wandering. The crowds suddenly seemed to thin out and the smell of cooking food over open fires became apparent.

Some people were still sitting in small groups along the river bank. Ray wandered between the houses until he could see the river. Down near its bed were groups gambling. The ones on the bank watched. Some mothers were trying to get enough money for tomorrow's tucker.

He walked back to the road. There were two old men sitting at a table playing draughts. A small crowd had gathered to watch the game. Martin had told him that some of these old men were very good at the game. He had said, 'Never play against the old guys; they'll have you every time!'

There were only five houses on the eastern side of the river street. They had spaces between them which were taken by humpies. Shanty town dwellings made of iron, wood and cardboard. Some would surely disappear as soon as the first rains of the monsoon came; they could not possibly survive the storms.

The sun was hanging, like a gigantic red ball, just above the horizon and slipping fast when Ray reached the end of the street.

An old man was standing at the side of the road waiting to meet him. He was wearing no hat, but had an old long sleeved shirt on. In the fading light it looked a dull brown; that was the impression left after years of wear. It was small on the man. Its sleeves flapped loosely on his forearms. His cuff buttons had been missing for a long time. The shirt tails reached the top of Jumbo's trousers. Ray could see initiation scars running across his chest like huge snakes.

The chairman was wearing baggy pants with no shape. He was taller than his guest and big in the chest. He had just begun to stoop with age. His white hair sat on his head like a fleece. His face was fairly smooth with the only lines running from his nose beside his mouth. Jumbo's eyes seemed to be rheumy. The hand that reached out to shake Ray's was large and strong. His bare feet were flattened from constant walking and very hard.

This future leader faced the, now, esteemed leader and smiled. He could smell the stale smoke that clung to the old man's body. Obviously he had not washed for some time.

Ray felt a real urge to have a drink, something that would calm his nerves. He wanted to dull his feelings and ease the pain in his stomach. He licked his dry lips nervously and looked over at the men drinking. He could see their relaxed faces in the firelight. With a supreme effort of will power he forced his mind back on the job. He winced as Jumbo grabbed his hand in a crushing hand shake.

The old man walked over to another fire and sat down. He sat in the dust, far enough away not to be unduly heated by the fire. It was only a small fire but the night was hot. Ray looked desperately for a seat. As the darkness began to enclose his field of vision he couldn't see anything.

Reluctantly Ray sat on the ground. His jeans were tight and he couldn't cross his legs; his testicles hurt.

The old man began to talk. His voice was quiet but dignified. Ray feared that things would not be as he had planned. He had hoped that his own presence would dominate the meeting. The older, uneducated man should automatically recognize his priority.

The exact opposite was true. This man had an aura of genuine wisdom about him; wisdom that could only be learned in a lifetime of hardship. He also possessed an augustness founded on his patience.

Our young man was uncomfortable sitting on the ground. He was nervous. Ray had lost his confidence and was thirsty for a long, calming drink of alcohol.

'Boss fellah, him tell me city fellah want to talk.' Jumbo's introductory remarks were straight to the point. This man might have great patience but he wouldn't waste his time on trivialities.

'Yes, I come from… the… er… big council in Brisbane.'

'What for youfellah come mefellah country?'

Jumbo was offended at this intrusion. These people didn't understand his country. They had no respect for the traditions. They were unwilling to wait for anything.

'We have come to… um… consider… ahhh… land rights.'

'What this land rights?'

Ray's nervousness was now beginning to come under control. He had heard this man's speech and felt sure that his debating skill would soon win. Suddenly he felt that it would be easy.

'We believe that Aborigines should have some control that is… er… ownership of their land.'

'Me b'long mefellah country, mefellah country b'long me!'

'That's right!' Ray mistook the statement for a question, 'We believe that the Aborigines should have the final say in the running of their land. We are the traditional owners of our land. The white men intend to rape this land and rape the original owners as well. Figuratively speaking, that is. They are vandalizing the culture by destroying the heritage that has grown over thousands of years. When these people still lived in caves our people were a proud and cultured race!'

Ray's confidence had fully returned to him. He had no sensitivity to his listener and did not see that the old man was not impressed.

'What youflah dreaming, young fellah?'

'We have a dream to see all Aborigines free and independent!'

Ray committed his first great error of the night. He was not prepared for the question. The old man wanted to find out his love for the land; he asked for his cultic subgroup. The young man did not immediately understand the significance of the term. Ray failed the test!

'You just yellah fellah! What youflah know 'bout mefellah country?'

'We have a dream of every Aborigine owning their own country.'

'You want themfellah woman, he come to sacred place?'

'Yes we are modern and believe in the liberation of all! We believe that every Aboriginal person should have full access to his or her heritage.'

'No woman, he not see my sacred place! No young fellah he bin come long time.'

Ray suddenly realized what he had said. He kicked himself for the blunder.

'Well maybe we won't allow women.'

'Youflah hab man marks? You bin hab man rights?'

Ray felt that the interview was going sour. He had an empty feeling in the pit of his stomach. He wondered what his boss would say. He felt the strong urge to drink, and forget again.

'Not exactly. I didn't have enough time as a young man.'

'You eber lib in humpy? Lib in bush b'fore?'

'No I've never done either. I have been mustering and droving so I've slept under the stars.'

'You know how to make spear; boomerang?'

'Not exactly… but I'm willing to learn!'

'You yellah fellah neber see me fellah country. This place b'long mefellah. Youflah make 'em dreamtime spirits angry!'

The old man got up and walked away. Ray tried to follow him, not believing that he had failed. Another man stopped him, 'That ol' fellah doesn't like you. You've got Buckley's chance of success now. Come I'll take you home now.'

The younger man took Ray to his old battered Holden and drove him back to Leichhardt, 'You stay here in the white fellah's world. Don't trouble us any more!'

Ray now felt that he must have a drink. He walked into the hotel and then into the back bar.

He saw a small balding men sitting at a table. There really wasn't a bar here. The customers could only buy bottles.

The man had red eyes and a swollen face. He looked like he had been crying.

'What's the matter mate? You look like you've found five cents and lost one hundred dollars. Boy do I need a drink!'

'Come and share my bottle.'

The two men sat together and drank their way through the bottle of claret that Adam Angel had been enjoying by himself.

Ray ordered a bottle of Jack Daniel's, after that they began to drink seriously. By the morning both men were sleeping at the table. Beside them were three empty bottles. Two of then were Jack Daniel's.

A Fool's Paradise

Bluey Walters woke up in his room at the Dornoch pub. It was hot and the sheets beneath him were soaking wet. He slept naked. The sheets, at least, were clean and he could not smell the stale sweat that was evident in his own bed at home. There were no covers on the bed. It had been 95 degrees last night, just before dawn. There was no breeze blowing to help cool him. The room was cool last night when he came in from the verandah, but that was only by comparison.

He stayed in this room every time he came through. This was his bed every second Monday night. Usually he shared this bed with a gin for part of the night. He wasn't choosy when it came to sharing his bed; his philosophy was: 'You don't look at the mantelpiece when you stoke the fire.' Besides he didn't have sex with a woman for her benefit but his own.

Not tomorrow though; he would make a real effort to give Bernice pleasure. He must be in love, or have a virus, he thought.

He didn't even want the woman last night. She had come to the door after he had gone to bed. The door remained shut and she was asked to leave.

Our mailman kicked the hanging mosquito net. A couple of months and you wouldn't be able to sleep without one of these. When the wet started, life began again; a three or four month season in which every insect bred frantically. They seemed to spend all their time trying to bite someone or get onto his Ford's windscreen.

This room was quite Spartan; American tourists did not frequent this hotel. Poor sods, didn't know what they were missing. The Garden of Eden would have seemed like a street in Calcutta after this place!

There were not any glass or screens, just wooden shutters to block out the sun. Problem with shutters was that they made the room stuffy. It was an upstairs room on the other side to the bar; too noisy above the bar for a man who had to work the next day. The bed had a hand made wooden frame and slats. On top of the slats was a tired sponge mattress. Too many people had done push ups on this bed. There was no rug on the floor, just polished boards. This room, along with one other, had the status of being executive suites; each had its own bathroom. The other four had to share a bathroom and the 'bulls' and 'cows' toilets downstairs. At least they didn't have to wander outside to the dunny during the night.

The early morning sun dragged Bluey from his slumber. His room was at the back of the pub and, therefore, facing west. This meant he didn't get the direct morning sun. Of course, this far west, it didn't get light until about six thirty so you could sleep in a bit. Here, at the back, he managed to sleep until seven.

Our door to door salesman lay in his bed and dreamed about his coming conquest. He imagined the smile on Bernice's face. His mind traced down her body till he enjoyed her vertical smile just before he took it. These stirrings of lust drove him from bed and into the shower. He took his time and washed his body carefully.

After he toweled himself attentively, he liberally applied 'Charm Pit' in the appropriate place. A shave brought his stubble into submission and then clean underclothes; a luxury not usually taken after only one day on the road. New Ruggers and a clean singlet completed his wardrobe. He may be meeting a woman but he still needed his work clothes. Bluey was prepared for any emergency.

His overnight kit was bundled into his black 'Tiger' bag. At seven twenty he went downstairs for breakfast. The dining room was at the back but there were also some tables out in the open.

'Give me steak and tomatoes, Rosie.' Bluey called to the cook as he went out to the tables. He stopped at the glass fronted fridge and took out a pint of orange and mango juice. By the time he had drunk the juice his steak was ready. It was a big slab of rump and there were four pieces of tomato. In a man's country a man must eat man's food!

After breakfast he chewed on an apple. Bluey read in a magazine that an apple was as good as cleaning your teeth. He settled the bill and then climbed into the big blue Ford. It was parked behind the pub and away from the trees. If you parked under the trees the birds would be sure to poop on it.

There was no 'Aboriginal' art on its blue duco. He heaved a sigh of relief. His big motor caught first try and its powerful rumble soon became regular. Our sly grog man sat in the truck and waited until the truck's air conditioner tamed the summer heat. For the first time since he had left its cool embrace the night before he began to feel comfortable.

The river bank was quite high here and the shade trees tall and strong. The ground was just damp underneath and the bank had green grass. This country would be the most productive in all the earth, if only there was more water.

The gear easily slid into reverse and he backed out. Bluey's mail van slipped around the side of the hotel and into the full blast of the morning sun. It was only eight thirty but already the mercury was tickling one hundred. It would be a hot day today, like a furnace. What was one hot day among so many? After ten or eleven weeks of forty plus every day, one survived. The temperature was unremarkable in a remarkable land.

Bluey had been nursing one of his pet ideas the day before and again he let his mind run. A man often took refuge in dreams when he had been through a difficult childhood. This man was always on the lookout for get rich quick schemes. The city slickers dreamed of colored balls falling in a pre selected numerical pattern. The man in the bush set his hopes on similar riches but longed to find them through his own talents.

There was one problem which troubled our man on many occasions. When a car was climate controlled it was comfortable to drive. Its batteries were not of the long lasting kind so that the climate could not be tamed while the engine wasn't running. Could there be a way to keep the car cool and maintain electronic security while the driver was away? In this land there was one unquenchable power source: that cursed sun, driving everything into untimely retirement.

Could the sun be used to keep the car cool, or warm in that God forsaken part of this land where warmth was needed? A second roof could be fitted and this would contain solar cells. This roof would, of course, be aerodynamically efficient. The second cover would leave a cushion of air above the car and that would help to insulate it. The solar cells would constantly recharge batteries which could run the air conditioner.

No more waiting for the car to cool down. First step; right into a cool blast of winter in the heat of summer. A good marketing slogan that! Must sell the slogan at the right time.

Our great inventor suddenly found himself dressed in a dinner suit. He was at a special function in Sydney. There was a large crowd clapping in the Opera House as he collected his award for excellence. The papers told of his genius. They also told of his rapid rise to fortune due to his clever marketing. This man is a real life example of business genius only seen before in novels and the movies.

It wouldn't take him long to get out of Sydney and back to his beloved North. He would buy both Lawn Hill and Escott; maybe Augustus Downs as well. He would be a millionaire cattle entrepreneur; the emperor of a prosperous Gulf Country.

Right beside him would be Bernice, bewitching in her haunting beauty.

The dreams seemed to flow in an unending river from his overactive imagination. He learnt to be a survivor early in life. His mother and father had fought continuously when he was very young. He had a couple of really good hidings from his father before the old goat had shot through. He went to the Territory and then west to do some prospecting. Bluey left school as soon as he could. Between his father's and his own departure he lived in poverty. His youth had been dreamed away in hope. The habit continued until today. Whenever he felt like it, he sat back and let his mind wander. It increased his determination to succeed. The mailman enjoyed his job, but driving in this country was hard.

The roads were long and tedious; the glare was constantly trying to bore into a man's eyes. He could remain alert and drive well while the genius within was pampered. His mind was carefully cocooned in sheer bliss while his body managed on the job. He found himself in many destinations without having felt the pain of the journey.

He was always fresh and a bit randy after one of these trips. There would be housewives to satisfy his needs in most places.

The road on the right looked familiar. Bluey recognized it in the subconscious part of his mind. His remarkable genius took over again; it was the turn off to the Leichhardt airstrip.

His enormous powers of concentration were now at their outstanding peak. He slowed the great beast down to a safe and legal speed. It would be folly to get caught by the police. There were too many investments to risk. The clothes would not survive an accident or even a spell in jail. The flagons of watered down port were not insured at all. They would be the major catastrophe in any accident.

The shame of being caught with all that drink for the boongs would be the worst. He would get time for that and lose all his investments. His boarding house would survive but nothing else.

Bluey had a real fear of losing everything. He despised himself, as a child, for being poor. Many times he reaffirmed his childish oath; 'I will be a wealthy man!' To end up in jail, with nothing, would be a good reason to shoot himself.

These horrifying thoughts were soon brought to an abrupt end. He stopped at the end of the great north-south road and eased left into the east-west turnpike. This second highway would soon feel his wheels but just for now it was time for parking.

Bluey's blue Ford came to an easy rest beside the cool inviting verandah of 'The Burke Arms'. This hotel would act as his base tonight. He would move on towards the west with the next day's sun.

Antonio was a good host. He was always glad to meet regular guests. The welcome afforded the mailman was breezy and genuine. The two men stayed beside the reception window and chewed the fat for about ten minutes.

When Bluey walked outside the front door and onto the verandah he was hit hard by more than the heat. There was a police truck parked in front of his own. Next to his truck was a man dressed in regulation police uniform. He was an incredibly tall man. Already there was a stain of sweat, dark on his grey felt hat. His blue shirt was wet all over.

When the policeman saw Bluey he removed his hat, took his foot off the fender of the Toyota and walked over. Bluey looked up and saw cold anger in the chilling grey eyes.

'This your truck, mate?'

'Yeah, nothing wrong with it either!'

Bluey resented authority and always fought against any representative of it.

'I want to have a look at it!'

'You got a warrant?'

'Listen, stupid, you been watching too much American TV. I can search your truck if I've got a suspicion of crime. Maybe I got a tip or something.'

'OK, go ahead. Don't put your sweaty back on my seat!'

'Have you ever heard of a man being hurt while resisting arrest?'

The policeman's eyes certainly had that killer look. Bluey imagined this cop would kill his own grandmother and then finish her beer for her. He told himself to play it cool. The guy didn't know anything. He had never come across this big guy before but the locals didn't seem to mind him. They all reckoned that he was fair and kept the boongs in their place.

'Look mate, I'm only trying to make some conversation. Don't get your nappy in a knot.' He couldn't help himself. The old mouth just ran away by itself. Perhaps it would be wired shut for the next few months if he didn't watch out.

*

Ernie ignored the last remark. He walked around to the driver's door and pulled it open. The trimming inside was light blue: to tone in with the outside.

The driver's seat was the first thing that caught his eye. It was like an expensive lounge chair, covered in lamb's wool. There were soft arm rests on each side, the one near the door had been folded back out the way. There was a soft lumbar cushion. Its back was contoured and firm. The man who used this seat spared no expense on himself; he obviously used it a lot. A business executive would have his seat designed for comfort, so did this executive of the road.

The steering wheel had a lamb's wool cover, as well. Behind this was an instrument cluster. Ernie didn't look at them for long, he examined the Pioneer stereo system. It had a six band graphic equalizer. There were two speakers in each door and two more high up in the back of the cabin.

An automatic air conditioning system looked after the climate. It was set at exactly 70 degrees. The controls were at on, obviously they were left set. Cooling air would begin to blow as soon as the engine was started.

There was another comfortable chair on the left of the cabin. Between the chairs was a passage way and a T shaped opening leading to a sleeping compartment. Ernie backed out of the truck and called his offsider, 'Dave, come here and check out the back of the cabin.' At 6 feet 7 inches he was too tall to fit comfortably into the back. His bad knee would hurt too much if he squeezed into the sleeping space.

Another man climbed out of the police Toyota. He was shorter, but well built. He was still quite a bit taller than Bluey. Dave Billings had blond hair and was well tanned. He was 5 feet 10 inches tall and must have weighed nearly fifteen stone He would make a great second rower in rugby league. He had the look of a man in good physical condition and his thick arms bulged out of the short sleeves.

'Get in there mate, will ya. I can't squeeze in and have a look. My old bones won't take the bending.'

The younger man climbed in the passenger side. He slipped across the seat and bent over into the space between the seats.

He was confronted by the T shaped entrance. It was about two feet wide at the bottom and went out to four feet at the top. The space inside was taken up by a comfortable bed. As Dave peeked in he could smell stale tobacco mixed with old sweat.

The bed had a yellowing cover and a crumpled pillow. At one end there was a small chest fridge. Its other end was taken up by a chest of three drawers. Above the fridge and drawers were darkly tinted windows. There was also a pop up window in the roof. A pile of girlie magazines was scattered over the bed.

There was very little dust inside the cabin. The driver must keep the old air conditioner going most of the time.

Dave jumped out, 'Looks all in order in there, Ernie!'

Bluey was starting to wonder if he had been dobbed in. He could feel spasms of pain playing up and down his guts. His throat was dry and he longed for a drink. Which swine had told the pigs about him? Perhaps they were on the wrong track; they seemed to think that something was in the cabin.

The big guy was saying something to him, 'Open up the back for us, mate.'

'Which back?'

'We'll start with the mail section.'

Bluey breathed a sigh of relief. He tried to walk in a relaxed and unconcerned way. He legs seemed stiff and he hobbled a bit.

The mailman opened up the back and a cloud of bulldust floated out. All three men coughed. The mail sacks were all there and covered in the fine dust.

'How many bags for us?'

'I think there's six for here and about eight for the boongs.'

'They can be dropped off later!'

Bluey was feeling slightly relieved now. They hadn't looked too carefully in this section. Only a very careful search would reveal the false bottom in the middle section. He was safe now for sure.

The big man in blue walked up to the middle section. Bluey opened the door and slid it over. Some dust fell down around the door but there was very little inside. The floor was carpeted and the dresses were hanging in plastic bags.

Ernie's eyes perused the boxes. There were toasters, toasting ovens, electric kettles and ghetto blasters. The stuff was probably not stolen. It wouldn't repay any effort to check it out.

'Shut the door!' Ernie commanded.

Bluey nearly collapsed on the ground. He reached out and began to close it.

The voice of the sergeant cracked out like a whip lash, 'Just a minute! I want another look in there.'

Bluey stared in disbelief as Ernie reached into the truck. He lifted the carpet and pulled it out onto the ground. Bluey felt weak in the legs. His guts turned to water. Fortunately he didn't disgrace himself.

The cover over the hidden compartment was quite obvious now. There was a small gap running around the edge of the wooden lid.

Ernie stood and looked for about three minutes. Bluey was ready to faint. His head was beginning to spin slowly. He could hear a buzzing sound in his ears. He struggled to breathe. He couldn't get enough air into his lungs. His world was being destroyed before his eyes. All his dreams went crashing onto the ground with that blue carpet. His worst fears were being realized.

Ernie spoke again, 'See anything in there, Dave?'

'Looks like there's some sort of cover on the floor.'

'Yeah, it does, doesn't it! Better pull it off and have a look.'

Dave Billings pushed his fingers into the small gap near the door. He easily lifted off the cover. It was quite substantial: a strong framework covered with five ply. Bluey was surprised; he had to struggle with that lid. Dave treated it like paper.

The wood clattered onto the verandah as it was flung aside. There was a layer of sponge rubber, next. The sponge rubber was quickly disposed of revealing thirty flagons. The red wine had been carefully placed in a shaped foam base. Foam had been injected into the bed of the compartment. It was covered in blue plastic.

Ernie whistled in disbelief. They were even using advanced packaging technology in the age old profession of illicit alcohol.

Bluey slumped down on the edge of the verandah. The light was too bright for him now. He couldn't get enough air into his lungs. The world had started to spin quite rapidly. As he hit the wooden boards he was embraced in comforting oblivion.

'Ernie, I think this crook has had a heart attack!'

'Nah, mate, he's just passed out. This bludger couldn't face up to the rewards of his skullduggery.'

'What shall we do now?'

Get him into the Toyota. I'll take the mail down to the boongs and then drop all the other bags up here at the PO. Nip over to the hozzie and get the sister to check him over. I don't reckon he's got heart trouble.'

'Rightio!'

The two men humped Bluey into the front seat of the Toyota. When they had strapped him into place, he seemed to recover a bit. Dave drove out to the west along the Escott road. As he drove, he heard an awful sobbing sound escape from Bluey's lips. The poor ex great man began to weep.

When Ernie had completed his trip, he piloted the Ford into the impound yard, behind the station. The blue beast wouldn't have too much use, for the next few days, at least.

Sergeant Collins checked into the station. Dave told him that Bluey was sitting in the cells weeping. Ernie's main regret was that he didn't get to put the cuffs on that scum.

A quick trip to the cells revealed the salesman lying exhausted on a bunk.

'You'll never touch another man's wife again!' Certain, less than savory, appellations were included at this point.

Bluey heard but he didn't bother looking up. His heart again plumbed the depths of despair. This whole set up must be revenge. He wondered which roughie, he had sampled, was married to his tormentor.

'If you keep your life you won't get away with your stones!'

Ernie returned to the front desk. Tony, from the pub walked in, 'You catcha that crook. I tell ya hesa been selling turpsa to the boongs longa time now. Taka all my business.'

'We try to do our job, mate.'

'Come to my puba later. I giva you a drinka two.'

Trouble Brewing

Adam Angel felt incredibly hot. He had just woken up. He tried to open one eye but the blinding flash of the sun was too much. His head felt ready to explode. The pain he was feeling now was far more intense than any he had ever known.

The little man tried to swallow. His mouth was too dry. It seemed as though every cell in his body needed liquid.

Somewhere a door banged. The sound seemed to bounce around inside his head.

He wondered where he was and just squeezed his eye open again. A flash of the bright burning sun burst on his eyes. He became aware that he was sitting up against a wall outside.

Antonio found them both asleep when he came down in the morning. Ray and Adam slumped over the table. There were three empty bottles and some of the alcohol was spilt. There was a stale smell of bile and Jack Daniel's that had been through the lips twice.

Tony unceremoniously dumped the two men outside the back door. Their clothes were stained with the excesses of the previous night. Tony carefully cleaned the back room.

Adam heard someone groaning close by. He felt a thud against his left shoulder as another body slumped against him. He struggled to remember what had happened. It seemed to hurt, just thinking.

Slowly his memory crystallized. The awful pain of rejection hit him again. He stifled a sob and longed to forget again. At least alcohol deadened his pain.

Adam chanced another look and saw the black and burnt yellow skin of his companion. A name fought its way through the alcoholic mist but couldn't quite find the surface.

'You all right, bud?' A man asked in a hoarse voice.

Adam tried to reply. His empty stomach lurched painfully and a foul taste filled his mouth. He spat some thick greenish phlegm.

'You in a bad way, mate. I get what you need.'

Ray's cultured accent and his eloquence seemed to have deserted him. He was a seasoned alcoholic again and knew the cure. There was only one thing capable of defeating a hangover. His cells were rebelling against the harsh attack of the liquor. Some smooth liquid would once again dull their rebellion and bring them under control.

'Get this into you, bud.'

Adam felt a cool hard object thrust into his hands. Its feeling was familiar.

'It won't help unless you drink it!'

A bottle was forced up to his mouth and he gagged on the first taste. Some spilt down his once immaculate shirt. This liquid seemed to slow the fire down inside his neck. He drank again, tentatively at first, and then deeply.

Slowly his pain began to subside as the sat there, against the wall. At last he was able to open his eyes. He was propped up against a wall in the sun. Directly in front of him were the legs of a water tank stand. The earth was dry and bare.

His companion, of the previous night, floated into view.

'Ray?' The man's name jumped into his head from nowhere.

'Yeah, bud?'

'What are we doing here?'

'We got drunk last night and the publican threw us out. We are at the back of the pub now.'

'What are doing in the sun?'

'He put us against the eastern wall of the outhouse. A couple of more hours and the sun will be gone.'

Adam didn't want to think any more. He had another drink from his bottle. This liquid had a magical quality. It didn't take long before a feeling of tranquility encased his whole being. Every time he drank a wave of peace seemed to flow around his body.

He could smell a pungent but familiar smell. His mind searched through its data bank. Sun burn! His arms were already starting to go pink and the top of his head felt tight.

Another mouthful of the fluid massaged his throat. Who cared about sunburn anyway? He was feeling great just now.

Ray tossed his bottle away and Adam took another refreshing draught. His bottle was now empty. He threw the bottle away and heard it clunk somewhere. He didn't even know what he was drinking.

'Must be your shout now, bud.'

Our special friend of powerful people felt for his bill fold. It was securely tucked away inside his back pocket. He was glad now that he always carried plenty of money. He carefully selected one of his three fifty dollar bills and gave it to Ray.

'Will that be enough?'

'Sure, bud!' Ray disappeared into the back of the hotel. After an age he returned. There was a bottle in each hand and three were pressed tight under his right arm. A sixth bottle was tucked away in his left armpit.

Adam jumped up and carefully unloaded his friend. The bottles were all put in the shade.

Adam didn't even care what was inside the bottles. Some of his self pity was welling up inside him again. He must drink more and feel that pleasant euphoria again.

A top was quickly unscrewed and discarded. He saw the name, 'Whiskey' somewhere; must be American. They spelled everything wrong. No time to examine the label. Must get the juice inside! This time his first swig was all swallowed.

Adam glanced at his watch, on his pink wrist. One o'clock! Where had the morning gone? It didn't matter anyway! Another mouthful just to keep his throat lubricated.

'Be careful, bud! That's not water, you know. Just take it slowly. There's more in the other bottle. If you drink it too fast, you'll be sick again.'

Adam leaned back against the wall and smiled to himself. He would be a strong force in the Union Movement again.

The camaraderie of the bottle gave him a feeling of kin with the man next to him. They both relaxed back in the shade and talked of inconsequential matters.

At three thirty Adam looked at his watch again. By that time there were two bottles each remaining. He reached for another bottle and took the top off. He glanced over at Ray and saw that he had taken another bottle, too.

Their quiet camaraderie was rudely interrupted by the arrival of another man who was quite big and half caste. He had some teeth missing and his face was scarred. 'Must be a fighter?' Adam thought. He had huge hands which were badly scarred across the knuckles.

'What youflah doing here?'

'We habing drink. What you want? This place belong me and little white fellah, aye!' Ray reverted to the habits of his childhood.

'You gib me drink, too?'

Adam was a physical coward. Even while he was quite drunk, he feared pain. Quickly he pulled out his billfold and extracted another fifty dollars.

'Go and buy yourself a drink with this.'

The newcomer observed the bottles carefully and then went inside. He returned with five of the bottles rather than six. Adam thought that he must be an easy mark. Still, he didn't complain. With the bottles here, they would have three each.

He didn't realize that on top of their current consumption the three bottles would almost kill him.

The newcomer put the bottles down. He quickly selected one for himself. With a conspiratorial gesture he called the other two men close. Norman showed them three small bottles of olive oil, 'This make you drunk for long time. You nebber get hangover. Make me feel real good in the morning.'

He pulled the top off his bottle and drunk it quickly. Ray said something about eating stopping you from getting drunk. He said that he wasn't drunk anyway. When he tried to demonstrate his claim, his legs just didn't seem to work properly. 'Legs must have fallen asleep while I was sitting down! Never mind, I show you later.'

Adam noticed that Ray gagged slightly as he drunk his oil. Both of the other men quickly chased their oil with large mouthfuls from the other bottles.

Adam took a swig from his small bottle. It caught in the back of his throat and he couldn't swallow.

'You wanna get big hangover?'

He held his breath and forced the oil down. He completed his bottle and then rinsed his mouth out with whiskey.

Norman began to talk to his two friends of the bottle. He sounded very angry. Obviously he had a chip on his shoulder. Adam felt safe, however; the big man seemed to have adopted them as family. They had given him a drink; although he did drink more quickly than the other two. His thirst must still be fresh, and he had some catching up to do.

Eventually Ray asked, 'What you call?'

'Norman King. I bin kick out of Mission.'

'I was there when it happened. I'm surprised you're still here.'

'I gotta wait for plane.'

'I certainly don't think you should be banished, it's an invasion of your basic human rights.'

Norman didn't understand philosophy; he just grunted. Rights were a foreign concept to him. He only knew about pain and revenge. He thought back to the day when he emasculated his Jesuit tormentor. The man wept openly; poor guy he was too scared to tell anyone lest his other activities be revealed. That Father passed on to his reward about two months after that.

Ray butted in at this stage, 'Black fellah got no rights in Australia!'

'You right, now'

'What do you mean by that?' Adam was interested.

'White fellah bin take country. No gib it back. We bin take it back, dreckly.' Norman was uncharacteristically loquacious.

'You should try to ventilate your feelings in the correct forums. The down trodden workers had to band together before they could demand any attention.' Adam's words were slow and slurred. He mind didn't seem to be working with its usual razor sharp insight.

'We bin try plenty. Black fellah doan wan help.' Ray tried to express his platform.

'What do you mean by that?'

'This man here, ol' Jumbo; he tell me, "Go away yellah fellah."'

'Jumbo bin tell me, "Go away!" too. You like we should get him?'

'Yeah, I hate that myall black fellah. We kill him, aye?'

Adam began to feel scared again. He knew that he would soon have to leave this place. He must not allow himself to be involved in any more trouble. A police conviction would ruin his good name.

'Come youflah, we go get him!'

Norman had already consumed his first bottle; he was now drinking his second. Ray was about half way through his bottle and Adam had only taken two mouthfuls.

Norman stood up easily though he swayed slightly when he found his feet. Ray was used to alcohol and managed to stand as well. It was five o'clock by now, the men would have to walk to the camp unless they could get a lift.

Adam tried to stand. He managed to reach his knees but his legs would not obey. The other two men reached down and picked him up. Once he was standing, he managed to stay that way. His mind seemed a little bit remote from his body. He lurched and his stomach grabbed. Once again some booze visited his mouth for the second time; a taste of oil was in his mouth once more. He took another drink.

Our two Aborigines set off on a meandering walk. Each of the men had a bottle in both hands. Adam saw a tap nearby; he washed his head and tried to regain some control. He saw his shoulder bag on the ground near where he had been. Quickly he picked up the three bottles on the ground and pushed them inside the bag. He was glad that he liked a big bag.

Norman and Ray were waiting beside the road. They were talking quickly. Adam couldn't catch what they were saying. He staggered towards them. The weight of the bottles combined with consumed alcohol made him unsteady on his feet. He caught up to his two companions.

An old Toyota came up the road. The men waved and called. The truck pulled up and they recognized Billy Ah Fat.

'Gib we lift to the camp, bud.'

Billy jumped out and helped the two Aborigines into the back of the truck. He carefully placed their bottles in the bed of the ute first. While doing that he extracted his fare from Ray's bottle. Billy only managed one mouthful.

When each of the men was pushed over the edge they fell into the tray. Norman sat up again and put the bottles between his legs. Ray lay where he fell.

Adam decided that discretion was the better part of valor. He made no attempt to enter the Toyota. As the car drove off he turned and headed towards his quarters.

His route covered exactly twice the distance it should have. Somehow he got inside the door and into the bedroom.

Adam's flat was typical Department of Works; a kitchen and bedroom side by side. A long lounge/dining room was at the front. There were a bathroom and laundry out the back. Adam had decided to make a fight about the accommodation when he got back to the nerve centre. He wasn't really concerned, right now, about industrial matters.

When he reached the bedroom he sat on the bed and finished the open bottle. It was quite a struggle to get the bag off, over his head. When that was done, he began another bottle.

Before long the Angel groaned and fell back onto the bed. His feet remained hanging over the side. His head hit the wall and stayed at an acute angle. His bottle dropped to the floor and broke spilling the last three quarters over the polished floor boards and through the cracks.

Adam’s bladder contracted as he lay. His stomach again rid itself of the poison. Fortunately his head was not prone. He didn’t drown in his own vomit as he may well have done.

A Little Bit of Sanity

The Smallbone family always enjoyed Tuesday night. Roger came home from work a little bit early. As second in charge of the station he was responsible for the staffing roster. Ernie was in charge of the station during the day and Roger was on call every week night. He also did a turn on call every fourth weekend.

When Roger was called out during the night, he could take the next day off. There were patrols during the week and liaison with the mission police. The men out here didn't have to walk or drive a beat as they did in the big smoke.

This time was sacrosanct for the family. It was four thirty when Roger walked into the yard and around the side of the house. There was a Clarke Rubber, above ground, pool in the yard. It was behind the house and could not be seen from the front.

The pool was rounded at each end and had parallel sides. Its long axis was at right angles to the house. The sides were four feet high while the dimensions were seven feet by four feet. There were aluminum sides and a blue plastic liner. The pool had a deck running along the side nearest the house. A small pump and filter system worked hard in the dust. Cathy usually vacuumed the pool every day. She didn't mind the extra work because the pool was so good in the hot weather.

Years ago someone planted a wind break of four Kurrajong trees. They were slightly out of their habitat. The trees had not grown to their regular fifty feet but were stunted at about thirty. The soil here was not limestone but ironstone.

Cathy often wondered how the trees managed to grow here. Being native, they must have some chance. They usually grew further south than this.

Someone with a trained eye could easily tell the local soil type. In the native bush the trees stuck to their preference of soil type. A bushman would have been fooled by these trees.

There was bare soil under the Kurrajong trees as the local grasses could not compete. Grass that had grown on a well watered lawn didn't like the shade.

These trees were stunted in the south where they faced the wind. During the dry season the winds blew from the south or south west. They were dry and quite cold in the short winter. Winter was a misnomer, much more pleasant, and warmer, than an English high summer.

The northern aspect of the trees was much more pleasant. Their leaves were thicker and the branches longer. While the southern branches pointed up, the northern ones grew parallel to the ground.

The back yard was sheltered by the trees and quite pleasant when the wind blew. The problem today was not the wind. It was 106 degrees in the shade. Even in this heat the ground under the trees was slightly damp. It was a hot day and the problem was compounded by high humidity.

The blustery south wind stopped blowing back in early October. It was very still just now, barely a breath of air. Sometimes, just on dusk, a sea breeze would ghost in and break the heat. This town was too far from the Gulf to get its full effect. The Gulf was quite shallow here, too. The water didn't stay as cold.

Roger remembered his trip to Mornington Island. They always had a lovely breeze by about three o'clock. It didn't help to dream about the breeze that only made you feel frustrated.

As Roger passed the corner of the house, he saw his family. They were sitting under a bark shadehouse. This shadehouse had been made by the boys in his senior Bible class. There were four sturdy bloodwood poles with crossbars at six and a half feet. The boys had made the shelter extra high so that he wouldn't have to bend. Its roof was built out of flattened ti tree bark. Underneath was a framework and chook wire. The latest technology was used alongside Stone Age methods to stop the roof from blowing away.

Cathy was sitting in a fold up aluminum chair and her two boys were standing. They were both wet and wearing their 'flotation jackets'. These were like vests with large blocks of buoyancy stitched into the upper chest and back.

Roger's wife was still dry. She used to laugh and say, 'I'll wait till you get home and we can swim together. Isn't that part of my conjugal responsibility?'

The boys looked up and began to shriek with glee, 'Daddy, Daddy!' They ran to their father and jumped into his arms. No one was concerned about wetting Roger's uniform; it had already been soaked with sweat.

Cathy poured Roger a large glass of juice from the jug on the card table next to her left elbow. The juice was made from freshly squeezed lemons and tank water. There were only two lemons and lots of water. The hint of lemon was refreshing and the water cool. She had learnt how to make this drink while a child in Africa. It was hot there, too, but no hotter than Leichhardt in November.

Roger sat down and drank his drink slowly. Both boys tried to balance on his knee. Drinking with a circus on your knees is a practiced art.

The boys prattled away about their respective days while Roger listened absent mindedly. There would be time later to listen to his wife.

After he had drunk, he took another half a glass and then went inside. He quickly changed into his togs and came outside again.

In North Queensland one did not have to take a breath and jump into the water. It was warm enough to jump in without any effort. Roger stepped over the side of the pool, using a cross piece on the deck framework as an aid. He stood for a moment and then dropped his shoulders under the water.

Cathy stood and Roger admired her body, modestly covered with a one piece bathing suit. The boys had already climbed up the removable ladder to the deck. They jumped down into the water with their father and began to play. There was a floating ring in the pool with a framework to make a basketball ring. Our three boys played this game for quite a while.

Cathy stood and watched. Her heart was full of love. She loved the boys and loved their father even more. He made her life complete. With Roger she felt a security which nothing could shake.

At about five thirty Cathy climbed out of the pool and dried herself. She went inside and had a quick shower. She dressed again in her plain cotton dress. It was time for her to cook tea. Her boys always woke before six thirty in the morning.

It was going to be a special meal this afternoon. Yesterday Sally O'Keefe came up from the camp. The old lady was fishing down below the falls on the Wills River with some friends. In the afternoon they had stopped on their way home and left two lovely barramundi.

Sally said, 'We bin catch big mob them barrows.' It was meant to indicate to her that the fish was just a small gift. These giant perch were a great gift! Roger didn't get too much time to fish these days and the family always enjoyed the bounty of the river.

Cathy took two large fillets from the each fish and then froze the rest. The larger fish looked like it weighed about twelve pounds while the other one would be about two pounds less.

Cathy cut the fillets into meal size portions and then lightly crumbed them before she fried them lightly. The delicate, sweet taste of the fish was preserved as far as possible by the minimum of cooking.

Cathy called her family in and soon Roger appeared carrying the boys. He entered through the side door and disappeared down the hall. The three of them showered together. The boys were dried first. While Roger completed his toweling Paul got their pajamas.

Cathy rubbed plenty of powder on both boys and they giggled with glee. Matthew had his nappy and pajamas put on and Paul dressed himself. Roger threw on some shorts and a T shirt. All this was done in record time because they all knew there was a treat tonight.

Cathy cooked chips with the fish; she was a traditionalist at heart. Their vegetable garden provided the rest of the meal. There were lettuce, tomato, sliced capsicum, radish and chopped cabbage. Roger liked his foods unadulterated so they never ate any coleslaw or other salads with dressing. The Americans and Europeans might despise English food as bland but at least you could taste the real vegetables when your mouth wasn't sated with salt and oil.

Their meal was capped of by a delightful fresh fruit salad. paw paw, diced mandarin, pineapple, apple, watermelon and passion fruit. Cathy put some cream on hers and the boys succumbed as well. Roger ate the fruit without additions. His motto was 'I like mine pure!'

This meal was completed by six twenty and Roger read the boys a Bible story before putting them to bed. Matthew's nappy was still dry so he sat on the potty.

Prayer and good night hugs and kisses ate up a further ten minutes before the boys were in bed. Paul took his green Care Bear while Matthew snuggled into his baby pillow and sucked his thumb. These boys had been on the go all day and were tired.

Matthew's afternoon sleep did not seem to affect his tiredness tonight. Roger switched off the light and they were asleep within five minutes.

Cathy was sitting at the table with a cup of coffee. Her husband got a glass of water and joined her.

'The church here is really starting to prosper.'

'Yes, I know. I am amazed at the maturity of the women at the camp. They seem to be really concerned these days.'

'That's right; since they took over the complete responsibility for the church themselves they have done a good job. Years ago when the missionaries ran everything there were only a few faithful Aborigines.'

'Angie Mick is starting to be a real Priscilla among the ladies. They have a ladies' meeting every Thursday morning. Recently the women have started a care program. Anyone in the camp who is in need is given all the help they can take.'

'I'm glad we are involved in this church. The people somehow seem to be more sincere than most of the folk back in Banyo.'

'You're right about that. I think it's because they are less materialistic.'

Roger paused and said, 'You know they mightn't want after things so much but they are all hard workers.'

'You can say that again.'

'I heard an interesting story from old Arthur, what's his name, the other day.'

'Arthur Dick?'

'Yeah, that's the one.'

‘His faith seems to be so real, doesn’t it?’

‘He is not ashamed to share anything. Remember he was away in August or September?’

‘I wondered where he was but the others didn’t seem worried.’ Cathy continued.

‘He went out to the Territory with some geologists. These modern people, with all their satellite navigation, still need to rely on the age old skill of the Aborigine. A man with a degree will die just as quickly as anyone else if he gets lost.’

Cathy just chuckled to herself. She respected this country and the people who knew it so well.

‘These guys were out on a trip in one of their Toyotas. They went down into a gully while trying to get to some cliffs. The gully was a dead end for them so they had to turn around. They couldn’t get out again. The truck was stuck half way up the bank. Their radio was masked by the hills. They had left the winch behind because it was broken. Arthur had gone with them in case they got lost. These three fellahs worked hard to try and get the truck out. They tried every trick in the book but didn’t get anywhere.’

Cathy butted in, ‘Like that time we got stuck at seven mile?’

‘Yeah, a bit like that. Anyway, after a while Arthur said, “How about we ask Heabenly Father? He get us out plenty quick!” The old guy knelt there in the dust and prayed. One of the young guys jumped into the truck to show him how stupid he was. He started the truck and drove it straight out!’

‘I’ll bet the geologists were cheesed off.’ Cathy added joyfully.

'That's right! I saw one of them when I was on patrol a week ago. He confirmed Arthur's story.' Roger looked at his watch. 'I'll have to go and get changed now.' He changed the subject. 'It's time I was going to the prayer meeting.'

He slipped into the bedroom and put on some blue Bermuda shorts and pulled on his white loafers over some white long socks. A floral Hawaiian shirt completed his wardrobe. Roger didn't need to clean his teeth. Fresh fruit and vegetables didn't give anyone bad breath. He grabbed his Good News Bible then kissed his wife fondly before jumping into his car.

One of the jobs the policeman had was to pick up Andy Pluto. He was a saintly old man who was blind and couldn't walk. Even in the days of the missionaries Andy was the shepherd of the local people. Many came to seek his wisdom over the years.

These two Christians went to the meeting in the village hall, together.

Mayhem Begun

Billy Ah Fat pottered along in his old truck. He couldn't drive too fast; the vehicle was beyond winning at Bathurst*. Billy didn't mind, he enjoyed driving this ancient ute. It was like a second home to him. Sometimes he even slept in the back. It wasn't hard to stretch out under a sheet of corrugated iron. If iron wasn't available he would use bark or some other bush shelter.

It didn't occur to him that his two passengers would be unwelcome at Boomallooba. This driver was working at his job when Norman was declared persona non gratis. He didn't care that Ray failed in his Sacred Sites bid!

This young man was not burdened with worry. He enjoyed living in Boomallooba. He hadn't seen beyond his own small world and had no desire to do so. As a boy, he watched every car and

---

* The Bathurst 1000 is Australia's premier car race.

truck he could, and spent many hours running around 'spinning de wheel'; the boys often pretended to be cars here.

Billy had taken his place as one of the superior people. He was in command of a vehicle. No man was greater than he!

He didn't dream about other things when he drove. He sat and enjoyed his status.

When Billy was about one mile west of his home town; he heard someone banging on the roof. When he looked back he saw Norman waving frantically. What could be wrong? Maybe that other fellah fell off. He squeezed on the brakes and came to an easy stop.

'We get out here!' Norman called in through the window.

'Okay mate, jump out.'

Norman carefully placed their bottles near the edge of the tray. He jumped out and hauled Ray over the side. When he had collected the bottles, he banged on the passenger side door. Billy smiled and eased in the clutch. He pulled away smoothly, leaving only a gentle cloud of dust.

Ray was able to stand now but was slightly unsteady. The sun was a golden orb suspended about two hand widths above the horizon. It was about the same time as his walk of the previous afternoon. The men meandered their way over to the southern side of the road and in among the trees. A car sped past; it was an old blue Commodore.

Ray was just beginning to realize what was happening. He didn't believe until now that there may be some substance to Norman's threats.

Norman seemed to have no doubt about where to go. He took a long swig from his bottle and gasped. The next long drink was enough to ensure that he needed to throw the bottle away. Ray drank the rest of his bottle as Norman stood and examined the bush.

His feeling of pleasant detachment evaporated. There was a feeling of fear wrestling inside his guts. Spasms of pain returned with gurgles as one side or the other seemed to embark on a foray. Adrenaline heightened his senses and seemed to overcome the effects of the alcohol. The bottle was unable to restore any equilibrium. He did, however, have a certain feeling of bravado.

Norman took the remaining two bottles and hid them under some scrub, 'We get these dreckly and hab good drink. Presently 'ol Jumbo be dead.'

Another kick assaulted the inside of Ray's abdominal wall. He swallowed to overcome his fear. He wondered how Norman would find the bottles again. The bush seemed to be without landmarks in this light.

Norman was not concerned. He knew exactly where he was so he set off towards the west and in about one minute came across an infrequently used cattle pad. There wasn't too much grass here for the cattle to feed on.

Our two men set off towards the south following the pad. Ray could vaguely tell the direction by referring to the sun. Norman didn't need to; he knew exactly where he was.

As the sun approached the horizon it seemed to gather speed in its descent. The trees were not thick enough to blot it from view. Norman stopped and listened. The sounds of a village preparing for the night could be heard over the bush. Some dogs barked and snarled in the south; they seemed to be much closer.

Norman wrenched up a small sapling. He seemed to possess super human strength. He broke off the top end and tore off the roots. He pulled his large knife out of its hiding place. Before long he armed himself with a vicious club.

Norman gave Ray his own weapon next. The alcohol, which helped him so much earlier in the day, had no comfort left in its embrace. He was fully aware. His anger once again blazed. The war inside was calmer now. It would be sweet revenge. Perhaps if the old guy died, he could negotiate with someone else and be successful!

He backed up in his mind and considered that without Jumbo he could start again! This idea was indeed appealing. Andrew might even elevate him to Vice President or Secretary of State. This whole episode began to assume worthwhile proportions for him.

It would be much easier to negotiate with a younger man. These older fellahs didn't understand what it was to be black. Imagine being called a yellah fellah! Someone with his intelligence and ability; there had been opportunities for him to become an academic or a successful politician. In spite of this he had chosen the hard road. He had given his life to serve his people.

They were so ungrateful. That old man couldn't even read! He could read the tracks of animals and remember the ancient traditions but what use was that when there was big money to be made.

Men could really make a name overseas if they played an issue correctly. Even if things didn't quite hang together here, his reputation would be an invaluable asset.

How dare that old fool refuse to give him the information that he could use so well. Surely the old guard must be removed. Jumbo Seven Emus must die!

Norman moved on stealthily. He seemed to be the moving shadow of a cloud. His bare feet carefully tested the ground before they took his weight. Ray stumbled after him in his heavy boots. He made a noise but Norman didn't seem to mind.

This big renegade had his own revenge to mete out. He hated anyone in authority. Too often those with power had corrupted their trust, at his expense. He had been used and abused by those who should have nurtured him.

In the mind of this man any leader was bad. He made no allowances for the fact that sometimes a bad apple must be removed from the box.

Jumbo was wise and careful. He acted for the good of his people. Others had not acted for the good of their charges. The chairman would soon have to pay for the misdeeds of people he would never know.

Norman seemed to be searching for something in the scrub. Ray wondered if his companion had some other surprise hidden.

Suddenly Norman paused and squatted down. He looked up to the stars and then looked around. It was apparent that he was searching for landmarks in the dark. The big man grunted. He sounded pleased with himself. He reached out and began to scrape away the earth, under a bush.

The earth was soft and moved away easily. Soon a large ammunition box became obvious. It had come into Norman's possession in a round about way. He could not have adequately defended his ownership in court.

Norman didn't take long to have the box out of the ground and on the path. He opened the box carefully. The smell of petrol was unmistakable. Inside were half a dozen bottles filled with fuel.

'We burn that ol' fellah house, aye!'

Ray nodded and smiled. That would do fine. They could wait till later and then barricade the doors shut. The gasoline would soon create an inferno when projected through the windows. Even the pope would not survive in there.

Norman shut the case and easily swung it onto his shoulder. He was, now, whistling in a tuneless monotone.

Norman and Ray emerged from the bush to the south of the village. Their path ran into the road which came from the tip. The scrub was heavy and the two men were able to walk without being seen.

These partners in revenge joined the aimless milling crowd. There was no television here and the electricity supply was poor. The power leaked out of the lines between the generator and the houses.

There were a few dull street lights. Inside the houses there were some lights. These globes only produced a dull glow. Reading was hard and few tried. All the people could do was wander up and down. Some followed a circuit while others just sat in the dust.

Darkness lent anonymity to our two conspirators. No one recognized them, no one seemed to care. The people wandered locked into their own aimlessness and misery.

Ray felt saddened by the sterility of the environment. There was no reason for the people here to long for education. The streets were unnamed and they had no signposts. This town had no newspapers or magazines. Its store didn't order any in from the south. Even the radio didn't really have anything to offer. No one here cared if the Barwon was threatening to flood. There was not even one person in the camp who had shares or grieved over the stock market crash. Their endless monotony was not relieved by the regular occurrence of an Australian cricket win.

The children knew nothing else and played in the dust unconcernedly. Unconcerned that the eggs in the dust would soon clog their little bellies with worms.

Two and three year old children ran past laughing and giggling. A four year old girl humped her younger brother on her hip. She called out, 'Youflah stupid…' The rest of the sentence was lost in the night.

The choking taste of the dust seemed to catch at the back of Ray's throat. He hacked and spat. He could feel the dust drying out the lining of his nostrils.

Alcohol in his blood no longer gave him a sense of equanimity. His heart pounded on, taking the fine powdered dust from his lungs to clog his arteries. A python within again fought to drive the life from his vital organs. He felt spasms of pain play back and forth across his abdominal wall.

The contrast with his last visit to these streets was marked. Last time there was a desperate longing to succeed; the prospect of meeting the unknown man; his hope of triumph. Today the bitterness of his rejection was sharp in his mind.

One part of him felt the weariness of his broken spirit. He felt kinship with these people. They, too, had no hope. They had no ambition. Forever condemned to the treadmill of rejection and prejudice. The once proud hunters were now worse than a white man's dog.

Could these people ever climb back to dignity from the ashes of their noble heritage?

Then again, why should they? He came with the offer of friendship and help. He alone could reach down into the mire of their degradation. Who else could drag them to safety? Who else could restore the venerability of the Dreamtime heroes?

Ray's hand of compassion had been bitten. The man eager to help was treated like a pariah.

That old man's ignorance was astounding. He was a fool not to recognize the greatness of his savior. Without the hard work of people like this future President these people would never rise again.

That antediluvian fossil should not have the right to impair the excellence of their future. One day, Ray knew, he would preside over the final expulsion of the white man.

Perhaps they could stage a coup. He could imagine the remains of this, once proud paper tiger, hero of fools, cowering under his bed. His trousers fouled, crying with fear. Ray the great black warrior ruthlessly eliminating any opposition.

The white man would be sent back to Europe. Asians would be forced to work as slaves. The black man would be dominant.

'Yellah fellah!' The words cut his heart like a knife. He was a black man; a proud traditional owner of this country. The man, who had the temerity to suggest that he had no affinity with this land, must die.

His death would create the solution. Surely the next generation of leaders was already plotting in the wings. They would be quick to act when he removed the old guard. Younger men would immediately recognize his sagacity.

Real Sacred Sites did not matter. What was essential was to claim sites where there was oil. That revenue was essential. It would certainly contribute to the final solution.

The new leaders would understand that a fine mind was more important than affinity with the country.

Ray looked up from his musing. Our two men were walking south, now. On his right was the village hall. Its lights were on and there seemed to be something going on. Outside the door waited a blue VB Commodore, and some even older cars.

The sound of a voice floated out through the door. They couldn't hear what was being said. Soon that sound was lost in the general hubbub of the street.

Ray and Norman came to the end of the street and turned left. There was a large group of people sitting in the dust. Even in the dull light one could see that they were beginning to be covered by a thin powdery film. The people in this group didn't seem to be doing anything at all. A few were talking but most sat listlessly inhaling parasite eggs without complaint.

Norman made no attempt to communicate. He was locked into his own private pain. Everyone who had hurt him in the past would be repaid tonight. This ageing man would soon represent the vampires of his childhood.

Both men paused and looked at the house they had come to burn. The feeble light inside fought against almost opaque window glass and just managed to spill out a few inches. It did nothing to illuminate the outside. There was a fire in the yard. Their target sat on the ground. Around him were about ten other people. A couple of large older women, maybe his wives. One younger girl was feeding a baby.

The family was eating. In this light it was impossible to tell what. Nearby a small boy was chewing the meat from a large bone. A dog came and stole the bone. The boy ran to the house crying.

Norman moved off again. He walked over to the river bank and put his box down. He sat in the dirt next to it. Ray went to sit on the case. Norman hissed angrily. Ray sat in the dirt.

Our avenger seemed to possess infinite patience. He sat immobile and watched. His hatred smoldered in his eyes.

Ray became uncomfortable. He felt tightness around his knees and along the outside of his thighs. Soon his back began to hurt. He uncrossed his legs and stretched them out, placing his hands out behind him and leaning back on them. This position was difficult to maintain. He stood for a while and then squatted on his haunches.

Norman growled, 'Doan move!'

Ray shuffled back into his own private misery. He couldn't understand why they were waiting. Wouldn't it be better to walk around?

Norman watched. He didn't need to walk around. This place was familiar to him. This deed had been carefully planned over the last weeks. He knew his banishment was coming and had set his goals in advance.

The old man would soon go into the house with his family. Then he could act! A crowd milled around. Down in the river bed some men were sharing a flagon of wine. They growled and scrapped, like a pack of dogs.

A group of young children wandered by; they looked about nine or ten perhaps a year or two older. Each one carried a milk tin. The smell of petrol wafted over along with that of stale smell of body wastes. These youngsters seemed lost and uncaring, totally given over to the fumes. Ray remembered back to his childhood, he had been told that the fumes would seep through into his brains. They would condense back to petrol. Then his brain would be dissolved. He heard, later, that this wasn't true. It didn't really matter; you died just the same. He shivered despite the heat.

There was a sensation of coolness as dusk came on, banishing the burning sun to oblivion. That feeling was quickly lost. The mercury was near eighty seven and the humidity was at ninety. The dense heat was almost like an unpleasant embrace. An embrace from an old fat aunty, her breath would make a person drunk. Her heaving bosom had suckled sixteen babies. The nearness was unpleasant, repressive, overpowering. Thought of that embrace activated one's flight fear response. There was nowhere to run;

nothing but humble submission and the subsequent feeling of defeat.

As Ray sat in the dust, afraid to move, he knew that the man next to him would not be persuaded by his superior intellect. His body became a furnace of pain. Years of chairs and comfortable beds in liberal homes had driven all hardness from him. It was demeaning to be the trained pet for these open minded hypocrites. Never the less his ends were achieved. They used him but he had used them as well. When the revolution came he would despise them as they begged. They would no longer patronize their trained primitive.

The sharpness of his pain drew his mind back to other painful days. Days of childhood deprivation; hunger had gnawed at his vitals as the writhing snake did now.

Howling winds blew incessantly from the south west. They were freezing. Frost was heavy on the ground. His bare feet throbbed and drove the hunger pangs from his belly. He fought to drag out the last ounce of warmth from his threadbare coat. His shorts were tattered with torn seams, repaired with fuse wire. This wire strove to devour his flesh. His teacher rescued him from the wire. He had to wrap up in a towel while the girls in the sewing room had laughed at him. Afterwards he had punched them. Later he punched them lower down as well.

Another memory floated through the mist in his mind. He was on a station living in the Aboriginal camp. Stockmen lived with their families, away from the homestead. Ray was living with his mother, poor stupid woman! He stayed with his mother once or twice. She was living with one of the ringers.

A big, white, head stockman came thundering down in the middle of the night. His stock whip was licking away at the darkness and dust. The cattle had stampeded. Every man was needed. Tomorrow the cattle would be yarded and then trucked away. His men stumbled out of their beds; each man's mind still wrapped in the cotton wool of sleep.

That monstrous man rode between two houses and collided with a clothes line.

Aboriginal clothes lines were made of barbed wire. There was no need for pegs, even on the windiest day. The only problem was three cornered tears on their moleskins.

The man crashed from his horse. Barbed wire clutched at him, like an aroused lover. Its orgasmic frenzy tore him to pieces. That man was broken that day. One day many white men would be broken in this land.

Ray remembered his own days as a stockman. A big bronco horse outside the yard, small stock ponies saddled and waiting patiently. The man on the bronco lassoed a young bull. His rope was tied to his saddle and went between two strong poles which were a few inches apart. A quiet word from the rider encouraged the strong horse to throw its shoulder against the rope. He hauled the beast up against the posts in a fighting frenzy. When its head was jammed one of the ringers roped a leg and the bull thrown. They tied branded and cut the animal. Sometimes they threw the stones into the fire. The meat was good and it made you strong!

Ray felt a strong hand, heavy on his shoulder. Hard fingers bit into his flesh. He looked around feeling angry. An oath caught in his throat; Norman's face was close to his.

‘We go now!’

Norman stood up and easily swung his box onto his shoulder. He was a truly powerful man. Bruises left by his grasp still burned into Ray’s shoulder.

The big man seemed to drift, like a shadow, over the bank and down into the river bed. It was much quieter here, now. All the drinkers were unable to stand. Some slept where they had fallen. One or two copulating couples could be seen vaguely in the shadows.

Norman walked with purpose. He knew where he was going. Ray tagged along stumbling while his feet sought to regain their circulation.

Abruptly Norman turned right and headed up the bank. He did not pause to check his way.

At the top of the bank was a small clearing among the scrub. Two paths led away from this space; one to the north and the other to the west. This clearing couldn’t be far from old Jumbo’s place; they hadn’t gone far along the river bed.

Ray felt something soft and slippery under his foot. He realized that this place was used as a toilet. It was easier to slip into the bush and squat than to sit inside those hot iron boxes. The dunnies were regularly used but everywhere else was just as popular.

Norman put his box to one side and opened it. He stood and listened. He seemed, to Ray, to be a wallaby trying to sense the wind.

*

Angie Johnny was eating with her grandfather. She loved old Jumbo, dearly. Her own parents, Jumbo's daughter and son in law, lived in one of the new houses. It was always good to get away from her father; he enjoyed too much grog, then he used to beat his children. Johnny would never beat his wife; she was sixteen and a half stone while he was only seven. Perhaps having thirteen children sucked all the flesh out of him, giving it all to his wife. This scrawny little runt did, however, seem to have incredible strength when he had a skinful.

Angie didn't pause to think about her father. She didn't really trouble her mind with any philosophy. The hoary headed sage had been in fine form tonight. Within his head was the entire cultural memory of his people. He, also, had the skill of a natural story teller, which was combined with a rare wit. His stories always entertained and often amused, as well. After some of the night time sessions Angie felt pain around her middle from laughing.

Tonight her heart was happy. She laughed again, to herself, as she remembered a mirthful episode.

It was too hot to use the dunny. A quick trip into the bush would be more pleasant.

There was a path heading southwards into the bush, behind the house. She took this path and headed for a clearing.

Norman reached out one of his massive paws and encircled Angie's neck. 'You bin call out, I kill you!' He hissed coercively into her ear.

'What are you doing? This is mad!' Ray croaked hoarsely at Norman.

'This one, him ol' fellah best chile! We gib it to him good! Then he plenty mad!'

Angie shrunk back from the overpowering animal smell. She was a tough woman and decided to wait. It would be no good to struggle now. She didn't want to be beaten as well. This man was close and large. She could sense the strength in his clammy hand. He could easily break her neck. His fetid breath seemed to run down her face. She gagged at its alcoholic fumes. It was impossible to swallow. His claw was almost crushing her glottis. Her consciousness began to ebb. She started to kick her feet to fight against this. There seemed to be bright lights popping on and off in the sky.

There was an absolute priority to remain awake. Blackness would swamp her pain, but she would be defenseless. Miraculously the hand let go. At the same time her bra and dress were torn from her with a swift flick of the tentacle. She was crashed down on her back, winded.

He groped blindly between her legs. She couldn't suppress the gasp of pain that sprang to her lips as he tore away a handful of hair and knickers. Angie was naked now!

Another man kneeled on her upper arms and pulled her hands back over her head. This brute was panting in wheezing gasps. His breath had the same sodden odor, now mixed with lust. The stench of stale sweat, wine and urine made her vomit. She spat it out so that she wouldn't choke.

The first man was trembling like an excited greyhound. He fumbled at his fly and seemed to get frustrated. The zip and stud burst open as he tore impatiently at them. His trousers tumbled down around his ankles. He would not be able to run now!

She tried to scream but couldn't. He was erect and pulsating. He forced her legs apart. Pain shot up and down inside her thighs and abdomen. He began to groan and pant, like a dog.

He tried to kiss her. She opened her mouth and drew in his lips. She bit his upper lip with all the force she could muster. He bellowed in pain and began to thrash at her arms. At last she could scream.

Jumbo went inside after talking to his family. The information inside his brain had to be passed on before he died. The vast treasury he contained within him must not be lost.

The old man saw Angie go back outside and followed her. The air was not so close out here. He sat beside a bush and meditated. He vaguely heard the sound of a struggle in the clearing and wondered. There was no more noise.

Suddenly he heard a man cry out in pain and a scream; a woman's scream. The sound was muffled.

He rushed back into the hut and grabbed his nulla nulla and boomerang. Jumbo didn't take his spear because with that he would be sure to kill.

He moved freely, like a much younger man, as he ran down the path. In the clearing there was a man struggling on the ground. His arms were waving around. Under the man he could see the spots of Angie's dress.

His nulla nulla whistled through the air. It crashed into the base of the man's neck. He grunted and fell forward, onto the girl.

Three hits across the buttocks had him rolling off the girl. She lay there naked and battered. A crashing blow to the bridge of his nose left the man immobile on the ground.

Angie cried out in anguish.

Nina noticed the old man grab his weapons and followed him. She sprang down and cradled Angie's head. Both women sobbed together.

Jumbo noticed another man run off along another path. He could tell from the tracks that the man limped and was wearing boots.

Nina called out for help as Jumbo padded off after the other man; the path re emerged at the bottom of Second Street. In a small pool of light beneath an underpowered street light near the hall he saw his quarry running.

The hunter paused and took aim. He threw his boomerang. It spun away through the air.

Ray was running desperately. He wasn't thinking about anything but escape. He had to duck and weave around the people. Suddenly he felt a blast of sharp pain in the back of head. A bright light flashed before his eyes as he fell headlong into the dust. He couldn't remember any more. Blackness swept him into its embrace.

Jumbo's years of hunting left him with incredible skills. His heavy hunting boomerang gave him a great advantage. He brought the running man down, with one throw, at fifty yards. The legend, when it was later repeated would state that Ray had been running through a crowd of people. The stalker picked his prey and brought him down.

An Aboriginal hunter must bring down the correct animal. It would do no good to hunt a fat wallaby and come home with a skinny one!

A Just Conclusion?

Roger was on his knees in the meeting house at Boomallooba, quietly meditating. He was thanking God for his wife and children.

Jimmy Joe, one of the men from this Aboriginal church, who was working as a missionary in the west, was experiencing some problems. An anthropologist and some half castes had been trying to silence him.

A carnal knowledge case had been brought against him by the local police. The magistrate dismissed the case against him out of hand. But that kind of pressure was hard for his family. On the other hand they were enthusiastically accepted by many of their own people. Erica had requested specific prayer on this matter.

There were some hoarse shouts projecting into the building now. Roger looked up and saw someone rush into the building. 'Policeman, plenty trouble, come now!'

Roger knew his job. He took the man outside and began to question him.

Edward Jack came running up. He was bareheaded and wore no shoes. He was still buttoning his trousers as he arrived. The poor man had gone to bed early. Norman King's trouble had kept him from bed most nights in the last three weeks. Eddie stoically carried on his job, refusing to lie down or take a break.

The two policemen looked over to the middle of the intersection. Lying on his face in the dust was a stranger. Eddie knew immediately. The man's clothes seemed to be a much better cut than those of the local people. He wore shoes which was unusual in this town.

The position of the prostrate mortal was, to say the least, extremely uncomfortable. His left leg was stretched out and twisted across his body. His right leg was splayed back the other way and bent. He lay on his right arm and his left arm was flung over his back. His face was pressed into the dust. He seemed as if he had been hit by a giant hammer and, as he fell, had vainly tried to twist and see his assailant. His new hat lay on the ground with its brim up, near his waist.

This man rolled over slowly, untangling his limbs. He groaned, tried to get up and fell back. Roger still did not recognize him.

Edward tapped Roger's shoulder and pointed to the ground near the edge of the puddle of light. A large, dark, heavy boomerang lay there. 'Must be one of the old guys, Eddie! None of the young ones could throw like that.'

Edward strolled over to the boomerang and picked it up. He examined it and said, ‘This one belong ol’ Jumbo.’

It was hard to concentrate. There was a growing noise storm coming from the southeast. The sound of angry women shouting seemed to dominate.

Roger didn’t bother with the boomerang but ran over to the prostrate man. There was blood on his neck and shirt. He had a large gash on the back of his head. Apart from being dazed, he didn’t seem too bad but he would have a headache for a day or two.

Two of the other mission police drove up in their police truck. It was a battered old Toyota long wheel base ute. The back was covered with a home made cage. The Aboriginal police used this truck for transporting drunks.

The man was sitting up now, his head cradled in his hands and hanging down between his knees. Roger had a closer look at the cut. It would need about six or seven stitches. He smelt the man’s breath; obviously drunk!

His nose wrinkled with displeasure. He called out to one of the settlement police, ‘Chuck him in the back, Roddie!’

The two new arrivals lifted the man and unceremoniously dumped him in the back of the ute. Eddie threw in his hat. They shot home the bolt and clicked the lock.

Old Jumbo stood next to them now. He was shaking with anger. His eyes gleaming hatred, ‘This yellah fellah, he rape my granddaughter!’

Roger heaved a sigh. This was going to be a hard night. When the state police were involved there was often trouble that could have been avoided.

The keening continued over in the south east. There seemed to be a great commotion. He would have to go over there and check the situation. It would be important to get statements.

'Come on Eddie, we've got to get over there and see what has happened.'

'Yeah, Roger, look like we better get ober there.'

'Jumbo where did this happen?'

'Happen bush, my place.'

'Were there any witnesses?'

'I bin see wil' fellah Norman King on top my girl. This yellah fellah he bin catching him.'

Roger felt that an eye witness was quite a good asset. He decided to investigate further.

Our two policemen walked over to the other street and then into the bush. Roger had a powerful torch with him. He always carried the light in his car in case of an eventuality like this. Edward also had a police torch.

Jumbo led the two men down the path. They came to the clearing. Angie was in a sitting position. She was leaning back on Nina who was sitting behind her. Both women were crying.

A group of women had gathered around. There were, perhaps, seven of them. One had an old kerosene lamp which threw a dull circle of illumination. They were all stunned at this assault. No one had made any attempt to cover Angie yet. There was blood between her legs and around her face. Roger thought that her neck looked swollen as well.

Next to them, and lying on the ground, was a man. His face seemed to be bursting out of its skin. There was a vicious contusion on the bridge of his nose. His bottom lip was torn as well. He had blood around his genitals.

Roger immediately realized that the force used to stop this man was necessary. His reputation was as well known to the police as his appearance. Even with his face so distorted there was no mistaking his identity.

He thought to himself of the times that Norman King had stolen a night's sleep from him.

'I thought that we had got rid of this man last week. Isn't he meant to be banished?'

'He bin staying in town ober weekend. Too much to drink, I think.' Eddie replied.

Roger sent one of the mission policemen up to the hospital. He asked one of the women to get a blanket for Angie. The poor girl seemed to be in shock, she was shivering. This was quickly done. The victim was gently wrapped up, by the women. Some of them began to shout abuse. It looked as though more trouble would follow.

Eddie handcuffed Norman while he was still stunned. There was no telling what trouble this man might create when he came to. The alcohol, which could easily be smelt, would anaesthetize his pain.

A procession of women took the crumpled girl to the hospital. Six of them carried the blanket in which she lay. Another had been thrown over her.

Nina led the marchers calling out in a loud voice. She let the world know exactly what would happen to Norman King if she managed to corner him.

Roger shuddered. He knew the ferocity of these women. When the ladies fought here it was awesome. Any men in the area hid until the tempest was over. If a group of women managed to corner the perpetrator he would not last long! His strength would not match their anger.

The old truck, with its unwilling passengers, arrived at the hospital. Ray was essentially unhurt, but required stitching. He would have a headache the next day.

A sister, on night duty, gave Norman some pain killers. The Flying Doctor would be called in to deal with his injuries. Most of the nurses here did not have great sympathy for those injured in drunken brawls. This man could wait. If the doctor were called out tonight a baby might die while he was on this errand. This nose job would take time and require care. Besides, who wanted to care for a rapist?

The two criminals were waiting on the hospital verandah outside the clinic. Ray sat on a bench while Norman lay on the floor. The mourning procession arrived outside the building. Two women went inside; they saw the men and began to abuse them. A night sister came to ask what was wrong. She was not feeling sympathetic to the two men either.

The women would not bring Angie inside while the men were on the verandah. The two thugs were led through the dispensary and into the men's ward. Both were still handcuffed. It was unlikely that Norman would do anything and Ray was too filled with shame.

One of the nurses was detailed to stitch up Ray's cut head. She was not particularly careful about this. His hair was shaved away roughly. Archie Daylight, the hospital orderly, sat on Ray's back while he was sutured without anesthetic.

Roger ducked in to see Martin Stone. He had been drinking beer in the white house. One of the nurses had come over for tea. The night had been looking good for Martin so he was not at all pleased.

The visitor was still unknown to the policeman. He was concerned to discover Ray's identity. Fortunately Martin knew all the details. His earlier friendship with this erstwhile statesman looked to be a liability. He felt that a frank disclosure of all the information would be his best course, at this stage.

The Council Member looked to be finished now. His influence could no longer help.

This man, however, could still provide Mr. Stone with the promotions he craved. The information he had obtained would lead to a commendation, at least, in his file.

The information, on the recently arrested, alleged, rapist, was now as complete as it could be. Roger felt that he ought to do a quick sweep of the village.

While the procession was making its way to the hospital; some young boys found Norman's petrol bombs. These boys took them to one of the nearby houses.

Within the camp there had been a long standing feud. It began up in the Northern Territory. Two men fought over the same woman twenty years before. There had been a fight and one of the men was killed. The other, larger man hit him and he didn't get up.

The feud now boiled between the next generations. It had disintegrated into a series of fights, one every few months. Both families had been warned that they were not to continue. The police had kept a close watch on the situation since their last fight. Two of the older teenage girls had a huge fight. This fight had been over a man.

The river side street had polarized into two groups after the fight. One of the girls had been cut badly by a knife.

The major protagonist was now the owner of the petrol bombs. He used them to exact revenge on three other houses.

As Roger ran to his car, he heard some noises and saw the glow of the fire. He drove down to assess the situation.

As he turned into the street he saw some brawls. The position was too unstable for him. The entire mission police force was up at the hospital.

Roger raced away to get reinforcements. Outside the hospital was a crowd of women. They were crying out in anger. Dust was being thrown in the air and the roof was being stoned.

A chant came from among the wails, 'Give us these men! They are outsiders! We will teach them how to act!'

It looked as though the two prisoners would soon be taken forcibly from their beds. Bush justice was rough. It was also final!

Roger sent Edward Jack, with his men, down to the village. He bundled the two men into his car. The local people respected Roger so his car was not attacked.

The rapists were quickly returned to the main station. They were put in one of the cells. Neither man caused any trouble as both were dazed from their misadventures.

Bluey Waters lifted his head from his cot. His eyes were swollen from his tears. Two men were placed in the other cell and their handcuffs removed. The larger man immediately slumped onto the floor while the other man sat on a cot and hung his head. He, too, it seemed, was weeping quietly to himself.

Roger woke Ernie. When he returned to the station, the entire force was mustered.

The men waited for Ernie to arrive. As they waited, riot gear was issued from the store.

Five policemen, including Roger, set out for the village. Ernie remained in the command centre. Reinforcements would not be available till the next day, at least. The situation would be more easily assessed in the daylight.

The Toyota stopped for a few short minutes so that Cathy could be advised of the situation.

It was a long and difficult night. These men worked well under Roger. He had a fine tactical mind. Eventually the warring parties were separated. An uneasy calm reigned in the village as the dawn began to struggle with the night.

Martin Stone had a direct link with the outside world. He was able to call Mt Isa on the radio phone. His calls were relayed to the regular phone system with complete confidentiality. He reported the situation to Brisbane for their evaluation. One of the calls, that night, was to Ted Stewart.

Ted had many contacts and seemed to get all the scoops. This time the report was not entirely accurate. Ray Walden was not only a rapist but the instigator of the riot. Martin Stone exaggerated the part he played in quelling the riot.

Too Much Anger!

Ernie decided to stay in the station overnight. His sleep had already been broken. Bernice was drunk and snoring. He would get no joy from going back to bed. As the station commander he was responsible to see that the station was always manned. All the men were now at the riot. He would have to stay, in case there was another emergency.

Things would be okay in the morning too. Angie would come up at sparrow's fart and they could have some time together. There were men in the cells. Perhaps it would have to wait. All of them would have to go out on Thursday. There was another boong, somewhere in town, who would have to go as well.

These two coco pops must have had a real fight. Both were a bit messed up. Funny thing was; the big guy seemed to be a lot worse than the other one. He was smashed up around the face. Wonder why they didn't put him in hospital?

He wouldn't have to worry about any official action. If there was a screw up Roger would get the strife. Squeaky clean, that Roger. It would be good to see him squirm for a change. So straight that guy; played everything by the book. Didn't drink either! Funniest thing about him was that he was a nigger lover!

The boong women were okay for satisfying one's lust but the men were useless; broken down, drunken, old fools. God left them in the oven too long. Their brains were cooked beyond any civilized thinking. Put them in the jungle and they'd talk to the monkeys. Do a lot more beside talk!

Just like the dingoes, couldn't really be tamed. Just get their skins full of grog and they returned to their true nature.

Ernie pulled out his 'Application For Transfer' form once again. He read through the questions. He was nearly ready for promotion. An inspector in Isa would be good. They had TV down there. Bernice could join a women's club or something.

Anger pounded through his brain as he though of Bernice. That man in there. His description was not so succinct or flattering.

The sergeant trembled with rage. He couldn't suppress his trembling. That man in the cells needed to be given a lesson in etiquette.

There was a small fridge in the secure room out the back. Sometimes samples were kept out there over night. He grabbed the keys and unlocked the door. The fridge also contained an emergency supply of XXXX. Officially it was evidence from some long completed case; smuggling grog onto the mission.

Some people even used a can or two as fire extinguishers in an emergency. Many shrewd Australians had a dozen or more fire extinguishers in their boot. When they left home, anyway! Poor guy who had a fire when he was almost home after a long hot day; just have to leave the car. No one could get foam from an empty!

Ernie was not going to muck up his case against Bluey. That home breaker and rapist would get his taste of the law. He had enough influence to ensure Bluey got a hard time in jail. The old lifers would happily push someone around if they got the chance.

Bluey had a small bruise under one eye. That came from the car door. Silly idiot, tried to push away just as he got into the car. The young constable would swear to that. That wog who owned the pub would too.

If he got hurt too much perhaps the case would get thrown out of court. That was too good for dirt like him.

His first can of XXXX helped Ernie to reassert his self control. The second eased the pain in his soul, which generated this anger.

The policeman limped out of the back room. He locked the door carefully. A mental note was made and filed. The remaining cans would not make a good case. He would have to get another box of 'evidence'.

Ernie sat down and tried to concentrate on the paper work before him. His pen didn't even find its way into his hand. The typewriter did not emerge from under the dust cover. He leaned back on the chair and put his feet up on the desk. It was going to be a long night. The clock showed 11: 35. A yawn escaped, he didn't fight it.

Fortunately, his chair was heavy and well balanced. It didn't tip over when he nodded off the sleep.

*

Ernie heard an insistent shouting; it seemed to invade his head. He shook himself awake. The noise wouldn't leave him alone. At first he didn't know where he was. He wasn't even sure what day it was. His mind wouldn't focus. He fought hard to control his consciousness.

It slowly dawned on him that he was in the station. He was sitting at his desk and had been asleep. He looked up at the wall: 1:47. What am I doing here?

Someone kept shouting at him. The noise was indistinct. Why don't they stop calling out? How can a man organize his thoughts with all that noise?

With great difficulty the sergeant focused his concentration. Someone was calling out from the cells, 'Norman is dying! He is spewing up blood!'

I wonder who Norman is. Why on earth should he be spewing?

Norman had been lying down ever since he had been hit. He lay in the truck. He lay in the hospital. He lay in the cells.

He woke up with a very heavy head. Clouds of mist rolled around inside. He couldn't make his way through the fog.

There was an enormous object on his face. It was like heavy dough. It covered all of his face. The weight pressed down and he couldn't move his face. It had invaded his nose and he couldn't breathe. His mouth tasted foul. The pressure was causing intense pain.

He tried to wipe his face. It was wet and painful. His touch was remote. He fought to open his eyes but they would not. His bladder seemed ready to burst. The big man began to panic. He struggled to sit up. It didn't help. He stood.

Everything began to spin. Nausea welled up within him. His stomach lurched violently. He fell to his knees and heaved convulsively. He kept it up until there was nothing left inside. Still he couldn't stop. By now he was lying on the floor rolling around in the sticky mess.

Someone was calling out somewhere. He couldn't make out the words. He mumbled to himself, 'I'm never going to come out again, Father!' and lapsed back into unconsciousness.

Ray was asleep against the wall when Norman began to thrash around. He woke up. He, too, did not know where he was. There was a bare light globe shinning in the ceiling. He was in the cells somewhere. Someone was playing drums inside his head.

He saw Norman try to stand up and then fall forward on his knees. He was violently sick. Ray forced himself to think. What can I do? He tried not to look at Norman. He couldn't stop himself. The man in front of him was vomiting blood. He screamed out in panic.

Bluey woke up. He thought the other men were just drunks, 'Shut up, Niggers!'

He rolled over and tried to go to sleep again.

*

Ernie came in and switched on the big light. The unrecognizable man was lying on the floor. He was lying there tensed up. There was red among the liquid on the floor. This was more than just a drunken aftermath. Alcoholic poisoning was not like this.

There was a local phone line between the station and the hospital. The sergeant dialed the nurses. It was answered by a night shift sister.

'Hospital here, can I help you?'

'Sister, it's Ernie here. I've got some sort of problem with one of the boongs. He has been badly smashed up. I can't imagine why they've put him here.'

'Find out if he's been given anything to kill his pain. It seems I'd better pop over for a look.'

'See ya in a copula minutes.'

'Rightio!'

Andrea Hilditch arrived at the police station five minutes later. She was the night supervisor at Leichhardt hospital. Andrea liked night duty and had the permanent roster. She was a nurse of considerable experience, having trained in the sixties and then spent four years in Viet Nam. She was not married and not a feminist; just fulfilled in her career and content.

It didn't take her long to decide that Norman had an allergic reaction.

'He must have been given something down at the mission. I expect he's allergic to it.

You don't know what it was do you?'

'Na! No idea at all.'

'Why is he here anyway? He should have been kept in the hospital down there.'

'There was some sort of riot. I don't really know why they sent these two Mars bars up.'

'Can you get in touch with the hospital down there? I must know what he has reacted to. I might make things worse if I'm not careful.'

'There's a radio here. I can contact the hospital or the main office. I'll get right on to it.'

Ernie went into the next room. He called the Boomallooba hospital, 'We've got a fellah here who's pretty sick. Roger brought him in earlier. He's badly smashed up.'

'We gave him morphine for the pain; must be allergic to it.'

Andrea had come in as well. She dashed back to the cell and gave Norman another injection; something to counteract his reaction. He was then cleaned up and put on the bed. She didn't want to move him just now. He would be worse for a journey, at this stage. This procedure took about fifteen minutes.

While Andrea was helping Norman, Ernie continued his conversation over the radio. He was interested in the reason for tonight's riot. It also seemed out of order to place two fairly sick men in the cells overnight. It would be good to haul Roger over the coals. Some extra information would not go astray.

He was disappointed. The facts showed that Roger had acted properly. He also found that Angie, his lover, had been raped. The anger which he had suppressed now began to surface.

Sergeant Collins had been quite fond of Angie. His relationship with her satisfied his basic needs. She helped him to maintain his sanity in a trying situation. His pride was also wounded. Once again a woman, who belonged to him, had been violated. His sense of strength and protection was now seriously under threat. Someone must suffer.

That cheeky boong, who had come up to the town recently, must be to blame. Old Norman needed to be provoked before he became violent. The yellah fellah from the big smoke was in for trouble; that was beyond doubt.

Some looney, abo activist group must have sent that young choco up to stir the pot. He had stirred the pot too! A bit too much! He had had too much to drink as well, from the smell of him.

Better get in there and teach him some respect for the establishment. These young coons thought they could come straight in here and take over the place. Not while Ernie Collins ran the show. He was the law up here!

Ernie had large and hard hands. Over the years they had developed calluses in the right places. He knew how to hit a man without sending him into unconsciousness straight away. More than once in his life this big man had taught a coco pop to mind his manners.

Ray was sitting on the edge of his bed. The smell was overpowering; he was also filled with a sense of deep shame. He had not been able to resist a drink. It was easy living the sheltered life of a future leader. Here in real life it was another matter.

Ernie unlocked the cell and then took Ray down to the last cell. He began by explaining to Ray that his actions were wrong.

He told Ray that, as an Aborigine, he had no rights at all. Men like him were worse than dogs.

When the man to man talk was over Ernie continued his lesson in a more physical way. Ray was systematically beaten for about fifteen minutes. After that time he was thrown on to the bed, like a broken rag doll.

Bluey watched the whole scene in stunned silence. He was overawed at the ferocity of Ernie's anger.

When Ernie threw Ray on to the bed he turned and looked at Bluey for about two minutes. He was filled with hate.

Ernie pulled the cell door shut and went to Bluey's cell door. He put his hand on the door and felt in his pocket for the keys.

Bluey gave a moan of fear and involuntarily evacuated his bowels.

Ernie shrugged, turned away and then walked into the office.

The remainder of the night passed uneventfully in the town police station. For the remainder of the garrison it was not so quiet!

A Straight Bat

Viv Swan was sitting in his office. It was Wednesday morning. Tonight he would be the guest speaker at a school speech night; a valuable exercise in flag flying. He should be so lucky! Would he even get there tonight?

His normally perfectly manicured hair was slightly awry. Last night had been an absolute disaster. He slipped down to his expensive flat in Southport. The parliament was not sitting and he wanted a weekend with his wife. Their children were well looked after by their Aunt in Sunnybank. Lenore, his wife, had an unmarried twin sister who lived with his family in their Brisbane home.

The first phone call came as he and his wife were asleep. His chief advisor told him about the riot at Boomallooba. Aboriginal Affairs was not normally his responsibility but, as acting Premier, he wanted to be in control of all emergencies.

He called a senior man in the Department of Aboriginal and Islander Affairs and told him to monitor the situation; so that he could stay in touch with things.

A second call came about an hour later. Viv decided to return to Brisbane then. It was essential for the Premier to have a good grasp of every situation. He, the future premier, would be in control of this situation!

Viv showered and then raced back to the executive building by helicopter.

There had been many calls since his helicopter arrived back in Brisbane. The Acting Premier continued to use his own office rather than slip upstairs to the top suite. He didn't want to have to move out of the executive office if the old guy recovered from his latest operation.

Every member of the team in his dull red and yellow office were tired and frayed at the edges. A pretender to the throne could well have all his dreams wrecked on the reef of such a crisis. The future of these minders was also at stake. They were riding the crest of Viv's wave.

Someone had alerted the press to their problem. There had been a long line of journalists on the phone all night. No 'exclusives' had been given; a press conference was due to begin in about five minutes.

Alan Nielson was on the phone now. He was in contact with Leichhardt. The Acting Premier would need all the latest information before this press conference. When this call was complete, the news was passed on to everyone else in the room.

Jimmy Watkins, Viv's press secretary, quickly revised the press release.

Viv drank another glass of water. His throat was always dry when he was nervous. He was glad of the warm weather. His bladder was much friendlier at this time of the year.

Three of the four men left the room and headed for the lift. The ghouls were waiting downstairs. They would need to be fed. Each of the men hoped that their own flesh would not be in the correct state to satisfy them tomorrow.

The pressmen were packed into the conference room. The political hacks were ensconced in their regular corner. There were the bright, young, 'honorary men' from current affairs in the front. These women were not the usual politicos but the investigators. An anchor woman from channel eleven sat aloofly beside them. Ted Stewart hunched in a beaten lounge chair down the back.

Viv walked through the parliamentarian's door. He walked quickly to the desk. He carried the release in his hand.

Ted noticed that he was not quite his immaculate self. His face was more shadowed than usual. Must have shaved at about three, he thought? His shirt was not white, as usual, but dark blue with white cuffs and collar. His tie was somewhat out of the ordinary, a mauve pastel pattern. A light gray suit completed the picture.

It looks like he's dressed to go out to dinner rather than come to work. That was true. Viv never wore his suits more than one day at the time. The only suit down at his Southport flat was his entertaining suit.

The veteran journalist laughed to himself. Viv's hair looked a bit askance. Every strand was not exactly parallel across his pate. There seemed to be about three different lines of hair.

Jock Williams slipped in the back door and stood with his back to the wall.

Viv coughed and began to read the prepared statement. There was no trace of nervousness in his voice.

'We have received information from Leichhardt that there was a riot in Boomallooba. Our policemen in the area have successfully contained this outbreak of violence. As far as we can tell the outbreak was instigated by outsiders. It seems, at this stage, that a member of the A.C.A.I.Q. was involved in the early stages of this disturbance. Our representative in the area informs me that this man had gone to the North to create trouble. There has been an interest in creating land rights claims on the new oil fields in the Gulf. This man was rebuffed and hoped to engineer a situation out of spite. I have been monitoring the situation since it first came to my attention. This is not an outbreak of universal discontent among Aboriginal people.'

'Are there any question?' Viv continued after a pregnant pause.

Immediately bedlam broke out. Viv raised his hand for silence and finally was able to select a woman from the Courier Mail.

'How can you be sure that this is not the first act in an Aboriginal civil war?'

'We have been in consultation with leaders, in remote areas, over a long period of time. Our experts, in the field, have found no evidence of discontent among the outback Aborigines. There is always discontent in the fringe dwelling areas where activists and agitators can work without leaving the comfort of their homes.'

Another journalist jumped up. Viv made no attempt to identify him.

'What evidence is there to suggest that someone had gone to the North to cause trouble? That strikes me as being paranoid!'

Viv paused and slowly answered carefully, 'That is a very good question… The man in question talked at length to our representative. He told him, in confidence, of his mission.'

'I heard, on talkback radio last night, a man, claiming to be an Aborigine, say that the young Aborigines were looking for a newer and more energetic leadership. Was this latest incident just a manifestation of this phenomenon?'

'We all know that people, in most cases, ring up talkback because no one else will listen to them. Those who ring up with something to say soon learn that, with some notable exceptions, the hosts don't want to listen to them. A host must be careful not to let anyone, who is too intelligent, speak or else they might look as stupid as they are.'

There was a chuckle from the non radio press. These parasites might earn big money but they made no worthwhile contribution to the nation.

Some more questions were asked and Viv began to relax. He had always been known for his eloquence or debating skill. Talking was a real pleasure to him.

Another journalist called out a question, ‘Why do you think the people from the A.C.A.I.Q. are determined to cause so much strife?’

‘Well… in real life there are many people who are unable to achieve the success they crave. Most people are able to reconcile themselves to that fact. Some, who can’t do that, slip off to join some minority and use that as a vehicle to success. The reason being that in the looney fringe there is not much competition.’

Ted sprang in, ‘Do you believe that Andrew MacDonald is a man like that?’

‘I’m sorry Ted; I don’t believe that that is a proper question for me to answer.’

Some more questions came in and the conference looked set to grind down to its inevitable conclusion.

A phone rang on the desk. Jimmy Watkins reached down and picked it up. He listened carefully. His face remained a mask.

‘Can you say that again, Allan?’

He listened again and then bent down to give Viv a message.

‘We have just heard that a young girl has died. She was allegedly raped and brutally beaten by Ray Walden of the A.C.A.I.Q. and one of his friends. She died this morning.’

Ted Stewart’s voice came out again, ‘Who did you say was involved in this rape?’

‘Ray Walden and another man were allegedly apprehended at the scene of the crime.’

It seemed like a good time for some of the old hacks to trot out some questions.

‘When something like this happens, do you believe that capital punishment should be reintroduced?’

‘Capital punishment is, at present, not an option under Queensland law.’

‘But wouldn’t you like to see these rapists hanged?’

‘Cabinet has discussed this option and, at present, we don’t believe that it is appropriate in this day and age.’

‘But what are your personal feelings on the matter?’

‘One’s opinion on this subject depends on their philosophical standpoint. There are basically two concepts: “Retribution” or “Rehabilitation”. If you believe that everyone is intrinsically good then you will believe in “Rehabilitation”, that is, to restore them to their innate goodness. If you do not believe that man is essentially bad then you will prefer “Retribution”. A man should be punished for his crime. The end point of the “Retribution” philosophy is capital punishment. It is difficult to argue against basic philosophy; “Barbarity” to one is “Injustice” to another. At this time the Government leans towards “Rehabilitation”. At some future point in time the people may choose “Retribution” and then capital punishment will be reintroduced.’

‘Do you believe that man is inherently good?’

‘I do believe that some journalists are bad. Perhaps you should experience “Rehabilitation”… Perhaps, “Retribution”’.

There was an undercurrent of laughter. Jock Williams walked out. The questions continued for a few more minutes.

Hot! Hot! Hot!

It was a barbarously hot night. Even without the fires it would not have struggled below eighty. The police officers were exhausted when they took stock the next morning. By nine o'clock all was quiet. It was hard to imagine that there had been any trouble as the police sat outside the store. From this vantage point the charred remains of the houses were invisible.

The men were dirty. Their normally immaculate, according to regulations, uniforms were stained with sweat and soot. It seemed that no one was moving in the entire camp. They had just completed their last foot patrols and were satisfied.

Of the five men, who came down to quell the riot, only three were still fit for duty. Ossie Schaub had been hit by a nulla nulla at first light. His jaw was badly broken and he would have to be flown out. The doctor was due, directly. David Cummings broke his arm at about one thirty.

There was an emergency at Mornington Island during the night. The Flying Doctor went there first. Three or four kids had been laid low by gastroenteritis. One died before the riot. The plane was in the air when David had been hurt and it couldn't be diverted.

Both men were comfortable in the hospital down the road. They would soon be sent out.

Roger was a hard man. He came through the night unscathed. He still had it in him to work all day, if needed. It would be good to sleep, though. He told the other young constables to have the rest of the day off. Roger would man the station with Ernie, if there were no reinforcements.

They heard the drone of a plane. It was the Flying Doctor coming, at last. Edward and Roger jumped into the truck and headed towards the west. There was a rough airstrip in the bush. It ran parallel to the river. The strip was only used by the doctor because there was a much better one in town.

The plane landed and the doctor and his nurse climbed out. Their plane taxied to the northern end of the strip where the truck was parked. The door swung down and the nurse seemed to stagger as the heat hit her. 'Boy, it's sure hot today!' she said.

'You're not wrong there, Barb!' Roger replied.

'What have you been doing? I'd have thought that it was too early for mud wrestling, yet.'

'Well you learn something every day.'

Now that the pleasantries were completed, the doctor and nurse climbed in to the cabin with Roger while Edward climbed into the back. This Toyota was the 'police truck', 'meat wagon' and 'ambulance'. The Federal government certainly got their money's worth when they brought this truck.

They drove back to the hospital. The doctor examined Ossie and decided that he would need an operation. He was heavily sedated and was soon transferred to the waiting truck on a stretcher. Dave walked to the truck himself. His arm was splinted but not set. Both bones in the left forearm were broken. He, too, would require orthopedic surgery.

The doctor examined the other patients in the wards. He diagnosed bruises, sprains and lacerations but no one else needed to be taken to Isa.

There was no reason for the medical team to stay any longer. Both the injured men were in the back of the ambulance. It was a bumpy and dusty trip out to the strip. Ossie grunted with pain a few times but arrived without too much discomfort. In the bush people had to endure more hardship than that.

Roger went back to collect the two remaining policeman. They moved from the ambulance into their own patrol vehicle. It was the grey, short wheel base, Toyota that Roger regularly used.

These three men sat across the front of their vehicle and headed west. It was ten thirty by now; the sky was clear of clouds. This was surprising as it was very humid. The temperature was about one hundred ten in the shade. Fortunately the police union was concerned for its men, in the not north of the state. The truck was air conditioned and the exhausted constabulary was given some relief from the heat. Roger suspected that there would be storm in the next few days. Hopefully, it would come this afternoon.

The two young constables tumbled thankfully out of the truck and into their barracks in Leichhardt. Both men were grateful that they had survived the night. They were now safe and comfortable. Their unmarried quarters were very nice. This whole building was cooled with ducted air conditioning. The men had five star, motel type accommodation with their own en suite bathrooms. Plenty of hot and cold water was available. It was a real advantage to have a river which flowed all the year round. There was plenty of sun to heat the water.

There was a story of an early sergeant, in this area, who tried his own solar heater in the early fifties. He put a forty four gallon drum on the roof. It wasn't long before the drum had to be wrapped in many layers of sacking because the water was boiling all day.

'See ya later, Bill, Dave.' Roger had to be careful not to say David to Dave Billings and Dave to David Cummings.

Neither man answered.

'Go home and have a good rest. You'll probably have duty tonight or tomorrow but nothing today.' Roger closed his car door and drove off.

When he arrived at the station, everything was quiet. Some flies buzzed lazily around an old dog sitting in the shade of the building. It seemed as though no one was alive in this part of town. The Toyota slipped easily into its place under the parking shelter. The policeman braced himself for the heat. He climbed out of the driver's seat and leant against the shut door. The heat was like a physical being. It struck him in the chest with a hard punch and took his breath away. He wearily staggered over to the station door.

He entered the charge room from the back and saw that everything was quiet inside. It seemed as though the post was deserted.

Roger walked into the sergeant's office, he was tired and irritable. It was hard to concentrate with the headache that pounded inside his head.

Ernie was sound asleep. Roger found it hard to imagine how he could sleep in that position. His feet were on the desk right up to his cocked knees. The chair was swung back to counterbalance this. Both hands hung down and touched the floor. He was gently snoring. There were half a dozen empty cans of XXXX on the shelf behind him.

Roger immediately felt extremely angry. He and the other men had risked their lives, in the line of duty, last night. Ernie had stayed here and got drunk. His boots were not cleaned. His shirt was undone and creased His thin, hairy chest and stomach heaved in peaceful contentment; perhaps it was inebriated forgetfulness. An ashtray was full of burnt out cigarettes.

Full of righteous anger, Roger reached back and slammed the door. Ernie woke with a start and fell onto the floor. He cursed soundly as he struggled to his feet. Fortunately, he had been relaxed when he landed and was not hurt. As usual his speech was liberally sprinkled with expletives.

'You silly idiot, Roger! What do you want to do? Give me heart failure?'

'Ernie, you were asleep on duty! You know that is against regulations to leave the station unmanned!'

'I was here!'

'But you were asleep! We were out last night and you slept at your post!'

'Listen to me, Roger. I'm your commanding officer! Insubordination is a grave offence!'

'I did your job last night! You were responsible for quelling that riot but I did all the work!'

'As commanding officer I ensured that the riot was handled. I sent my men out and manned headquarters myself. I guarded the prisoners all night. I dealt with an emergency. I remained on duty. Would you like to clean out the cells?'

'You haven't gone and beaten one of the prisoners, have you! I said last time that I couldn't keep quiet any longer with a clear conscience!'

'They were both beaten when they arrived. For all I know, you could have beaten them yourself!'

'Come on Ernie, you know I'm not like that!'

'I would have to tell any investigation exactly what I believe!'

'You'd lie to protect yourself?'

'I might say the same thing to you!' Ernie snapped back.

'What happened to the prisoners last night?'

'One of them had an allergic reaction or something. He was quite sick.'

'Which one was that?' Roger was interested now.

'The big renegade.' Ernie answered.

'What about the other one? Is he all right?'

'He's beaten up a bit.'

'What! He shouldn't be marked! Did you beat him?'

'How should I know what he's like? I saw he was beaten first time I looked at him. Maybe someone hit him in the riot.'

'We got him out before the riot!'

'Go home now Roger. I'll watch the station. Some reinforcements should be sent in tomorrow.'

'They should be able to send some in before that! Are you trying to hide something, Ernie?'

'Roger, you are tired. Your judgment is unsound at this time. Why should I want to hide anything?'

'I'll go home now and come in tonight. I'll make a thorough search of everything then! If you have done anything wrong, I'll find it!'

Roger walked out onto the verandah. His head was aching. So was every muscle in his body. He already felt bad about losing his temper with Ernie. He'd have to apologize tonight. Trouble was the old guy was always cutting corners. He acted like some sort of autocrat; like he was above the law.

The younger man had always felt bad about that. Sometimes he talked to other people about his feelings, as well. That was wrong.

Ernie was incompetent. He just didn't manage his section properly. Roger had to clean up his mess and complete the paperwork every week.

The older man remained at his desk and thought long and hard. That young guy didn't seem to understand police solidarity. He was always a threat. All that painful honesty!

Ernie was also concerned. He bashed a man in the cells. There was a white man who had seen him do it! The guy he bashed looked like he was dead. He hadn't moved. He lay there with his head and arm hanging over the side of the bed.

He'd better do something about it. With Roger he could always bluff his way through… Pity the renegade had been sick. He could always blame him for the bashing. No! The wowser cop would have to be got out of the way as well.

A Windfall

Rick Walcott was a happy man. He lived in the country he loved. His job was better than a hobby. Every day he did what he loved. For this bachelor, life was uncomplicated.

He wanted to be a truck driver all his life. Now he was. He started the hard way; driving the big road trains in the Territory and the West. Finally after eight years he had enough to put a deposit on his own rig. The rig belonged to him, now; not the bank.

As a boy he was very big so he wanted to get his license as early as fifteen. The cop at Bedourie gave it to him without any trouble. This big boned, gaunt, blond haired boy seemed to be of an indeterminate age. He was burned dark brown and his blue eyes stood out in his face. His hands were already hard and horny. He was six feet tall at thirteen but hadn't grown since then.

Rick's father was a drover. One day the old drover and his son camped out near the Bedourie. They had already taken a mob down from the Territory and were now heading south. The old man decided to work in the opal mines. Rick wasn't keen to live in a hole. All his life he had been on the plains. He decided to try for his license. After a few lies he paid the money and walked out.

That blond haired boy hadn't changed much. These days his eyes had more creases around them. He was still as thin.

Today was the same as any other day in the last few years: perfect. He didn't own anything but the truck and a few items of clothing. It had a bed in the back but he slept outside. He ate his humble beef and damper on the ground next to a camp fire.

There was a girl who lived with him for a few years but she had, eventually, wandered off. Now he had a dog. A white coated bull terrier called Deefer. It wasn't original but he liked it; an abbreviation for 'D for dog'.

Rick pulled into Leichhardt and camped his truck next to the pub. He had two dogs* behind the bogey. Each one had four tanks of Diesel or petrol. The tanks contained 6,000 gallons each.

In the bush petrol tankers weren't used. This system was more versatile. He could unload the tanks and pick up empties, or pump the fuel out. The stations usually could only manage one tank. He left four tanks here behind the pub.

The petrol man had not had a day off for sixteen months. He was quite content to drive and sleep. There was a bucket of water and soap in the back. Each stop he put his dirty clothes and some washing powder in the bucket with some clean water. The clothes

---

* In the Australian bush the trailers pulled by an articulated vehicle are called "dogs' because they follow along behind.

already in the bucket were taken and rinsed before being hung out. His attire was unvarying: King Gee shorts and a blue Bonds singlet. He wore elastic sided boots and ex army socks. He never wore underpants; there was not a chance of him getting testicular cancer.

Rick was quiet and content. He didn't smoke and rarely drank. He used to read extensively, including many of the classics, in his time off the road. When he spoke he was articulate.

His main vice was the same as his father's. The old drovers would often spend many months on the track. They would have little sleep and hardly any food. Often breakfast was a cigarette with some tea and damper. When the cattle were being driven there was no time for a drink.

At the end of the run the old drover used to have a binge. He would collect his money and drink hard for a week or so. Sometimes these men, with sad, far seeing eyes, would get violent; sometimes they would wax eloquent.

Rick often remained sober for one or two years then he would get a powerful thirst. He was reaching the time when his safety valve would pop. He turned the truck around and parked it facing east. A drink or ten had become his top priority. A couple of days hard drinking would be enough to put the gremlins inside him to sleep for another year or two.

He parked the rig and crossed the road into the bar. His big bony hand flattened a hundred dollar bill onto the bar, 'Tell me when that's finished, Tony! I'll have XXXX from the tap and nothing else.'

His first three beers where chugga lugged. Tony was amazed at the speed. They didn't even touch the sides.

This publican had not seen Rick on a binge. He didn't know that this quiet, taciturn man would remain as gentle as a mouse. The only irritation would be his quoting of poetry. This would start after a few hours. The truck driver's knowledge ranged from Shakespeare and Donne to Lawson and Judith Wright.

Tony sent a message to the police station, telling the sergeant of this binge. He hadn't seen one before but had heard the legends.

A Glimmer of Hope!

Ernie sat in his office and tried to think. He was still shaking with the adrenaline of his argument with Roger. His mind was a bit foggy but he fought hard to clear it out. Alarm bells were ringing inside his brain.

There would soon be trouble. His young second in command would make sure of that. All the public anger at the recent Aboriginal deaths in custody would soon pour down on his head. That trouble maker would also ruin his own career. No one in the police force ever dobbed in his mates and survived. The real cause of concern for Ernie was his own reputation.

Too many people could testify to the condition of the boong. The other one had been too sick to do the damage. If they could close ranks then they would all survive the inquiry. If there was any hint of bashing then everything would fall apart like a house of cards.

As he sat and brooded he got Tony's message from the pub. A glimmer of hope began to appear on the horizon. There had been another binge just the day before. It had lasted about twenty four hours; Tony missed seeing that binge because he was inside the hotel serving other customers. Those two men in the cells had gone binging with a white fellah.

The pieces began to fall into place for Ernie. The other guy in the binge was the poof. He was meant to fly out on today's plane. It would be a good idea to make sure that he was on that flight. He'd man the radio in his vehicle. It wouldn't take too long. The plane was due in about an hour. The Trilander would connect with the Brisbane plane in Isa.

He could get one of his mates to pick up the poof. They could keep him 'on ice' as a witness.

The sergeant got a line to Mount Isa. One of the sergeants down there owed him some favors. A few more calls confirmed the fact that Adam Angel was booked on the Brisbane plane with Ansett. He also checked that the same man was on Bushy's to Isa today. There would be a policeman in Isa to put him on the Brisbane flight. Another colleague would meet him in the city and escort him to a hotel. They could act officially as he was a material witness. His superiors would consider these precautions as foresight on his part. The man would be needed in any inquiry. He was due to leave and could easily get lost. People like that Angel pervert, were not trustworthy.

When the sergeant arrived at the public service residences, they looked deserted. It was a normal school day and no one should be there. Ernie had made it his business to know everything there was to know in town. He knew which flat belonged to Adam.

Ernie went straight to the door. It was ajar. He pushed it open and walked in. There was an overwhelming smell. The small, bald man was lying in his own mess on the bed. He was still and prone. His head was propped up, drunkenly, against the wall.

Ernie felt sick in his stomach. He went into the bathroom and ran the shower. He picked Adam up and put him under the cold shower. The teacher gasped then groaned. Adam swore profusely and tried to get out of the water. His tormentor pushed him back in. Adam looked up and saw who it was. He started to weep silently. He stripped off his dirty clothes and washed himself.

The sergeant told his witness to rinse out the dirty clothes and then dress. Adam's bed linen was still on the bed but that would have to stay. The school principal was empowered to employ someone to clean the room at Adam's expense.

As Adam dressed himself, Ernie took a bag and told him to pack it. All the other goods could be sent to Brisbane. Everything would be charged to the Education Department. That was not the policeman's worry.

They drove to the airstrip when everything was ready. Adam sat uncomfortably. His head was very sore and he was burnt in other places too. Ernie nearly switched the air conditioner off to make him squirm a bit more. Trouble was he didn't like the heat much himself.

They didn't have to wait too long for the plane. Ernie had decided to see the man right on to the aircraft. He sat inside his cooled cabin and waited till the door of the Trilander was shut.

With a satisfied sigh he started the engine and returned to his station.

He was confident that in about four hours he would receive the call he was waiting for. Right now his mind was contemplating that truck waiting outside the pub!

More Good Luck

It was always relatively cool at the twenty mile outstation. The homestead was built among the thick river trees. It was almost like rain forest here along the water course. Tall, shady trees cut out most of the sunlight. The thick undergrowth seemed to climb onto the house itself.

The residence here was not much more than a shed on stilts. It had been built beside a water hole which ran parallel to the river. It was only sixty yards from the flowing water. In the wet the channel next to the house flowed as well. The outstation buildings: house and work shop, were on a small ridge. It would not flood here unless the whole country was inundated.

There was a wide shady verandah and four rooms inside. Two were bedrooms and the others: a kitchen and a general purpose room. There was also a bathroom with the luxury of a septic system.

Water was pumped up from the billabong, into a tank which rose above the height of the roof. Another tank was there to collect rainwater.

As the sun rose, it began to filter its way in through the trees. Ritchie Arnold woke as its rays caressed his face. He was sleeping on the verandah of his home. He had not slept inside a house since he was a baby.

He lay stretched out on an old wire bed base. It was covered with a retired saddle blanket. He slept, naked, on top of the blanket which passed for his bed linen.

He rolled over and groaned as his back caught. His feet hit the floor and he winced while he stretched the knot out of the middle of his spine.

He walked around to the western reach of the verandah and woke his brother. While Paul lay and tried to wake up, Ritchie climbed into the shower. Paul was wearing a tired, old pair of cotton shorts.

The younger brother went inside and boiled a billy. He threw in a handful of tea leaves when it began to bubble.

The brothers ate their breakfast in silence. There was no special, cooked food here. Just damper and a slab cut from a roast rump of beef.

Outside the dull murmur of their generator was just loud enough to hear. It ran the freezer and its accompanying fridge.

Their damper had been cooked by Noreen, their mother, at the main Covent Garden homestead. She had also sent out the beef. The boys usually ate roast wallaby or wallaby stew. They had plenty of fruit sent out for them as well. Bananas and oranges were the main staple here. Beef and bread filled the space left by wallaby and damper, if it was there.

It was a meal which did not violate the pristine as far as the silence of the environment was concerned. Both of the eaters were scared.

It was Tuesday morning and they were due to meet with the policeman in Leichhardt. He was an awesome man. The glint of his cold grey eye would turn even the belly of their father to water.

The week had been hectic since their last encounter with the law. All the marijuana plants had been sprayed with 'Roundup'. They were already starting to die. Some of the undergrowth had been sprayed as well. These were also looking sick as well. Never mind the plant life would soon grow back.

It would take a few hours to drive into town. The men would go along the river. They could also head over to main road but that way was hotter; no shade!

Their battered, old Toyota four wheel drive was carefully swept out first. Paul wanted to make sure there were no seeds in the tray.

The track headed north for about three hundred yards. It swung away to the west and over to the river bed. Somehow it found its way through the heavy foliage on the large island. Their own road met the main highway heading into town. 'Main highway' may have been accurate twenty years ago. It serviced the home of one of the members of the Shire Council in those days. Today it was just two tracks with a mound of grass between. On the black soil it was very rough. When there was rain the cattle gravitated towards the road. Later the churned up mud turned into a concrete like mass.

Ritchie and Paul arrived in Leichhardt. They went to the pub first. Both had dressed as well as they could. R M Williams riding boots, jeans and fancy western shirts were topped off by Akubra hats on both heads.

In this country most people knew each other. Sometimes underage drinking was allowed, sometimes it wasn't. Not for any respect of the law; just bigotry.

Paul went straight to the back door of the pub and called out while Ritchie parked the beast. The circumstances were serious. Both boys ordered double scotches, Black Douglas, to settle their nerves.

Then they drove around to the police station. Ernie was back by this time. There was still only one policeman on duty, rather than the regular three.

The sergeant rang the head office in Mt. Isa. There would be four extra constables on a charter plane tomorrow morning, first thing. It would be good to have extra men for a while; after the riot. Sometimes these things simmered for a time and then blew up again.

He felt satisfied that he had another night to deal with his own problem. This satisfaction increased, almost to ecstasy, when the two brothers walked in. Both of them were a didgeridoo short of a corroboree, for sure. They would do exactly as they were told.

Their fear was strong in the air. Ernie smelt it with distaste. Stupid boongs! No brains to do anything! They got themselves into trouble but then they couldn't handle it.

At least they would do whatever he told them. It wouldn't hurt to get them a bit more into his power, though. A small spell of bullying would knock any remaining resistance out of them.

The sergeant sat at his desk and continued to study some papers. He always kept some manuals and papers on his desk. It didn't hurt to look like he was working sometimes.

The paper on his desk was actually blank, but that didn't matter. The two boys stood before the desk and fretted. Neither was brave enough, perhaps foolish enough, to speak.

Casually, Ernie reached for a pen and began to write. He wrote his own name and his wife's name five times each. His mind was neither adept nor nimble enough to create any literary masterpiece at this time.

Eventually he looked up; Paul was almost crying, 'What do you boongs want?'

'Er… ah… h… uhmm… you wanted to see us.' Ritchie was the mouth piece.

Ernie read through the list on his page again, 'Oh… that's right… you are the drug boys!'

'We didn't mean it, sergeant!' The answer jumped out rapidly.

'Well… did you earn any money from the drugs?'

'Yeah… w… w… we earn some beer money. You like we should give it to you, boss?'

'Are you trying to bribe me?'

There was nothing for them to say. It could be construed as offering a bribe. The poor young man was so confused because of his fear.

'That is also a very serious crime! Do you understand that?' Ernie continued, striking while the iron was hot.

'We doan wan to bribe anyone!' Ritchie managed to gasp.

'What would your father say… if he found out that you tried to bribe a policeman?'

'Doan tell our father! He kick us for good! He not wan anything with policemen!'

'There is the drug trafficking as well! You grew a prohibited substance for sale!'

'Boss… if the old man fin out about that, he goana kill us dreckly!'

'Well… what do you think I should do? You will have to do a lot of work for me if you want me to forget what I know.'

'Sergeant, we even kill a fellah if you like!'

'I'm sure that won't be necessary. Firstly you can go and clean out the cells while I consider your case.'

Ernie took the two frightened youths into the cell block. Norman still lay on his cot. He would be groggy from the drugs for a while yet. His smashed nose would keep him quiet as well. He was due to go to Mt. Isa the next day.

Ray lay as he had been dropped; broken and askew, on the bed. Ernie felt the fear churn inside his stomach. That boong certainly looked dead.

Bluey was utterly depressed. He lay in a state of lethargy on his bed. He had not yet cleaned up his trousers. He was so full of self pity that he did not notice that it was well past breakfast time. In fact, lunch was not only due but slightly late.

The whole block had the pungent smell of stale, alcoholic vomit.

Ernie took the syringe of Pethidine that the nurse had left last night. He very carefully injected Norman in the thigh. It was intended to kill his pain but had the advantage of immobilizing the big trouble maker.

Bluey didn't even seem to notice the intruders. Maybe he didn't realize that a murder had taken place last night. It would be too much of a chance to assume that he didn't know.

Ernie took Ritchie and Paul through to the cleaner's room and showed them the equipment.

While the boys cleaned Norman's cell Ernie stood guard. He had locked them in. Both boys had learnt to wash floors when they were younger. Sometimes Ambrose Da Silva had insisted that they clean the house for him. He would take their mother aside and make them work so that he would not be disturbed.

Before long the first cell was clean and smelling of disinfectant. Ernie let his charges out to clean the buckets; he sent them to get some fresh water.

Bluey's cell was cleaned next. He didn't seem to notice. Soon the whole block was clean. There was a strong smell of 'Pine O Clean'. It was much nicer than the odor of human excrement.

Paul looked up at Ernie and said, in an almost inaudible whisper, 'That fellah dead!'

They were quickly hustled into the cleaner's room.

'That's what will happen to you if you break the law! Last night that man tried to bribe a policeman.'

There was nothing to say to that. If they were killed for their crimes the old man would find out for sure. The old goat would be sure to punish their mother.

The three moved back into the cooler section, 'Boys, there is a job you can do for me.'

'What you want?' Ritchie stammered.

'Did you see the truck outside the pub?'

'That big ol' petrol truck b'long Mr. Walcott?'

'Yes that's the one.'

'We do anything!' Paul butted in.

'I want you to get into that truck and drive it for me. Do you understand?'

'How far we take it?'

'Listen carefully! I don't want you to do anything wrong.'

'We listening!' Both boys spoke together.

'The key will still be in the ignition.' Ernie knew that Rick Walcott would not take the key out. He wouldn't lose the key if it was ready to start the vehicle.

'Sure thing.'

'I want you to take the truck and drive it towards Boomallooba. Go over the bridge and drive a quarter of a mile. There is an old track going off to the right. On the left there is a big gum tree and just before the track there are two ant beds. After the track is an old tree which was struck by lightning. You understand?'

'Yes.' Paul repeated all the landmarks precisely. These youths had been brought up in the bush. The land marks would be as familiar to them as street signs to a city boy.

'Take the truck down the track until you come to an old grid near a dam. There used to be a homestead there. You will see the stumps and some big ol' trees. Turn the truck around and park it there. Go and hide in the old shed behind the ruin.'

Ernie asked the boys to repeat his instructions half a dozen times. At last he was sure that they knew exactly what to do.

They went outside and climbed into their battered old Toyota. From an early age their father had trained them to obey instructions. Both of the boys had stock whip scars on their lower abdomen and upper thighs.

Their old ute was parked in the shade behind the pub. Ritchie purposefully walked over to the cab of the truck and climbed in. The engine was still running. Often diesel engines were left running over the lunch break. The engine would cool down too much and then have to be warmed up again.

Rick had not turned off his engine; he only intended to drink for a short while. Once he got the taste, however, he wouldn't stop until he was paralytic.

The big rig had eighteen gears. It was very similar to the Covent Garden cattle truck. Ritchie had taken cattle to Isa and the rail head before. He had no trouble selecting the correct gear while Paul climbed in.

It took exactly thirteen minutes for the truck to be parked beside the old homestead ruin. Paul had jumped out when the truck left the road and swept away the tracks. The old track had not been used for many years. Even after the petrol tanker had gone in the track looked unused.

The boys remained in the shed until they were called for after dark.

Another Emergency

At about four thirty that afternoon Ernie left the police station and entered his vehicle. He heard, from the pub, that someone had taken the petrol truck. Rick Walcott hadn't noticed anything but Tony had seen two Aborigines drive it away. Ernie mentioned the possibility of theft to the publican, registering surprise that it had been taken away.

The petrol man was slouching over the bar. He had a schooner of beer half finished in front of him. Next to that was a full one. Rick had let Tony know that he didn't want to wait between drinks.

The truckie was still coherent when Ernie came to see him, 'Did you ask some boongs to drive your truck away?'

'Naah, I shertainly wounnut let any boongsh dshrive my shruck.'

He turned back to the bar. At this stage of his life the thirst in his soul was more significant than anything else. He would certainly have rushed out at any other time.

'Too drunk to realize!' Ernie winked at Tony.

'Yeah mate.'

'It looks like it has been stolen. I'd better do something about it, I suppose!'

The sergeant drove over to the police barracks. He walked in through the front door and into the shared recreation room. Both the first constables were slouching in easy chairs. They were watching a video of 'The True North'. Dave looked up and saw Ernie, 'Good movie this, mate. I've seen it six times and it still makes me laugh.'

'You'll have to switch it off now. Some boongs have stolen the petrol truck.'

'Fair dinkum, mate! I didn't think anybody would be that stupid, up here.' Dave replied.

'Well it's true mate. As far as I know it was full of petrol. That would be like heaven for the coon kids, wouldn't it!'

'Yeah, they could sniff that till the end of time.'

'We have to do something about it! Get into your uniforms and come over to the station.'

The sergeant drove over to Roger's house next. It was only about twenty yards, but in this heat no one walked anywhere if they could help it.

Cathy was sitting in the lounge with her two boys when Ernie walked in. They were all sitting on the floor eating watermelon. It was too hot outside.

He stripped the young woman with his eyes. ‘Wouldn’t mind having my knees between hers’, he thought.

Cathy shuddered. He was a loathsome man.

‘Where’s Roger?’ Ernie didn’t bother using her name. Women didn’t matter anyway, unless they were on their backs! They should be chained to the bed, with leash long enough to reach the kitchen.

‘He’s asleep, Ernie! Surely you don’t want to disturb him now. He was up all last night. He has only had four hours sleep now.’

‘Well, there’s another emergency!’

‘Not another riot?’

‘No, some boongs have stolen the petrol truck. Roger’s due to come on duty soon, anyway. Tell him to get over to the station on the double.’

Ernie turned and walked out. He climbed back into his car, drove back to the station and parked in his spot. He dashed inside to the cool of the office. He checked his watch; it was five thirty.

It was about time for a feed but he couldn’t leave his post. If he wasn’t here, the other men could easily nose around the cells.

He slipped inside and gave the big coco pop another injection of Pethidine. Norman wouldn’t cause any trouble. The guy who raped his wife didn’t seem to notice anything at all. He just lay on his cot and stared at the roof. They wouldn’t get any tucker tonight. People like that shouldn’t get fed anyway. It was a drain on the honest guys, like him, who worked.

The other three men arrived at the same time. There was no time for any small talk. ‘The truck was stolen sometime this afternoon. There are only two ways it could have gone: east or south. Tony saw it head off to the east, but didn't see it again.'

'How long has it been gone, Ernie?' Roger was always practical.

'At least a copula hours.'

'Will we stand any chance of catching it then?'

'Yes, I'm sure we will. Listen to my plan:' the three younger men nodded their heads and waited.

'We have to try and track the thing down. I want Bill and Dave to head south. They can check the road that cuts away to the west. Look for any tire tracks in the soft mud near the crossing. If there is nothing there get down to the Dornoch. See if they have seen anything. If the truck hasn't been there head back. Wait at the bridge over Beame's Brook. Don't worry about blocking the road west. The truck couldn't take that crossing with both dogs. You will hear anything that comes by.'

'That sounds Okay, Ernie. How long do you want us to wait?' Bill asked.

'You'll have to wait all night, I'm afraid. Keep in radio contact with me. Get some tucker and camp out for tea.'

Bill and Dave walked out the back door and took their short wheel base Toyota Land Cruiser. They would do a thorough job. Of course, they wouldn't find anything!

'Roger!' Ernie turned to his second in command. 'You'll have to go out alone tonight.'

'I should have one of the replacements with me if you weren't so slack.' Roger couldn't hide his animosity towards his supervisor.

'Well, that doesn't matter, mate.' Ernie felt that he could afford to be magnanimous.

'Well, what's the plan for me?'

'Take your vehicle and go up to the boong camp. Ask them up there if the truck has gone through. If there has been no sighting use your vehicle to block the crossing at the camp; right across the road. You'll have to camp out as well. Go home and get some tucker but don't take too long.'

Roger sighed and walked out. Tomorrow he would investigate some of Ernie's activities; lucky for him that the truck was stolen. It would only delay the inevitable, anyway!

Ernie waited in his office for fifteen minutes and then he walked over to his home. He told Bernice that he would be at the station again tonight. He wanted her to bring his tea over soon.

Roger found himself frustrated with Ernie. He felt that the sergeant didn't do his job. Tonight he had to admit that his superior had done the right thing. It was a good Christian witness if he could be nicer to his boss in future.

He went home and explained the situation to Cathy. She was disappointed that he would have to spend another night away from home. Being essentially optimistic, however, she soon busied herself with preparing food for Roger.

She made half a dozen sandwiches with beef, lettuce and tomato. These were wrapped individually and put in an Esky.

‘Roger, darling, I’ll put some bacon and eggs for you to fry tonight. Make a campfire and then cook them. That will help you stay awake and it will take some time.’

‘That's a good idea, love. I could do with a feed of fat tonight. Don’t pack a flask of tea or coffee. I’ll brew up a billy as well.’ Roger usually didn’t take any of the family drugs. At night, however, when he was on patrol, he drank weak coffee with lots of milk and sugar.

It would be a good idea to make a fire and cook something. It would take at least an hour to cook and eat. Then he would have to clean up.

Reading wouldn’t be very pleasant. Any light would attract mozzies and if he shut the cabin he would suffocate. Perhaps he could run the motor and use the air conditioner. All the police four wheel drives were diesels these days.

He put in his Bible and one of Ironside’s Commentaries. He was studying Galatians now.

Cathy had all the food ready in a small Esky. Roger kissed his wife fondly and then the two boys before he went to the car. He reached over the driver’s seat and put his Esky on the passenger seat. He climbed in slowly. It was as though he was loathe to leave this time.

The young policeman drove back towards the west before turning right and then right again onto the highway. The sun was low in the west and he had to squint as he drove. He was glad that most of the trip was to the east.

This trip was uneventful. Roger did not notice the slight disarrangement of the scrub on the right. He had not been brought up in the bush and his eyes were not trained to see this.

His first stop was on the left. He pulled into the space between the post office and the store. He walked into the police office at the back of the mail centre. Eddie Jack was sitting at his desk. He looked very tired. Poor man he had worked all night and then been on duty all day as well. His dark, full blooded skin looked slightly pale.

'Have you seen the petrol truck today, Eddie?'

'No mate, that fellah hasn't come through here today.'

'Are you sure he hasn't come through?'

'I been outside neely all day, long time, anyway. That fellah not been here today. We been needing fuel for a copula days.'

'Someone stole the truck. He wouldn't have stopped in to deliver.'

'Come, we check with some other fellah. Maybe they seen that fellah.'

The two men walked out into the heat again. They chose to check with some people at the hospital. No one had seen any trucks at all today. The office staff were equally sure that no one had come through in the petrol truck. The store was not a good place to check. There were no windows looking out onto the road.

Some of the people were sitting in the shade of the trees. They had no memory of the fuel truck, either. Roger and Eddie also checked with some of the folks in the houses. This whole excursion took about an hour. By that time Roger was sure that no one had seen the truck during that afternoon. It was obvious that the truck had not come through that day.

Eddie suggested that they walk down to the crossing. There was a low concrete causeway; it was about twenty feet long. Underneath were four large pipes; at this time of the year the water ran through these pipes. At each end of the crossing were two large concrete posts. The posts at each end were joined by guard rail supported by metal posts.

The local people had many stories of drivers trying to cross over during the wet. Sometimes the judgment of these travelers was not good. About a dozen people had been drowned when their cars were washed into the river. These rails were a recent addition to eliminate this possibility.

There was enough room for one car or truck to drive over the crossing. At each end there was some wet mud. Eddie checked the mud carefully. His eyes were good and he said that no truck had been through that mud for about three or four days at least.

Roger heaved a sigh of relief. At least he wouldn't have to drive any further. He went back up and collected his own vehicle. His shirt was completely soaked by now. His heavy police trousers were also clammy around his upper legs.

He sat in his Toyota and fired the engine. The air conditioner was running and he waited for the cabin to cool down.

The young policeman drove down to the crossing. He swung off the road to the right and engaged four wheel drive in the low range. Roger looped around and placed his vehicle across the road. He eased as close to the posts as he could. No one would use this road tonight.

Roger remained in his cabin for another half an hour. By now it was eight o'clock and the sun was beginning to sink in the west. It would be dark in another hour or so.

He called over some of the kids who were playing in the river. He gave two of them ten dollars and asked them to get him some wood. There was none lying around this close to camp. These boys would not take the money and run. They knew the policeman well. He would be able to catch them later.

The boys soon returned with quite a large pile of wood. There would be enough for a good fire. It would last most of the night.

Roger made his fire close to the back of his car, on the south side of the road. When the fire was set, he took out his frying pan. This fry up was delicious.

When he had eaten his food, he boiled up the billy and made a nice cup of coffee. It was now fully dark. Roger sat on a stone and watched the fire. It was slightly cooler now, perhaps eighty five to ninety degrees. Most people would be hot in this temperature, but it had been fifteen degrees hotter earlier that day. There was also a very gentle breeze coming up the river from the Gulf.

Paperwork

A completed, accurate report would be essential tomorrow. A second report must also be drafted on the drug raid and that the two boys came and reported. Their small drink at the back of the pub was noted. They cleaned up the cells but essential business had lured Ernie away. The boys were alone with the prisoners for about ten minutes. Ernie made no mention of the truck in this document.

It was duly noted, in the charge book, that the boys were told to remain in town. They, it was reported, were told to fly to Mt. Isa to face the Magistrates court.

Ernie noted in the daily log that the petrol truck was stolen during the afternoon

It was about ten o'clock when Ernie finally completed the paperwork. Everything was dated and signed. To all intents and purposes the log was up to date. Any inquiries would show an efficient and effective administration. So far Roger had not committed any of his concerns to paper.

The hard slog with the pen was punctuated by regular communication with the men on the south road. The second in command made no effort to report on the radio.

At ten thirty the whole town seemed quiet; all the workers should all be in bed. Others would, by now, be under the table. Some of the town folk were still glued to their videos watching something obtained from Johnnie's video parlor, near the store.

Ernie told the men on the radio that he had some problems to sort out. He would be unavailable for about an hour.

He drove out to the two boys in the bush. When he arrived at the unused homestead he took Ritchie back to the station. Under the cover of the car shelter he sent the young man to get his truck. He was told to take his vehicle out to the deserted homestead. The tracks of the boys ute were all around the station.

The sergeant went into the cells. He told Bluey to pick up Ray's body and put it over his shoulder. He injected Norman again.

The mail contractor staggered out to the sergeant's vehicle. Bluey dumped the body in the cage at the back. He was still depressed and not thinking well. They left the back of the paddy wagon open; Ray would not run away.

Ernie and Bluey picked up the prone body of Norman. The fifteen minutes it had taken to stagger out with the body had given the drug time to take effect. When the unconscious man was dumped on top of his friend the slave was pushed into the back and the door was locked.

The station commander put on some gloves. He took a crow bar and pried out the windows at the back of the cells. This metal rod was thrown under the station.

Our man in blue took his place in the cabin of his vehicle. He drove out to the petrol truck.

While Ernie sat inside his air conditioned cabin the boys opened the back. They put Ray and Norman in the bed behind the driver's seat of the fuel truck. Bluey obediently put on the gloves that Ernie had been wearing and took his place in the front compartment.

The instructions given to the drug growers were precise: take the petrol truck out onto the road. The older boy was to drive it towards the east. He was to go as far as he could and not stop for anything.

Ritchie took the truck out onto the road. He worked his way up through the eighteen gears as the big vehicle picked up speed. It took him nearly two miles to get through the gears. By the time he reached the village the monster was moving at ninety miles an hour. The driver had forgotten all about the steep dip at the crossing. He made no attempt to slow down.

I'm Okay Anyway!

Roger remained in his car for a long time. He didn't bother checking the time. It would not be hard to tell when it was morning. He sat in the passenger's seat and read for a while. Later on he put the seat back as far as it could go and stretched out. He felt quite comfortable with the diesel engine ticking over and the air conditioner running.

He did not feel bad about having a quick sleep. Nothing would go past him. Later on he stirred, feeling uncomfortable. It was time for a brew of coffee. He got out and stoked up the fire. He slipped down to the river and filled his billy with water. Before long he had the pot on the fire.

Our ambitious young policeman heard the buzz of a truck in the distance. He jumped into his car and tried to contact his superior. He left his door open while he used the radio. He called three or four times but couldn't get through. Roger clicked his fingers with frustration. He had been told by the sergeant not to call for about another hour.

The throaty roar of the big motor became louder and more insistent. That big beast must be fairly shifting along by now. The young father was not really concerned yet. He said to himself, 'He'll have to stop soon, or crash!'

Roger called the station again. There was still no reply. He could see the glare of the headlights in the air above his head.

Suddenly the monster popped out of the skyline at him. Eight large headlights glared at him.

The prime mover left the ground. It seemed to float gently in the air for about ten feet. The first trailer followed it.

The policeman remained transfixed in his seat. He could see nothing but the bright lights. They filled his whole vision.

The truck bounced and behind it the first trailer bounced. Its coupling broke and jammed into the back of the cabin.

With a screech of metal, the lorry crashed into the Toyota. Roger was killed instantly. Bluey and Paul smashed their faces into the glass. Ritchie crushed his chest on the high steering wheel.

On the two dogs, the chains groaned and snapped. Each of the eight tanks flew forward to the tangled mess. The first hit, stopped and burst. The next two burst as well. There was petrol and vapor in the air.

This dangerous mixture suddenly exploded as the petrol reached Roger's fire. This was followed by a series of flashes as the other tanks ignited in a cacophony of sound.

At four o'clock the next morning there was a large storm. It came from the west and moved through Leichhardt down to

Boomallooba. The storm lasted one and a half hours. The fireball was extinguished; all the tire tracks were washed away.

Ernie was back in his office when a shaken Edward Jack reported the accident to him. This was during the storm. Eddie was a broken man; he wept unashamedly. Roger had been the first policeman, that he could remember, who had cared for the local Aborigines.

Epilogue

An inquiry was made into the riot and its aftermath. Five badly burned bodies were found in the shell of the truck. Roger's body was identified from dental records. Forensic scientists were unable to positively identify any of the five bodies in the cabin of the truck. Their bones were so badly charred that nothing definite could be concluded. It was assumed all had died of the fire.

The ute belonging to the Arnold boys was found in the bush by one of the replacement constables. The sergeant had made an off handed suggestion at one of the station meetings.

Roger was awarded a posthumous medal for bravery. He was buried with full honors.

Ernie was commended for exemplary behavior throughout the crisis. He was promoted to the rank of inspector and transferred to Brisbane where he was transferred to the Public Relations Unit.

Bernice could not give up the drinking and died three years later from alcoholic poisoning. Ernie was convicted of corruption after a Government inquiry into the police force and sent to prison. He was knifed in a brawl and died four months after his wife.

Adele Andrews was so impressed by Cathy's quiet dignity after the death of her husband. She took Cathy's advice and read the Gospel of John to find out why. She became a Christian and went to work in a hospital in Zaire.

Cathy returned, with her sons, to her family in Katoomba. She went back to Sydney University and completed her Doctorate in Computer Studies. She accepted a post in the University of Beijing, on cultural exchange.

Adam Angel took his posting to Palm Island and completed his doctorate. He later died of AIDS, while living in Canberra as senior Public Servant.

For the people at Boomallooba nothing changed, except a few white faces; a well known humanitarian judge wept when he saw the town, a battle hardened reporter took a child on his knee and cried in front of the nation, the Prime Minister even shed a few tears. All these tears were nothing compared with the tears of the local people, whose hearts continued to bleed from the gaping hole left when their dignity was torn from them. No one really cared; after all, they were just boongs.

Other Books From Bekasume Books

Leonard and Dorothy Akehurst are examples of being living sacrifices for the Lord.

They didn't just volunteer at a soup kitchen twice a week and tithe into the offering plate on Sundays. They did more than send MERE PENNIES A DAY TO HELP A STARVING CHILD IN A THIRD WORLD COUNTRY!!!

They gave their lives.

Not in the sense of dying but in the sense of living. For God. And the spread of the Gospel.

This story is told in Doug McNaught's episodic *Other Days, Other Ways*, published by Bekasume Books.

In bringing the gospel and gospel kindness to Aboriginal people in Australia, they faced discomfort, disease, the elements of nature, starvation, primitive culture and religion. Pressure from fellow Caucasians who weren't so kindly disposed to the native, and other travails.

Not only did they bring the message of the Lord to a people starving for spiritual truths but they also brought basic human needs. Dorothy found herself many a time functioning in a medical capacity, treating ailing aboriginals.

Often nature made travel impossible, leaving the missionaries stranded and waiting for food to arrive. Malnourishment often resulted in sickness among white missionaries.

Monetary funds were far from in abundance. That, of course, brought problems in other areas.

The Akehursts serve as a spiritual challenge to us cozy and supremely blessed Americans who think that going to church is our duty to God.

Though missionary nonfiction is not my kind of reading, there were times in this book when I achingly felt the beauty of living with nothing but feeling the abundance of God in that nothingness. Of having joy despite despair.

The ‘Other Ways’ of the title is presumably a reference to the interesting and unusual culture and customs of the primitive natives. The Akehursts, in witnessing, had to deal with a people whose mores were not our own.

The book is also chock full of light-hearted anecdotes about the Akehurst children and the often-childlike native converts.

I think people who are interested both in missionary work and the aboriginal people of Australia will find some merit in McNaught’s labor of love.

Kristofer Upjohn, *Religion Section*, Pine Bluff Commercial, Saturday November 9 2002

Order through your local book store (ISBN: 0 646 16777 4) or send $AU 25.00 to bekasume.books@optusnet.com.au through PayPal (www.paypal.com). Don’t forget to include your name and address in the notes section. If you would like the book signed include the inscription you would like in the notes section after your name and address.